DARK GUARDIAN'S MATE

THE CHILDREN OF THE GODS BOOK 13

I. T. LUCAS

Also by I. T. Lucas

THE CHILDREN OF THE GODS ORIGINS
1: GODDESS'S CHOICE
2: GODDESS'S HOPE

THE CHILDREN OF THE GODS

DARK STRANGER
1: DARK STRANGER THE DREAM
2: DARK STRANGER REVEALED
3: DARK STRANGER IMMORTAL

DARK ENEMY
4: DARK ENEMY TAKEN
5: DARK ENEMY CAPTIVE
6: DARK ENEMY REDEEMED

KRI & MICHAEL'S STORY
6.5: MY DARK AMAZON

DARK WARRIOR
7: DARK WARRIOR MINE
8: DARK WARRIOR'S PROMISE
9: DARK WARRIOR'S DESTINY
10: DARK WARRIOR'S LEGACY

DARK GUARDIAN
11: DARK GUARDIAN FOUND
12: DARK GUARDIAN CRAVED
13: DARK GUARDIAN'S MATE

DARK ANGEL
14: DARK ANGEL'S OBSESSION
15: DARK ANGEL'S SEDUCTION
16: DARK ANGEL'S SURRENDER

DARK OPERATIVE
17: DARK OPERATIVE: A SHADOW OF DEATH
18: DARK OPERATIVE: A GLIMMER OF HOPE
19: DARK OPERATIVE: THE DAWN OF LOVE

45: DARK SECRETS UNVEILED
46: DARK SECRETS ABSOLVED
DARK HAVEN
47: DARK HAVEN ILLUSION

PERFECT MATCH
PERFECT MATCH 1: VAMPIRE'S CONSORT
PERFECT MATCH 2: KING'S CHOSEN
PERFECT MATCH 3: CAPTAIN'S CONQUEST

THE CHILDREN OF THE GODS SERIES SETS

BOOKS 1-3: DARK STRANGER TRILOGY—INCLUDES A BONUS SHORT STORY: **THE FATES TAKE A VACATION**

BOOKS 4-6: DARK ENEMY TRILOGY —INCLUDES A BONUS SHORT STORY—**THE FATES' POST-WEDDING CELEBRATION**

BOOKS 7-10: DARK WARRIOR TETRALOGY

BOOKS 11-13: DARK GUARDIAN TRILOGY

BOOKS 14-16: DARK ANGEL TRILOGY

BOOKS 17-19: DARK OPERATIVE TRILOGY

BOOKS 20-22: DARK SURVIVOR TRILOGY

BOOKS 23-25: DARK WIDOW TRILOGY

BOOKS 26-28: DARK DREAM TRILOGY

BOOKS 29-31: DARK PRINCE TRILOGY

MEGA SETS

THE CHILDREN OF THE GODS: BOOKS 1-6—INCLUDES CHARACTER LISTS

THE CHILDREN OF THE GODS: BOOKS 6.5-10
—INCLUDES CHARACTER LISTS

TRY THE CHILDREN OF THE GODS SERIES ON AUDIBLE

2 FREE audiobooks with your new Audible subscription!

ANDREW

*A*ndrew closed the file he was working on, put it back inside the metal cabinet by his desk, locked it, and then logged out of his station. One could never be too careful —not even in a secure government facility that was wired to the max. For all he knew, there could be a double agent among them.

Not paranoia.

Reality.

One had been caught in a similar facility on the East Coast.

Security had been upped, which made his life difficult. In a way, he was a double agent himself. Not working against the U.S., he wouldn't do that even for the clan. By law, though, using government resources and databases for the benefit of another entity was almost as bad and probably carried the same jail sentence.

With a sigh, Andrew grabbed his gym bag off the floor and headed out. His days of training downstairs in the office gym were long gone, the place couldn't hold a candle to the one in the keep, but with security being so tight it was the only place he and Roni could meet and talk without raising suspicion.

At the end of a workday, the gym was at its busiest, but Roni had his own designated corner. As the only employee in the entire building who'd been assigned a private trainer, the boy genius could claim that spot for himself without anyone grumbling about it.

Spotting the kid and his fitness trainer, Andrew smiled and waved before walking over. "Roni, Jerry, how are you guys doing?" He offered his hand to the trainer, a stocky dude with the patience of a saint. No one else could've tolerated Roni's attitude day after day and kept on smiling.

The trainer clapped Andrew on the shoulder. "Living the dream, Andrew. Want to join us?"

The guy was either the most optimistic, upbeat fellow Andrew had ever met or was high on something other than life.

"Sure. I just need to change out of the monkey suit."

Roni put down the weights and sat up on the bench. Bracing his elbows on his knees and his chin on his fist, he looked up at Jerry. "I'm thirsty. Could you get me a drink?"

The trainer rolled his eyes.

Andrew slapped Roni's back. "I'll keep this dick company until you come back."

"Thank you."

"I need to talk to you," Roni said as soon as Jerry was out of earshot.

Andrew put his foot on Roni's bench and pretended to re-tie his shoe, bending closer to Roni's ear. "Sylvia. Tonight. Eleven."

Roni nodded and picked up the dumbbells off the floor. The kid's troubled eyes betrayed the storm raging in his head. Something must've happened, but to say more was to take unnecessary risks. Until he saw Roni later that night, Andrew would have to be patient.

---

*a*s Andrew eased into the parking lot of the Starbucks that had become his and Sylvia's meeting place, she was already there, waiting for him in her car. Meeting that way saved Sylvia from having to explain to her mother why Andrew, a married man, was picking her up and dropping her off in the middle of the night or early hours of the morning.

"Thanks for doing this for us," she said, buckling up.

"You're welcome. But I'm not doing it out of the goodness of my heart. Your boyfriend is giving me valuable services in exchange."

"I know. Still, I feel bad about keeping you away from Nathalie all night. She probably hates me."

Nathalie had had a few choice words to say on the subject, but the romantic in her couldn't stay mad at him for helping out the young lovers. He'd promised to make it up to her.

But how?

What would make Nathalie happy?

Another dinner date with just the two of them?

It would be nice, but he wanted to be original—to surprise her with something he hadn't done before. "I'm trying to figure out how to best make it up to Nathalie. Any ideas?"

Sylvia shrugged. "Every woman is different. If it were me, I would want chocolates. But that's me."

Nathalie loved chocolate as much as the next woman, but she wouldn't be happy with just that.

When they arrived at the office building, Sylvia

performed her magic, momentarily disabling the cameras and whatever other electronic devices were monitoring the parking garage, the hallways, and the stairwells.

As usual, her freaky control over electronics worked beautifully, but regardless of how many times they'd pulled the same stunt, Andrew's heart pounded against his ribs until Roni's door closed safely behind them.

One of these days they would get caught, and the shit would hit the fan.

Not that he should lose any sleep over it. Worst-case scenario, Kian and his Guardians would have to bail his ass, thralling everyone concerned. The incident would get erased from memories and databases as if it had never happened. But the thing with anxiety was that it had little to do with logic. Andrew's response was on the gut level, instinctive, a leftover from his human days.

Roni wrapped his arms around Sylvia, pulling her to him and kissing her as if he hadn't seen her for a year. When the girl responded in kind, Andrew looked away, searching for a place to disappear to and give them privacy.

He ducked into the bathroom, used the toilet, and then spent the next ten minutes washing his hands. When his fingers started to prune, he came out, right as the young lovers were breaking apart after their marathon kiss.

"I need to talk to you for a minute." Roni turned to Andrew. "It's about the special project I was working on." He glanced at Sylvia, then back at Andrew, indicating that he wasn't sure he could talk in front of her.

Andrew would've preferred not to, but there wasn't much to be done about it. Even if Sylvia went into the bedroom and closed the door, she would still hear everything they were talking about. But Roni didn't know that. He thought she was just an ordinary girl, and that Andrew was the genius who'd found a way to avoid detection by the monitoring equipment in the building.

"It's okay. You can talk in front of Sylvia. I'll make sure she never tells anyone." He winked at the girl.

She rolled her eyes.

Roni looked horrified. "How exactly would you do that?"

"That's between Sylvia and me."

"Seriously."

Andrew chuckled. "Come on, Roni, can't you take a joke? As if I'm going to harm a single hair on her head."

Roni nodded. Taking Sylvia by the hand, he led her to the couch. The two sat close to each other, the fingers of their hands entwined, their thighs touching.

Cute.

Andrew pulled a chair from behind the desk and put it down facing the couple. "I'm listening," he said as he sat down.

"First of all, this is yours." Roni handed Andrew the flash drive. "I looked at the matches. There wasn't a lot of them." He ran a hand through his short hair. "I recognized one. The same face on three driver's licenses. Different names, same woman. One from thirty-eight years ago, another one with a different name from five years after that. The third one, with yet another name, is from nine years ago."

"Who do you think it is?" Sylvia asked.

"I don't think. I know. That's my grandmother. The first driver's license is under her name. The other two are not."

The implications were astounding. Andrew saw the moment the realization dawned on Sylvia. Her eyes peeling wide, her hand flew to her heart, and she exclaimed, "Oh my God!"

Roni cast her a bewildered sidelong glance.

Sylvia recovered quickly. "I assume something bad must have happened to her."

Roni nodded. "She died when my mother was twelve."

"How?"

"She drowned."

That could've been a perfect cover-up for an immortal. With powerful arms and lungs that could go without air longer than those of a human, Roni's grandmother could've fooled people into thinking she'd gone under, only to resurface somewhere down the shoreline where she'd stashed clothing and other necessities beforehand.

Exchanging knowing looks with Andrew, Sylvia patted Roni's knee. "That's terrible. I'm so sorry."

He nodded and then turned to Andrew. "So, what does it mean? For whatever reason, my grandmother faked her own death, then twenty-five years later pulled a driver's license under an assumed name, using an old picture?"

Andrew rubbed the back of his neck. Should he tell the kid? Based on Roni's incredible hacking talent and Sylvia's reaction to him, Syssi had called it weeks ago, deducing that Roni was a Dormant. If his grandmother was an immortal, then the guesswork was over.

Still, he needed to get Kian's approval.

Besides, even though Sylvia assured him Roni's apartment was clean of listening devices, talking about immortals and Dormants in a government facility that was wired through and through wasn't smart. There was always the remote chance that she was mistaken. If his illegal use of government databases for a private investigation was discovered, it would mean trouble for Andrew. If the immortals' secret got out, it would mean an existential threat to the clan.

"Let me take a look at it. It might be nothing. Just a doppelgänger. It happens."

Roni nodded. "Yeah, that must be it."

A few moments later, when the couple disappeared into Roni's bedroom, Andrew stretched out on the couch and turned on the television. He had hours to kill until Sylvia was ready to go.

A pity. He would've dragged William out of bed if necessary and had him look at the results.

Discovering that Roni's grandma was an immortal was big, but the implications of it were huge. It seemed that Eva wasn't the only Dormant who'd been accidentally activated.

EVA

*S*o far so good.

Two weeks had passed since Bhathian had moved into Eva's house, and she was still okay with that. His arrival had been unobtrusive. It hadn't affected Eva's routine or that of her crew in any way. No big announcements had been made, and no new furniture had been delivered. One bag of clothes and another one of weapons was all Bhathian had brought with him.

If things didn't work out, his exit would be just as quiet as his arrival.

On the one hand, it wasn't a big vote of confidence in the success of their cohabitation, but on the other hand, Eva was grateful for Bhathian's cautious approach. It hadn't been an easy step for her, and perhaps that was the reason he'd been treading lightly.

"When is Bhathian coming back?" Nick poked his head into the office.

Eva looked up. "Why?"

"I'm hungry. He said he's bringing burritos today."

Shaking her head, she pulled out her phone. "I'll check with him."

Bhathian was spoiling her and the kids rotten. Every day on his way back from the keep, he was stopping by one fast-food place or another and getting dinner for everyone.

As she selected his contact from her favorites list, Eva chuckled. Her man had found a sure way to make everyone happy to see him come home.

"Yes, love," he answered immediately, the sounds of traffic hinting he was on his way.

"How soon are you going to get here?"

"Why? Do you miss me?"

"Nick does. He can't wait... for his burrito."

"Tell him I'm almost there."

Bhathian hadn't chuckled or snorted like she'd expected him to.

Could her teasing have offended him?

"I can't wait either. For you, not the burrito."

This time he laughed. "Yeah, yeah, yeah." He ended the call.

"Well?" Nick tapped his foot.

She kept forgetting her crew didn't have her immortal hearing. Yet. "He'll be here in a few minutes."

Nick turned on his heel and strode out. "I'll open the door for him."

A rush of footsteps down the stairs meant that Sharon had spotted Bhathian's car. "He's here!" she shouted.

Eva wondered if the girl had beaten Nick to the door. "Aren't you joining the welcoming committee?" She cast Tessa an amused glance.

"I'll set the table." Tessa pushed up to her feet and headed for the kitchen.

Smiling, Eva reclined in her office chair. The hunter was coming back home to feed his grateful family. No one could navigate the dangerous jungles of the fast food industry as well as her man.

She'd better get off her butt and join the celebration.

In the kitchen, Tessa was almost done setting the table when her coworkers rushed in, plastic bags full of takeout in their hands, with the smirking Bhathian sauntering sinuously behind them.

For a big, muscular man, he moved with surprising grace and fluidity. Almost like a dancer, or rather a big, predatory cat.

Disregarding the bunch of hungry hyenas, he walked up to Eva and crushed her against his chest. "Give me those lush lips of yours, woman."

Obligingly, Eva lifted her head. He took her mouth in a hungry kiss, his tongue seeking entrance, his roaming hands turning her boneless.

Shifting his attention to her ear, Bhathian nipped at the soft fleshy part, sending pulses of desire coursing through her breasts and straight down to her core. "Do you mind skipping dinner?" he whispered.

Eva stifled a moan. "I don't. But I don't want to look at their snickering faces either." She pointed her chin at the kids.

He kissed her again. "Later."

"Definitely."

God, she was starving, and not for a burrito. It was a strange and unexpected phenomenon. The more sex she had with Bhathian, and it had been a lot since he'd moved in, the more she craved it.

It was starting to affect her work. Who wanted to read reports and devise strategies when such pleasure awaited her? The only evenings she'd worked this week had been the ones Bhathian had been teaching a late class at the keep.

Which reminded her. "When are you going to teach me

those self-defense moves we've talked about?" She meant thralling, but Bhathian's deep frown meant that he'd either forgotten or was bad at reading clues.

"Could you teach me too?" Tessa butted in. "I was thinking about enrolling in our neighbor's Krav Maga class, but I would much rather train with you."

Bhathian rubbed a hand over his square jaw. "I don't think it's a good idea. I'm used to training strong men."

Not really, but the immortals in his self-defense classes, even the most sedentary males and females, were as strong as or stronger than the average human male. Tessa was too small and too fragile.

"Oh." Deflated, Tessa bit into her burrito.

"I'll go with you to check out Karen's class," Sharon offered.

"Sure," Tessa mumbled around a mouthful.

Eva ate several tortilla chips dipped in guacamole and took a few bites from the burrito before rubbing her tummy. "I'm full. Are you about done, Bhathian?"

He dropped the burrito he'd been eating onto the plate and pushed up to his feet. "I am. For now." He turned to the gang. "Write the names on the wrappers before putting the leftovers in the fridge. I want to eat mine later."

Nick saluted. "Sure thing, boss. Thanks for feeding us."

"You're welcome." Bhathian took Eva's hand. "Come. I'll show you those moves."

Sharon chuckled, Nick snickered, and Tessa sighed.

Eva shrugged. She'd tried to be circumspect about taking Bhathian to bed, but if it didn't work, she could live with that. Shyness was not an affliction she suffered from.

Upstairs, Bhathian closed the door behind him and pulled her into his arms. "So, what moves are we talking about?" He nuzzled her neck.

"Thralling. You promised to teach me."

"I will, right after this." He scraped her neck with his fangs.

"Ah…" With her body taking over, her brain was too busy processing all the physical sensation to leave any room for thought.

Bending, Bhathian slipped an arm under her knees and lifted her up, then carried her the short distance to the bed.

Slowly, he began undressing her, starting with her shoes, then the skirt, and lastly the blouse. When she was down to her bra and panties, he took a moment to admire her lingerie. It was one of the sets he'd seen her wearing before, and Eva wondered if he'd paid attention enough to remember.

"Turn around and lie on your belly," he commanded.

"Are you giving me a massage?" She was starting to get addicted to those. Bhathian had a way of kneading out the tension from her muscles as no professional masseuse could.

"Do you want one?"

"Always."

"Let's get you naked first." He hooked his thumbs in the two strings holding her bikini panties together and pulled them down her legs, showering her butt cheeks and thighs with kisses and nibbles as he went. The bra clip was in the front, and Bhathian reached under her to unhook it, then peeled it off her shoulders.

"Beautiful." He ran a thick finger all the way down from her cleft and up the seam of her buttocks, spreading the moisture that had gathered there to her rear.

Eva gasped. It was such a sensitive spot, and she loved when he rubbed against it, but no more than that. As uninhibited as she was with most things sexual, there were some lines Eva couldn't cross, and frankly, had no desire to.

As usual, Bhathian read her body's responses as if she had

spelled it out for him, his hands leaving her bottom only to return to her back covered in lotion.

The massage didn't last long, though. With both of them short on patience, it soon turned into something else. Flipping her around, Bhathian dove between her spread thighs, bringing her to a fast and furious climax with his tongue and his lips and his fingers. No slow buildup, no teasing, zero to sixty in under a minute.

She was fine with that.

The spicy appetizer guaranteed a smoking-hot main course. As always, Bhathian didn't disappoint, driving into her with the force of a battering ram. She winced as he hit her cervix.

"Did I hurt you?" He stilled. "Am I going too fast?"

She surged up to meet him. "No, that's how I want it. Fast and furious."

Instead of answering, he gave her exactly what she'd asked for.

CAROL

"*S*ee you tomorrow, Carol," Onegus, the last customer of the day, said on his way out.

Finally.

"Have a good evening," she replied.

"I will. You too."

As if.

Onegus was probably going clubbing later that evening, and Carol would've loved to do the same, but after a session with Brundar, all she could think about was soaking her sore muscles in a bath and going to sleep.

Even her immortal body wasn't strong enough for that much abuse. Working harder than she ever had in her entire long life, Carol was exhausted.

Between running the café and training with Brundar, she was too tired to even go clubbing, which was a big problem since Robert was no longer at her beck and call.

According to the rumors, he was shagging Ingrid.

Good.

Maybe.

Given that Carol had been trying to get rid of him for

months, the ping of jealousy was unexpected. But after all the time they'd been together, she couldn't help feeling possessive of him.

Ingrid was enjoying what had been hers.

Not that Carol regretted giving Robert the push out the door. It had been the right thing to do, for his sake more than hers.

If he hadn't been such a romantic sap and wanted more than she was able and willing to give, she could've been still enjoying him in bed. Robert hadn't been the most exciting of lovers, but after all, he was an immortal male—the only one available. What he lacked in skill he more than compensated with stamina, fangs and venom.

Carol was going to miss it.

Not for long, an insidious little voice whispered in her ear.

After arriving at Passion Island, Carol was going to get more than her fill of immortal males. Could she handle it, though?

A courtesan wasn't the same as a whore. Carol could conceive of being with one or two, maybe even three males a day. But what if more was required of her?

She should find out exactly what her future job entailed. Fortunately, she had two ex-Doomers to answer her questions. Robert was too angry with her for taking on such a dangerous assignment and wasn't going to cooperate.

Which left Dalhu.

But to get to him she needed to go through Amanda, who intimidated the hell out of her.

Carol shook her head. What kind of a superspy was she going to make if talking to a relative made her nervous?

Pitiful.

Rag in hand, she attacked the table surface, scrubbing for all she was worth even though it wasn't particularly dirty.

Stop it. She commanded herself to leave it be and move to

the next one. The poor table had done nothing to deserve such harsh treatment.

From the corner of her eye, Carol glimpsed Onidu, who was almost done cleaning up the prep area, and came up with a perfect solution to her problem. Instead of initiating the contact and risking Amanda's snickering response, Carol could have Amanda's butler deliver a message for her. "Onidu, could you please tell Amanda that I need to talk to her? I'll write down my phone number for you."

Onidu bowed. "If mistress tells me her telephone number it will suffice."

Right. It was easy to forget the guy was a glorified machine. Once told something, he would never forget it.

When they were done with the cleanup, Onidu headed up to Amanda's penthouse, and Carol went down to the basement where her next shift awaited.

It wasn't easy running the café and training with Brundar—a merciless, heartless taskmaster. Carol would've gladly dropped the café in somebody else's lap. But there were no takers, and Nathalie was in no hurry to get back to work.

Not that Carol could fault the new mother. Phoenix was still too little for daycare. Besides, taking her out of the keep and entrusting her to some human babysitter was too scary to consider.

Carol was stuck with the café. If she didn't do it, the place would close.

It would be a shame. Everyone loved hanging around there.

She sighed. If only Kian would agree to employ humans.

Her phone rang, ending that line of thought. "Yes?"

"You wanted to talk to me, darling?" Amanda sounded amused.

"Actually, I need to talk to Dalhu, but I wanted to check

with you first that it's okay. I have a few questions for him about the island."

Amanda chuckled. "Thank you for being so considerate, but I'm not the jealous type. Dalhu can talk to whomever he wants."

"Thank you. Could you please check with him when is a good time?" Damn, now she was treating the princess as her secretary. Bad move. "Or you can give me his phone number, and I'll do it myself."

"Just come on up. We're home."

Unfortunately, it wasn't going to work. "I wish I could, but I have a training session with Brundar scheduled in five minutes. Can I come after? Like maybe in two hours?"

"That's fine. Say hello to Brundar from me."

"Thank you so much. I really appreciate it."

"No problem, darling."

An hour and fifteen minutes later, Carol left the class barely able to move her arms. Brundar had had her train with a wooden sword. She'd laughed at the toy, but half an hour into the lesson she'd laughed no more. By the end of the class, she could swear the thing had gotten much heavier. At least twenty pounds.

After a quick shower and a change of clothes, she headed up to the penthouse.

Never having been to the top floor before, Carol imagined it would be fancy, but the vestibule she stepped out into was absolutely gorgeous. A round table made of stone stood on top of a circular mosaic, holding a vase with a fresh flower arrangement the size of a hotel's centerpiece. Across from each other, there were two double doors.

But which one was Amanda's?

She was about to pull out her phone to look for Amanda's number in the recents, when one of the doors opened.

"Come in, darling." The princess waved Carol in.

"Thank you for inviting me." She stepped inside and followed Amanda to the couch.

"Dalhu! Carol is here!" Amanda called out. "Can I offer you something to drink?"

"No, thank you. I'll try to be as brief as I can."

Shit, she hadn't thought to ask Kian if it was okay for her to talk to Dalhu about the mission. Should she excuse herself and call him?

Was it okay to call the regent at eight o'clock in the evening?

Or maybe she could cross the beautiful vestibule and knock on his door.

Right. A tiny snort escaped Carol's throat.

"What's funny?" A smile lifted Amanda's lush lips, turning her beauty from gorgeous to blinding.

Intimidating as hell. It didn't happen often that Carol wasn't the prettiest and sexiest female in the room. Make it never, unless the princess was around.

Carol waved her hand. "It's nothing. I just remembered something embarrassing."

As Amanda regarded her with a penetrating stare, Dalhu walked in.

He was a big one, but men didn't intimidate Carol. Except for the sadist, may his dark soul rot in hell. Regardless of status, physical attributes, or even smarts, males were putty in Carol's hands.

A dubious talent, but one that might prove more beneficial to the clan than a slew of others.

"You wanted to ask me some questions." Dalhu's voice was deep and smooth.

Heck, she was a sucker for deep voices...

Bad girl, Carol.

Not the right time or place to go lusting after a male.

Especially one who was taken by a powerful mate who was sitting right next to her.

"I hope it's okay, but I wanted to know about the girls in the island's brothel. How well or badly are they treated? How many clients a day are they required to service? Are they given contraceptives? And what about sexually transmitted diseases? Are the human clients screened? What about days off?" Out of all the questions she was asking, there was one she was particularly interested in the answer to. The rest were for general information and to cover for the one she'd come here to ask.

Dalhu frowned. "Why do you want to know?"

It was on the tip of her tongue to say professional curiosity, but she bit on the inside of her cheek to stop from blurting it out. Amanda knew about Carol's infamous past, but Dalhu didn't. There was no reason to educate him right then and there. "I think it's an important aspect of life on the island that we need to know more about."

Dalhu seemed unconvinced by her answer, but that didn't prevent him from supplying the information she'd asked for. After all, it had nothing to do with him. She hadn't asked about his own experiences in the brothel, which she was sure there were plenty of. A virile male like Dalhu had most likely been a frequent customer. "I don't know what being treated well means. They are well fed and have a doctor examine them once a week to make sure they are fit and healthy. They get a day off every two weeks. I don't know how many clients each one services a day. Their typical shift is six hours long. So maybe six?"

"That's a lot," she blurted out.

"I guess. I don't know. They have access to mild drugs and are allowed to drink moderately. But they have to pay for that with the tips they get. An incentive to do a good job."

That was good to hear. Being high helped. Still, servicing six men a day was tough.

"What about the commanders? Do they get special privileges? Like keeping their own harem? Or demanding exclusivity with a particular girl?"

Dalhu chuckled. "Except for Navuh, who keeps his own harem, everyone else has to pay. Reserving a girl for the day costs triple. So if one of Navuh's sons, for example, wants to keep a harem, he can do it provided he pays a fortune for the privilege."

Interesting. And somewhat disconcerting. Carol was hoping to charm her way into an exclusive arrangement with a high-placed Doomer. But if the bastards had to pay extra for it, it would be harder to pull off.

She pushed to her feet and offered Dalhu her hand. "Thank you. That was very informative."

He shook it for about half a second before pulling away. "I'm glad I could help."

Amanda escorted her out. "I apologize for you know who." She tilted her head, motioning back at the apartment. "He doesn't like talking about it. Wants to put it behind him."

"There is nothing to apologize for. I appreciate his help." It hadn't escaped Carol's notice that Dalhu hadn't offered to answer any future questions she might have. But she couldn't complain. He hadn't been friendly, but he hadn't been rude either, just coldly polite.

The important thing was that she had gotten what she'd come for.

4

ROBERT

"*Hello*, handsome." Ingrid sauntered into Robert's office. "What keeps you so busy that you don't come visit, don't call..." She sat on a corner of his desk and crossed her legs, her skirt riding up to reveal a shapely thigh.

The woman had great legs, long and strong, and she loved to wrap them around his waist while he had her propped against the wall.

Searching his brain for an excuse, Robert winced. It had started as casual sex, and Robert would've loved for it to remain that way, but Ingrid was trying to make it into something more.

The irony wasn't lost on him.

He was doing to Ingrid the same thing Carol had done to him.

Had Carol felt as indifferent toward him as he felt toward Ingrid?

Maybe indifferent was too strong of a word. Robert liked the woman and didn't want to hurt her feelings, but other than sex he didn't enjoy her company.

"I'm trying to solve some problems with the Malibu

project. Kian put the whole thing on hold until we figure out what to do. The sooner we come up with solutions, the sooner the work will resume."

"Who are we?"

Robert shifted in his chair. The truth was that Kian hadn't assigned any of it to him.

"William and me."

William was the one who was supposed to come up with the solutions. But the guy was busy with other things. Whatever he was working on must've been damn important, because evidently it took priority over timely completion of the clan's safe haven.

With the project hanging in limbo, Robert had nothing to do, which was driving him crazy, and he had decided to start searching for the solutions himself. It was amazing what one could find on the Internet.

Ingrid huffed. "And what am I, chopped liver? No one thought to ask me?'

As he'd discovered, Ingrid had a somewhat inflated ego. "Do you know anything about gardening? Or trash disposal?"

She smiled. "I know about trash compactors and the best spots to put potted plants. Does that help?"

He shook his head. "Sorry, but no."

She got up and walked around the desk. "When am I going to see you?" She put her hands on his chair's armrests and leaned in, waiting for him to kiss her.

"Not here, Ingrid. What if someone walks in?"

With a miffed expression on her face, she pulled up and tugged her skirt into place. "So they'll see us kissing. But I guess you're too embarrassed to be seen with me."

"It's not like that. I'm supposed to be working. I don't want Kian thinking I'm slacking on the job."

Ingrid's eyes were cold as she cast him a parting glance. "I guess I'll see you when I see you. Call before you come over, though. I might be out clubbing." She sauntered out and let the door slam shut behind her.

Robert braced his elbows on the desk and let his head drop onto his fists.

Women.

He was never going to understand the way their brains worked. Carol kicked him out because he cared too much, and soon Ingrid was going to do the same because he didn't care enough.

Work was so much simpler. He'd been able to find solutions even for what at first glance had looked like insurmountable problems.

Done printing the last few pages for the portfolio he was preparing, Robert stapled them together with the rest of the printouts and headed for Kian's office.

"Come in!" Kian called when he knocked on the glass door.

"Do you have a moment?" He sat down even though Kian hadn't told him to. It had taken him a while until he was able to force himself to do so without being told.

Old habits were damn hard to break. Kian's casual leadership style was so different from the strict adherence to protocol that Robert's superiors at the Brotherhood had demanded.

Kian eyed the file Robert had put on his desk. "What do you have for me?"

"I've done some research, and I think I've found solutions for some of the Malibu location's challenges."

Kian leaned back in his chair. "Go ahead."

Robert opened the plain yellow folder, pulled out the first stack of papers, and handed them to Kian. "I got the idea from an article about large cruise ships and how they handle their trash. They incinerate it. So I started searching for small incinerators that could be used in individual dwellings." He pointed at the papers Kian was holding. "There are several brands to choose from. I picked the top two. They are not meant for home use, but I guess we can modify them to fit what we need."

Kian nodded. "Good work. What else do you have there?"

Robert pulled out the next stack and handed it to Kian. "Self-cleaning windows. Ingenious. I had no idea something like that existed. They are pricey, and we've already installed regular windows. Replacing them with the self-cleaning type will cost a fortune. That's a lot of money to spend only because your clan members are too lazy to wash their own windows." Robert might have been overstepping his boundaries, but he couldn't help pointing it out.

Kian flipped through the pages, his brows going up and down as he read the scientific explanations. "I'll think about it. In the long run, it might be the right thing to do. People's time could be spent doing more pleasant things than washing windows. I know that I don't want to do it, so I shouldn't expect others to."

Robert wanted to shake his head but refrained out of respect for Kian. There were those whose job was to lead and those whose job was to follow. Just as not everyone could shoulder the same level of responsibilities, not everyone should enjoy the same privileges.

"It's your decision, sir."

Kian rolled his eyes, but unlike Sharim didn't comment on Robert's use of the honorific. "What else do you have there? I must say that so far I'm impressed."

The compliment was unexpected. Kian wasn't the type who dispensed praise with ease, which made it so much more meaningful when he did. Robert pulled out the next stack and handed it to Kian.

"Sustainable landscape. Long-living plants, trees, artificial lawns, etc. Those are just a couple of articles on the subject.

To actually design a self-maintaining environment, you will need to hire a landscape architect specializing in this."

Kian nodded. "Next?"

"Street cleaning. I checked the slopes for drainage purposes, and we are good. The rain will take care of the loose dirt. One street cleaning robot should take care of the rest. Hopefully, people will not throw trash on the streets."

"They will not."

"The next two are more, how shall I say it, inventive." Robert smiled. He had kept those for last for a reason. If Kian hadn't been so impressed with the simpler solutions, Robert wouldn't have mentioned them. But it seemed that Kian loved every idea he'd presented so far.

"I can't wait to hear them." Kian put down the last stack Robert had handed him and folded his arms over his chest.

"Malibu is very close to the ocean, but it's on a higher elevation. We can have an unlimited water supply by building an underground pipe and pumping water from the ocean and then desalinating it. Economically, it doesn't make sense, but as a safety measure it does. We've already taken care of the power supply with the solar panels and the wind turbines and the battery array to store the surplus for when the sun and wind are down. I thought that adding an independent water supply would be a good idea too."

Uncrossing his arms, Kian leaned forward. "I looked into it and it's cost-prohibitive as compared to other solutions. We are searching for underground water. If we find anything in the vicinity, we'll use it; if not, I'll consider the ocean water pumping and desalination."

Robert felt his ears heat up. He should've researched it more and not embarrassed himself by presenting Kian with a half-baked idea. If Kian called something cost-prohibitive, then it probably was close to undoable. "My apologies. I should've researched the costs involved."

Kian waved a hand. "Never let it stop you. You can shelve ideas to use in the future. Tomorrow there might be a technology that will make it cheaper and doable. The important thing is to keep an open mind and think outside the box, which you do." He tapped his head with a finger. "Now, what's the last thing you've got there?" He pointed at the folder.

Robert would've preferred to stop and not embarrass himself further, but Kian wanted to hear it all. "I didn't research this one at all. So I don't know what's involved, but I know the technology exists."

"Just spit it out. I love crazy ideas. Today's science fiction might be tomorrow's reality."

Robert took in a deep breath. "The transportation problem. People don't like the idea of having to wait for someone to drive them out and then pick them up. They want to be free to come and go as they please, which is a problem since the location of the compound and the road leading to it must remain secret."

Kian drummed his fingers on the desk. "If you have a solution for that, you'll become everyone's hero."

A ray of hope blossomed in Robert's heart. Maybe that would be his ticket out of the keep? He couldn't wait to be allowed some freedom.

"Self-driving cars, but with a twist. The vehicles are controlled by a computer. What if they are programmed to do more than drive themselves? Like darken the windows until the car reaches a certain predetermined location?"

Encouraged by Kian's rapt attention, Robert got more animated. "Imagine a guy getting inside his car at the compound. He inputs his destination, and the car takes over. As soon as it leaves the compound, some kind of film coats the windows from the inside or the outside, so he can't see where the car is going. Once it's on a public road, the film or coating or whatever recedes, and the guy takes back control of the car. The same happens on the way back."

Kian lifted his hands and clapped three times. "Bravo, Robert. This is genius."

Was Kian mocking him?

"Do you think it's possible to make cars like that?" Robert asked hesitantly.

"I don't see why not. I'll run your idea by William and see what he thinks. And as it happens, we just bought a car manufacturing facility. Not self-driving, flying, but I'm sure modifications can be done quite easily."

5

ANDREW

"*Y*ou look like hell," Kian welcomed Andrew.

"Thanks, man. Between work and more work and a baby, I don't have time to catch up on my beauty sleep."

"Come on." Kian clapped him on the shoulder. "Let me fix you a drink."

"No, thanks. I'm actually looking forward to one of Syssi's cappuccinos." Andrew glanced around. "Where is she?"

"At Amanda's. They'll be here in a few moments. So what is it all about? You said it's something about Dormants."

Andrew nodded. "I'd rather tell the story when Amanda gets here, so I don't have to repeat myself."

"No problem. Grab a seat, and I'll turn the contraption on. I can press the button just as well as Syssi."

Andrew cocked a brow. "But do you dare?"

Kian glanced at the cappuccino maker and then raked his fingers through his hair. "On second thought, Syssi loves playing with that thing so much, I wouldn't want to rob her of the pleasure. I'll leave it to her."

Stifling a chuckle, Andrew planted his butt in an

armchair. "Whatever, man. I'm married too. You don't have to explain."

Kian cast him an annoyed look. "I'm fixing myself a drink." He walked over to the bar and pulled out a new bottle of Lagavulin.

The door opened, and Amanda walked in with Syssi. "Good evening, darlings. To what do I owe the pleasure of this invitation?"

Kian saluted with his tumbler. "Andrew has something he wants to tell us."

Amanda walked over to her brother and kissed his cheek. "I know that, Sherlock. Andrew called me. Remember?"

She sauntered over to Andrew, and he pushed up to his feet to greet her. "Thank you for coming."

He got a kiss too. "Of course. I'm so curious."

"Cappuccinos, anyone?" Syssi asked.

Andrew lifted a finger. "One for me."

"I'd rather have a drink. Can you mix me something sweet, Kian?"

"Sure." Her brother got busy at the bar.

Once everyone was seated, drinks and coffees in hands, Andrew cleared his throat. "Roni, my infamous hacker, is a Dormant."

Amanda crossed her legs and started swinging her foot up and down. "You sound very sure about that. How come?"

"He ran the driver licenses database through William's face recognition software, and one of the few faces it spat out was of his long dead grandmother who got a license nine years ago— under a different name of course."

"How did she die?" Syssi asked.

Andrew chuckled. "That was the first question that popped into my head. She drowned."

"Convenient." Kian put his drink on the coffee table. "But

it's not proof. What about a recent driver's license? Did she renew?"

"William is on it. But for now the answer is no. William thinks that she might have smartened up and used someone else's photo. Someone who looked like her but not exactly—similar enough to fool the naked eye but not identical, so as to avoid detection by the machines."

"Smart," Kian said.

"Yes. William suggests that we start doing the same. He also thinks that we don't have much time before the others realize it and follow suit. We have a very narrow window of opportunity to find matches."

Amanda put her drink down on the coffee table. "Pretty soon we will have to start wearing fake noses and other prostheses like Eva. With all the cameras everywhere, Big Brother is not only watching but also recording everything."

It was a sobering thought, one that had crossed Andrew's mind before. The days when immortals could hide in plain sight were nearing their end. Soon, they would have to move and make their bases of operations in less advanced places, like South America or Africa.

"What about the other matches? Anything interesting?" Syssi asked.

"William is working on it. He has the geek squad investigating. Aside from Roni's grandma, there is only one additional confirmed match. The other four are still a work in progress."

Amanda snapped her fingers to get everyone's attention. "So what do we do about Roni? That's what we are here for, right?"

"First of all, I called this meeting to ask if I can tell the kid. That's the first step."

Kian got up and walked over to the bar. "Did William confirm that it was indeed Roni's grandmother in the newer driver's license picture and not someone who looked a lot like her?"

"Yes."

"And it wasn't the same exact picture? Because we all know someone might have used it to make a fake one."

"It's not. William assured me the photo was taken at around the same time the license was issued."

Kian nodded. "I understand that Sylvia has been seeing Roni for a while now."

"Yes."

"Does he love her?"

"Seems like it."

"Then let her tell him."

Andrew rubbed the back of his neck. "Here is the problem. I sneak her in to see him, which is bad enough. But I don't want any talk about immortals and Dormants in a building wired through the nose. The thing is, Roni can't go anywhere without his handler. I can arrange a meeting in a coffee shop, but someone would have to be there to handle the handler while Roni and Sylvia have the talk."

Amanda smirked. "I'll come with you and make sure that the handler will be too busy ogling me to pay any attention to the young couple. Unless it's a woman. Then I suggest Anandur."

Andrew put a hand over his heart. "You wound me. Am I not handsome enough to distract a woman?"

Amanda laughed. "You are, darling. But not a fellow agent. Unprofessional, right?"

"Good save. The handler is a guy. Still, I don't think you are the best choice for that. You're somewhat known. We need someone who is not recognizable."

Kian chuckled. "Take Carol. No one can do it better than her."

Amanda crossed her arms over her chest. "Now, I'm

offended."

"Get over it." Kian poured himself another drink and went back to the couch to sit beside Syssi, who posed the real question.

"What about later? What do we do once you tell Roni? If he is a prisoner how are we going to bring him over here for sparring?"

"I thought about it, and I think I have a solution. Roni has been training in the gym for months. He even managed to get himself a private trainer paid for by Uncle Sam. I can suggest an outside martial arts class. Naturally, he would have to come with his handler, but we can have Carol or some other hottie do her magic and distract the guy. We'll have one of the Guardians pretend he is the dojo master who is giving Roni one-on-one training."

Amanda lifted a finger. "You're all forgetting one important point. What if Roni doesn't want to do it?"

Andrew frowned. "Why wouldn't he?"

"Because, darling, he is treated like royalty in that facility, and he sits on an unparalleled treasure trove of data and equipment."

It was all true. Roni even had a throne-like chair in his glass-enclosed throne room. "But he is not free to do as he pleases."

Amanda lifted her drink and took a sip. "Neither is a king or a prince, and yet most people wouldn't mind being one. Some would even kill for the privilege, as we all know from observing history."

True.

Andrew rubbed his hand over his jaw. "Let's start with step one—a meeting with Roni, Sylvia and another girl or two in a coffee place or a restaurant—and then take it from there. Worst case scenario I'll have Sylvia thrall Roni to forget all about it."

6

BHATHIAN

*A*s they strolled down Eva's quiet street, she leaned her head against Bhathian's shoulder. At moments like that, he felt at peace with the universe. No unease, the constant irritation gone, replaced by a sensation of well-being that was almost unsettling. He was too old to get used to new feelings, to a new way of looking at the world around him. It was as if the gray lenses in his glasses got replaced by yellow ones, and all he could see was sunshine.

What a sap, he berated himself.

All of that because he finally had the woman. His other half. But only from his perspective. He didn't have her, not yet, and not fully. Eva was fighting hard to keep her emotional independence as if it was a priceless treasure.

He could tell her it was worthless.

Life without emotional entanglement might have been simpler, but it was also less fulfilling. Except, contrary to what most people believed, love wasn't for the faint of heart. To give yourself to someone required more bravery than charging into battle. Bhathian wondered if his warrior woman would rise to the challenge if he told her that.

But knowing Eva, she would think he was trying to manipulate her and close off completely. She was exceedingly good at that, going from warm and fuzzy to cold and distant in the blink of an eye.

A cat darted in front of them, its nose down to the ground and its tail folded tightly against its bottom.

"Is it possible to thrall animals?" Eva asked.

"It's possible, but it's very different from thralling humans. You can send out feelings, intentions, make a dog stop barking and come for a pat on the head. But I wouldn't try it with a hungry wolf or a tiger. When a predator is poised to pounce, its concentration doesn't waver and you don't have enough time to play mind games with it. Shoot to kill. That's your only course of action. Hesitate, and you'll get mauled."

Eva's eyes followed the cat as it jumped onto a windowsill and then shimmied inside the house through a narrow crack between the sill and the slightly opened window. "I wonder if this is its home or if it is going in to steal food."

"If it comes out with a big fat fish in its mouth, you will have your answer."

Watching the window, Eva halted. "Can you thrall the cat? I'm asking because I want to practice, and I don't want to do it on some unsuspecting human."

Bhathian had promised to teach Eva, and it was about time he made good on his promise. The only problem he had with that was imagining what she would do with it. Eva was taking serious risks as it was. If she possessed the ability to thrall, she would get even bolder.

"You can't practice on a cat. It's much easier to thrall a human than an animal. It doesn't have to be anything invasive or harmful. You can look at a person and have them check their teeth, or tie their shoes, or look in a certain direction. It's nothing."

A smile brightened her beautiful face. "Great. I was afraid it was against the rules."

He winked. "Rules are meant to be bent. But it's okay as long as you don't manipulate anyone in a harmful way or to gain an unfair advantage."

"Got it."

As they reached Venice Beach boardwalk, Bhathian looked around for a good candidate to practice on. The sweet tune of a classic violin gave him an idea.

"You see that violinist over there?"

Eva nodded.

"Go up to him and drop a few bucks in his hat, then look at him and smile but don't say anything. Think hard about a piece you want him to play. Make him hear it played, make him read the name on a billboard, anything you can think of that would translate in his head as this piece."

Reaching into her purse, Eva pulled out a twenty dollar bill and strolled over to the violinist. "Lovely playing, Maestro. Thank you." She dropped the bill in his hat.

Not exactly what Bhathian had told her to do. But then Eva never did what she was told.

"Thank you, beautiful lady, God bless," the old man said. "Is there anything you would like me to play for you?"

She dazzled him with a smile. "Surprise me."

"Very well." The guy tucked his instrument under his chin and started a famous Bach sonata.

As Eva closed her eyes and swayed gently to the music, Bhathian walked up behind her and pulled her against his chest. She leaned into him, her hands holding on to his arms around her. They swayed together until the end of the sonata.

Eva clapped.

The violinist bowed his head. "Thank you, Ms."

"No, thank you. That was beautiful. Have a wonderful evening, Maestro."

"Well?" Bhathian asked as they got farther away from the violinist.

"It worked." Eva almost shrieked with glee. "I want to try another one. Tell me what to do."

Bhathian glanced around, his eyes landing on an ice cream stand.

"Go get yourself some ice cream. Don't tell the girl which one you want. Ask her to recommend something, while thinking about a specific brand, the wrapper color, the taste. Let's see if this will be the one she suggests."

Eva practically skipped over to the stand.

As he watched her thrall the ice cream seller, it crossed Bhathian's mind that Eva was enjoying this a little too much. Hopefully, she was just excited, and the novelty would wear off. He hated to think that Eva could be one of those who got addicted to the power rush that controlling minds provided.

She came back with two Choco Tacos and handed him one. "Worked like a charm. You should've told me it was easy. What's next?"

He unwrapped the treat. "I think we are done for today."

"Why? It's so much fun, and I'm not tired at all."

Kissing her ice-cream-chilled lips, he licked off the little bit of chocolate that had gotten smeared around them. "Because before you know it, you'll turn half the boardwalk into zombies." He did a zombie impression, squeezing a throaty laugh out of her.

Then her eyes narrowed, and she regarded him from under her long, dark eyelashes. "You think I'll get carried away?"

"Don't look so incredulous. Some people get addicted to the power rush. I'd rather you took it slow."

Eva's expression turned serious. "You should know me better than that by now."

Oh, damn. He'd said the wrong thing. "I know it won't happen to you. You're such a strong woman. It's just a precaution." He sounded desperate as he tried to dig himself out of the hole he'd dug.

She shook her head. "It's not about being strong. I don't have an addictive personality. I don't smoke and never did, I don't do drugs of any kind and never did, I drink in moderation and never get drunk. Except that one time, but it could have been a thrall. What could've made you think I'll get addicted to this?" She waved her hand at the ice cream lady.

"I'm sorry. You're right. Am I sleeping in the dog house tonight?"

Eva's tensed shoulders slumped as she gave him a tentative smile. "No. But I expect a lot of groveling."

"I can do that." Bhathian's voice turned raspy as he imagined the kind of groveling he was going to do at Eva's feet and between her legs.

She batted her eyelashes. "I know you can."

7

EVA

*a*s they strolled down the boardwalk, Eva reflected on her flare of anger.

Why was she so trigger happy about every little thing Bhathian said or did?

She should've been the one to apologize.

It was almost as if she was eager to catch him doing something wrong to prove to herself she was right to keep him at arm's length. Eva was a firm believer in the old saying that if someone seemed too good to be true, then he probably was.

But the truth was that Bhathian's little stumbles were just that. Insignificant things that shouldn't have even irritated her. Eva wasn't a silly young girl, expecting perfection and getting disappointed when her poor guy couldn't measure up to her impossible standards.

At this rate, Bhathian would stop talking to her at all, turning into one of those beaten up guys who just nodded.

She'd seen couples like that, where one partner became practically mute because of the other's over-the-top reactions. More often than not, it was the male half who adopted silence as the best strategy for a peaceful coexistence. Not a big surprise since the typical guy's verbal communication skills were inferior to that of his female partner.

Bhathian wrapped an arm around her waist. "Ready to go home?"

"Not yet. Let's walk a little longer. It helps me think."

"What are you thinking about?"

She tilted her head and looked up at him. "I just had an interesting thought. Most men are not that good at verbal communication."

Bhathian looked puzzled, but said nothing in response, nodding in agreement and confirming her suspicions. She was turning her man into a bobbing head.

"But then there are those men who are exceedingly good at it, and they are typically more successful than others. I suspect that this vital quality is a big factor in that success. Those who have an advantage in that area rise higher in the ranks."

Bhathian shook his head. "Kian is an excellent leader, and he is as charming as a pit bull."

"I'm not talking about charm. I witnessed him with Tessa. He was concise, clear, and compassionate. How is he at motivating people?"

"Good."

"You see? I'm right."

Bending down, he kissed the top of her head. "You're always right."

"Except when I'm not. I'm sorry for before. I shouldn't have chewed you out like that over nothing."

"It's okay. I deserved it."

"No, you didn't."

Again, he said nothing.

Great job, Eva.

She'd better drop it and move to a different subject. The one that was at the root of her unease. "I have a new lead."

"You mean on a target?"

"Yes. But this one is more than a middleman. Not the top, but close. That's why I want to learn how to thrall. He has a bodyguard with him at all times, but just one. It's not that I can't take out the bodyguard, I just don't want to. He's not my target. Thralling him, however, would make my job much easier."

"You're quick, but I don't think you can master the technique in time. I can come with you and take care of the bodyguard."

His answer was so predictable. Bhathian always wanted to help, especially in situations where he believed she would be in danger. What he didn't realize, though, was that his so-called help might actually compromise her.

"As a last resort, I might ask you to come. The thing is, my mode of operation is based on solo performance. If I include you in my plan, I'll have to change how I do things, and that could be dangerous. I have a proven method that works. Adding new variables might mess things up for me."

Bhathian stopped and turned to face her. "I don't want to do anything that might endanger you. How about you skip this one and wait until you get a lead on an easier target?"

The thought had crossed her mind, but for a different reason. "I'm still in the research and planning stage. If I decide that this is over my head, I will drop it."

Bhathian's facial muscles relaxed for a moment but then tensed again. "You're not just saying it to ease my mind?"

"I would never do that. You're my sounding board. I can't lie to you. What would be the point? Besides, as I told you before, I'm not gung-ho about this. I have too much to live for to take unnecessary risks."

And here was the crux of the problem. Eva was losing her

edge. To do what she did required a certain level of darkness, but lately, it had been rapidly receding. All the love in her life was pushing it out.

Phoenix was like a huge generator of love and joy. One afternoon with that adorable baby lightened Eva's spirits for days. And her love for Nathalie was shining brighter than ever.

If she also let Bhathian into her heart, she would become useless. Her day job didn't require as much darkness as her vigilante gig, but she still needed some to keep going.

One couldn't slosh in crap day in and day out wearing pink shoes.

Looking into her eyes, Bhathian cupped her cheek. "Keep me updated. I want to know your plans."

"I will. Come on, let's head back."

As they turned around and strolled toward home, Bhathian was silent. His brows pointing down in a deep frown, he seemed to be mulling over something.

"Penny for your thoughts," she said.

"If there was an organization with similar goals to yours, doing everything they could to stop the slave trade, would you consider dropping your solo operation and join forces with them?"

She eyed him curiously. The only organization Bhathian was part of was the clan. Were they planning a war on slavers?

"Hypothetically speaking?"

"Yes."

Bhathian was such a miserable liar. It was good for her, but made him totally unsuitable for undercover work. There was no way she could take him on a mission.

"It depends in what capacity. A hit woman?"

"Let's say detective work, like the research you do on

your targets. Would you be okay with someone else doing the dirty work?"

It was on the tip of Eva's tongue to start berating Bhathian again for assuming she was a bloodthirsty bitch. But she'd done enough of it already. The man wasn't a great communicator, and sometimes what came out of his mouth sounded offensive, but she was certain that wasn't his intention.

Bhathian loved her.

She needed to remember that before letting her fuse ignite.

Taking several calming breaths, Eva forced a small smile. "As long as the job gets done, I don't care who does it. But I'm not a hypocrite. If I believe the scum need to die, I need to be willing to do so myself. Keeping my hands clean by letting someone else's get dirty is not my way."

"What if you're better at the detective stuff and that person is better at executing? Would you still insist on doing it yourself?"

"No. I'll always choose the best final outcome. If collaborating and specializing would mean getting more done, I'm all for it."

The deep creases between Bhathian's brows smoothed out. "That's what I needed to know."

With a chuckle, Eva threaded her arm through his. "You're funny, talking in circles about some hypothetical organization as if I don't know who you're working for. Is Kian declaring war on slavers?"

Bhathian cast her a sidelong glance, a smile crooking one corner of his sensuous lips. "Maybe."

She laughed. "Tell him that maybe I'll consider joining forces with him. But I need to see what he's maybe planning first, and find out what he is willing to maybe offer me."

8

JACKSON

"*I* can't believe you did all that." With her hands on her hips, Tessa turned in a circle, looking at the acoustic material covering the walls of his room.

It wasn't pretty, and it made his room look even smaller, but it was the best he could've done with his budget. As it was the project hadn't been cheap or easy. The isolating panels were pricey, and it had taken him and the guys an entire Sunday to cover the walls.

Mainly because they had no idea what they were doing.

The end result, though, was worth it. If he and Tessa kept their voices low, they could have some privacy.

He pointed at his ears. "Immortals have exceptional hearing. I can't keep throwing Vlad and Gordon out whenever I want to be alone with you. This way they can stay and we can still have some privacy."

"We could've gone to my place. Nick and Sharon still have their limited human hearing."

Jackson cocked a brow. "And what about Eva? Or Bhathian? Do you want them listening in on us? They can't help it."

"We could put on loud music." She waved a hand. "One of the horrible bands you like listening to."

They had very different tastes in music, but she liked the stuff he and the guys played, which was all that mattered to him. Tessa came to most of their gigs to cheer them on.

"You'd hate it." He leaned to whisper in her ear. "When I'm with you, I prefer to listen to some soft, romantic tunes."

Not that those were helping. He and Tessa were stuck in one place.

They'd had a small breakthrough when Tessa had let him kiss her. She had even dared put her hand on him over his pants, but that was as far as she was willing to go. For now.

Sometimes, she couldn't even tolerate a kiss.

As long as they were sitting or standing, he could kiss her as much as he wanted, she was fine with that, but not while she was lying on her back. Rarely, she could tolerate him looming over her, or even lying on top of her, but more often than not she freaked out and he had to back off.

A naughty smirk bloomed on her face, one he hadn't seen before. "You can come during the day. Most of the time I'm all by myself in the house. Bhathian is at work, and Eva and the gang are busy with the detective work."

Sounded great. But there was one problem. "I also have to work during the days."

"Can't you leave Vlad and Gordon in charge?"

"Not really. The place is too busy for one person to do dual jobs. I'm at the register and making coffees, Gordon is in the kitchen making sandwiches, and Vlad is doing the baking early in the morning and helps with cleaning up at the end of the day. I can ask him to step in for a couple of hours once, but can you imagine him at the register?"

She chuckled. "You'd have no business."

"Exactly."

Tessa glanced around again. "Maybe we can hang something over these ugly panels. Like colorful blankets. Talk about unromantic. No offense, but this looks like a badly done recording studio."

Jackson took her by the hand, led her to the couch, sat down, and pulled her into his lap. She loved it when he did that. For some reason, it made her feel safe. "When I dim the lights, all of this will disappear." He waved a hand at the walls. "I think I can get you in the mood. I'll put some romantic music on, pour us some wine, and feed you the chocolates you love so much."

Tessa wrapped her arms around his neck and leaned to kiss him. "Did you buy more?"

He'd discovered Tessa's greatest weakness. Godiva chocolates. Her eyes rolled back whenever she bit into one.

Of course he'd bought more.

He had a stash of them hidden in the pantry, but she didn't need to know that. They would be all gone, and Tessa would end up in the hospital from a chocolate overdose. He had to ration them.

"Yes, I did."

"Where are they?" She sounded breathless, the way he hoped she would one day when talking about sex. With him, obviously.

"Do you want me to get them now?" It was a rhetorical question. Of course she did.

"Please. And the wine. And when you come back you can dim the lights, but not too much."

Jackson chuckled. "As you command, my lady." He lifted her off his lap and repositioned her on the couch. "Don't go anywhere."

"I won't." She kicked off her shoes and stretched out on the sofa.

For a moment, he just stared at her, admiring the beautiful curves she was starting to show. Her stomach no longer formed a little concave when she lay on her back, and her hips were no longer two jutting bones. Even her breasts had gotten a little plumper.

Jackson swallowed. Those were like magnets for his hands. He fisted them, holding his arms by his sides to avoid reaching for her.

Maybe he should visit the downstairs bathroom and release some pressure. Not that it was going to do him much good. Lately, the need to sink his fangs into something was becoming more and more urgent, especially after jerking off. Hell, the mere thought of Tessa caused them to elongate and venom to drip into his mouth.

Sometimes it happened during work hours.

He couldn't go on like that. But what choice did he have?

The Fates were testing him to see if he was worthy of a true-love match. Like any other immortal child, growing up he'd heard the stories about how rare and how precious a true-love match was, about how Annani had lost her one and only and vowed to never love again. But he'd thought they were the equivalent of human fairy tales. Bedtime stories to keep kids entertained.

"Jackson?" Tessa's voice startled him. "Are you going or not?"

"Yeah, I'm going. I'll be right back with your chocolates."

9

TESSA

*a*s Jackson left the room, Tessa sighed, the smile she put on for him melting away. She was living on borrowed time, and the ticking clock was getting louder by the minute.

And yet, despite all the self-talk, she couldn't push through the barrier that kept her from moving forward. So much rested on her ability to overcome those paralyzing fears.

It was an impossible loop.

If she could have sex with Jackson and take his venom bite, she could transition, which would make her stronger, which in turn would make her less fearful. But to get there, she needed to overcome the fear in the first place.

It wasn't only about her either.

The wait was costing Jackson. It hadn't been the first time he'd zoned out on her, lost in whatever went on inside his head. Worse, he was losing control over his glowing eyes and elongating fangs. At random times, one or the other would make a sudden appearance even around the café's customers.

He was hurting.

Because of her.

She was forcing him to jump through impossible hoops, and the guilt was eating her alive. It was one thing for a guy to abstain when keeping his distance, but to do so while necking was another.

Jackson was sporting a gargantuan case of blue balls immortal male style, complete with fangs and glowing eyes. Bound by his promise, he was selflessly allowing her to experiment and touch him while he was keeping his hands to himself and awaiting her permission to make the slightest move.

No matter what, today she was going to push through another layer of resistance and give Jackson the hand job she'd decided on weeks ago. If she could touch him over his pants, she could touch him without any barriers.

It wasn't as if she'd never seen a dick before.

But maybe that was the problem.

Her biggest fear was that it would trigger horrific memories, and instead of helping her break through her fears, it would sling-shoot her back to the starting point.

But as the saying went: no guts, no glory. Drawing it out was unfair to Jackson and not beneficial to her. The sooner she became immortal, the sooner she would feel safe. She didn't even have to enjoy the sex, just power through it. Pleasure could come later, after the fear was gone, or at least subdued.

When Jackson came back, Tessa had a smile on and what she hoped was a come-hither look in her eyes.

Holding a small box of chocolates in one hand, and a wine bottle and two wine glasses in the other, he halted at the doorway. "Is that hungry look for me or the chocolates?"

"Both."

He put everything down on the coffee table, except for the box of chocolates, and sat next to her. "What will you

48

give me for this one?" He pulled a piece out and held it in front of her mouth.

"A kiss."

"You've got yourself a deal." He put it in her mouth, waiting until she finished chewing and rolling her eyes in pleasure before putting his mouth on hers. "Mmm." He smacked his lips. "Decadently sweet."

"Me or the chocolate?" she teased.

"Both," Jackson teased back.

"Give me another one," she demanded.

He pulled another piece from the box. 'What will you give me for this one?"

She pretended to think. "I don't know. There are six pieces in the box. I can keep trading one kiss per chocolate, or I can trade something better for the remaining five." There, she'd done it. She'd put it out there, and there was no going back.

Jackson lifted a blond brow. "What do you have in mind?"

"How about you lie down beside me and I'll show you?"

"What about this chocolate? Do you want an advance?"

Tessa shook her head. As much as she loved those, her throat was too tight to swallow saliva, let alone anything edible. "Later." She sat up, making room for Jackson to lie down.

When he toed off his shoes and stretched out beside her, she took a moment to admire the beautiful man who was putting himself at her mercy. Lean and muscular, he was almost too tall for the couch that served as his bed. The top of his head was touching one armrest, his feet the other end.

The button-down shirt he had on was perfect for a slow unveiling, and she wondered if he wore it with that specific purpose in mind. Jackson was a T-shirt and jeans guy. Tessa doubted he had more than two dress shirts in his closet.

His chest was going up and down, his breaths getting

deeper and more ragged. Did he suspect what she had in mind?

Slowly, she popped the top button of his shirt, then the second, her hand trailing along the opening before opening the next one. Jackson's incredible blue eyes began glowing, the inner light intensifying with every patch of skin she was exposing.

When all the buttons were undone, she parted the two halves, letting them fall sideways. His hairless chest was smooth, his muscles well defined but not bulging. There wasn't an ounce of fat on him anywhere.

Tessa shook her head. "I don't know how you do it. Other guys have to watch everything they eat and lift weights for hours to look like you."

"I guess I'm lucky." His words sounded slurred as if he'd had too much to drink, when in fact the wine bottle he'd brought remained unopened.

Sucking in a breath, he hissed when she trailed a hand down his pectorals to his flat stomach. A glimpse of white protruding over his lip made her realize that his fangs were the cause of the slur, not alcohol.

The funny thing was that they didn't scare her at all. What would've terrified any other woman drew Tessa in like a moth to a flame. She couldn't wait to feel them embedded in her neck. So strange. With her past she should've been terrified of anything that promised pain, of an act that spelled out submission on a level she'd never experienced before.

When she'd submitted in the past, it hadn't been by choice. She was small and weak and couldn't do anything to resist. Letting the monsters do as they'd pleased saved her from more injury and more pain.

But this was different. The choice was entirely hers. The problem was that Tessa wasn't sure she knew what to do with all the choices that were hers to make.

What would feel the best?

What would scare her the least?

One thing at a time. One small step that would lead to another small step and sooner or later she'd find herself on the other side, discovering what suited her best.

Jackson wasn't wearing a belt, which made the next step easier. Popping his jeans button, she quickly lowered the zipper before she had a chance to change her mind.

"What are you doing?" Jackson groaned.

"Something I've wanted to do for a long time and chickened out every time."

As she reached inside his boxer briefs and closed her hand over his shaft, Jackson's eyes rolled back. He lifted his torso off the couch, making it easier for her to tug his pants and briefs down.

He felt good in her hand. Satin smooth skin over hard steel, long but not too thick, warm but not too much.

Perfect.

Not scary at all.

Jackson opened his eyes and looked at her hand holding his shaft with wonder in his eyes, but he said nothing, probably afraid she'd panic if he moved a muscle.

Oddly, she felt the need to reassure him. "You're beautiful all over, Jackson."

His lips lifted in a smile bordering on a smirk. "I'm glad you think so." He put his hands behind his head, the elevated angle providing him with a better view.

When she cupped his balls with her other hand, Jackson pushed up, groaning as if he was in pain.

"Did I hurt you?"

He shook his head, his fangs biting on his lower lip and drawing blood.

"Good." She smoothed her hand up and down his length,

marveling at how amazingly natural it felt. Being in control rocked. The certainty that Jackson wouldn't do anything she didn't allow was so liberating, so exhilarating, she felt giddy with it.

A few more up and down strokes and Tessa realized she was hurting him. He didn't say a word, but the pained expression on his face told it all. At first she'd thought it was excitement, but then it dawned on her that without a lubricant, it wasn't as much fun for Jackson as she wanted it to be.

There were only two options. She could go searching for a lotion or use her tongue and mouth.

Tessa swallowed, the memory of being held down while one of the monsters shoved his dick down her throat causing a choking sensation.

But this was Jackson, he would never do that. Besides, she didn't need to take him into her mouth, she could just lick him up and down like a lollipop.

"What happened?" Jackson asked, his words free of slur. She looked up at his worried face. Even his eyes had stopped glowing and were back to normal. In her hand, his shaft had gone flaccid.

Damn, did she hurt him while making the very unpleasant mind journey into the past?

She panicked. "What did I do? Did I squeeze too hard?" She might have hurt him while zoning out.

One of his hands left its resting place behind his head and he reached for hers, closing his palm around the one that was still holding on to his manhood. "You didn't hurt me. But you looked like you'd seen a ghost. The revulsion on your face..." He looked away. "Is it too much?"

Tears brimming in her eyes, Tessa cupped his cheek. Bringing his face around, she leaned and kissed him hard. Talk about a difference. Where the monsters had gotten off on hurting and humiliating her, Jackson had lost his erection at the mere thought of her not liking what they were doing.

"A nasty memory did it. Not you. Never you. I adore every inch of you, but mostly what's between your ears. My angel." She kissed him again, then leaned back and looked at the damage she'd done.

Jackson had regained his erection, but he was nowhere near where he'd been when she'd let the past spoil the mood.

No problem. She knew what to do to fix it.

Scooting down, she leaned and licked him from top to bottom and then up again. His shaft twitched in her hand, getting thicker as soon as her tongue touched it for the first time.

With trepidation, Tessa waited for the revulsion to kick in and for her gag reflex to act up, even though she hadn't taken him inside her mouth. But none of that happened.

Jackson was breathing heavily like a locomotive and hissing through his fangs, but he was keeping his butt firmly planted on the couch. It must've required iron will to stay motionless while she was doing all that to him. But that was exactly what he needed to do to make her feel safe. One day she would treat him to the whole nine yards, but today it was the best she could do.

"I'm going to come!" Jackson half shouted and tried to pull away.

Tessa shook her head and kept on pumping. She felt his seed go up his shaft and then shoot up like a geyser, covering her and Jackson and the couch in hot sticky mess. Tessa didn't mind. All she wanted to do was grin from ear to ear, until she looked up and saw Jackson's face.

Feral, dangerous, his fangs extended to their full length and dripping venom. There was only one thing on his mind, and she was going to give him what he needed even if it scared the crap out of her.

Tilting her head, she offered him her neck and held her breath.

He struck like a cobra.

Before she knew what was happening, he grabbed her and dragged her over his body, holding her head in an iron grip as he sank his fangs into her neck.

The pain was so much worse than Tessa had expected, the two sharp incision points burning like hell. Instinctively, she tried to pull back, but Jackson's grip was so incredibly strong that she couldn't move at all.

Panic seized her. She whimpered, tears sliding down her cheeks. But then as suddenly as the pain started it vanished, replaced by the most amazing feeling Tessa had ever felt, but there was something off about it. A sense that none of it was real. That she shouldn't be feeling such euphoria.

She was drugged.

The sensation intensified as a coil started tightening inside her, more and more until it sprang loose and she orgasmed for the first time in her life.

Amazing, but unreal.

Through the haze, she felt Jackson cradle her in his arms and whisper apologies, but all she could do was smile at him as she drifted off.

Artificial or not, it had been the best experience of her life.

10

JACKSON

*T*essa had fallen asleep, looking more peaceful and relaxed than Jackson had ever seen her before. But that was the venom's doing. Nothing he could take credit for. Damn.

He lifted her off him and laid her down on the couch, then went to the bathroom for some wash cloths. He must've ejaculated the equivalent of two quarts of whipped cream. At least that was what it looked like.

Not wanting to wake her, he wiped the mess off her hands and her shirt and pants as best as he could, then covered her in a blanket and went back to the bathroom.

In the shower, Jackson stepped under the hot spray. Mindful of the limited supply, he went through the motions as fast as he could. The old water heater could barely manage two showers one after the other. If Tessa woke up and wanted to take one too, he was making sure she'd have enough hot water to wash up without having to rush.

He'd scared her at the end. After all the self-restraint he'd practiced, all the patience he'd mustered, he'd lost it at the worst possible time. Tessa had been doing so well, and then he had to ruin it by attacking her and holding her immobilized. But that was the only way to keep her from jerking away and tearing her flesh on his fangs.

The thing was, that was the best he could do. Replaying the scene in his head, Jackson knew that he wouldn't have done it differently a second time for the simple reason that he couldn't. Maybe he could've held back if he'd been sated, and it hadn't been so long since his last time.

But not like that.

Not when she'd offered him her neck.

From that point on, there was no going back.

Could he have refrained if she hadn't?

Maybe. He wasn't sure. Damn. He was no better than an animal.

When he was done, Jackson wrapped a towel around his hips and went back to his room.

Tessa was still sleeping and would probably stay asleep until morning. From experience, he knew that the first venom bite had the most effect. It became less of a knockout the second and third time. But if the second bite happened after a long break, the knockout effect was the same.

He shouldn't have known that, wasn't supposed to have sex with the same girl twice. But Jackson had broken the rules on occasion, not only because he'd been curious and wanted to experiment, but because some of the girls had been too good to let go after one time.

Normally he slept in the nude, but with Tessa in his room he had no choice but to put on underwear and training pants. Jackson didn't own any pajamas.

Eyeing the couch first, he then glanced at the floor. Even with how tiny Tessa was, there was not enough room on the sofa for two. Not unless he lifted her up and put her on top of him. But he doubted they could sleep like that. His only other option was the floor. The thing was, Jackson didn't even have an extra blanket or pillow to make himself comfortable.

With a sigh, he pulled out a few sweatshirts from the closet to make himself a makeshift pillow.

Tossing and turning on the hard floor, Jackson had to acknowledge that he wasn't warrior material. Bhathian would've probably fallen asleep a long time ago, as would any other Guardian. Soldiers had to learn to make do with the hard ground and open sky, and he was complaining about sleeping on a floor in his own room.

You're a soft male, Jackson. You need to toughen up.

With that, he closed his eyes and forced himself to fall asleep. Finally drifting off, he was rudely awakened by the sound of his cell phone going off.

Jackson snatched it off the dresser without checking the caller ID. "What?"

"Where is Tessa?" Eva asked, her tone cold enough to freeze water.

"She fell asleep at my place. She is right here on the couch."

There was an audible exhale on the other side. "She should've called me and let me know she was staying with you. When I woke up and didn't see her car outside, I freaked out."

"Understandable. She didn't plan on falling asleep. But I should've called you. Next time I will."

"Is everything all right?"

Jackson ran his fingers through his long bangs, smoothing them backward. "I hope so."

"What happened?" The freezing tone was back.

"Stand down, Mother Goose. Everything is fine. I can snap a picture of Tessa sleeping with a blissed out smile on her face and send it to you." That was the most he was willing to tell Eva. The woman was smart enough to catch the hint.

She chuckled. "Congratulations. Tell her to call me when she wakes up in the morning."

"I will."

"Good night, Jackson."

On second thought, he should snap that picture as a souvenir, a reminder of Tessa's first venom bite. Zooming in on her beautiful, peaceful face, he took several pictures, then looked at the results.

If Tessa woke up tomorrow morning mad at him for what had happened tonight, he could show her the pictures as proof that despite the first few unpleasant seconds, she had enjoyed his bite.

11

AMANDA

*E*ntering the elevator at the garage level, Amanda glanced at the mirror and grimaced. Tired wasn't a good look on her. It had been a busy day at the lab. Two new immortal volunteers had shown up as scheduled, thankfully, and needed training. Hannah called saying that something had come up and she couldn't come in. As a result, Amanda and Syssi had their hands so full that they had both skipped lunch.

There was a nice dinner waiting for her at home, her butler made sure of that, but Amanda's day wasn't done yet and she was starving. A quick snack to tide her over through the meeting with Kian was in order. Dealing with her brother while tired and hungry was a really bad idea. They would be at each other's throats over nothing in no time.

The cafe was closed this late in the evening, but hopefully there were some pastries left over in the vending machine.

Amanda glanced at her watch.

If she hurried, she could stop by the lobby before heading to Kian's office and be only a few minutes late. No big deal. She could always blame traffic.

As she'd expected, the place was deserted, except for Robert. Pastry in one hand and a newspaper in the other, he was sitting with his feet up on one of the chairs.

"Hey, Robert. How are you doing?" She rushed by him on her way to the vending machine, not really interested in getting an answer. But it would've been impolite to just pretend he wasn't there.

He sighed. "As well as can be expected. How about you?"

"That doesn't sound so good." Amanda stuck her credit card inside the slot and selected one of the few remaining pastries. "What's wrong? Are your new roommates giving you a hard time?"

She'd heard he was rooming with the two young pilots. They were both nice guys, but maybe they weren't too happy about sharing an apartment with an ex-Doomer.

He chuckled. "No, not intentionally. But they are so young."

Amanda collected her pastry and turned to him. "Meaning?" She unwrapped the foil and took a bite.

So good. No matter how many times she had them, biting into one always induced a blissful eye roll.

"Loud music, language that belongs in the gutter." He sighed again. "I don't want to be the old fart who rains on their parade. So I either stay in my office or hang out here for a little quiet time with the newspaper."

She saluted him with the pastry. "You do what you need to do to stay sane. Right?"

He nodded.

"It was nice chatting with you, but I have to run."

"Have a good night."

"You too."

Robert was a genuinely nice fellow if one could forget his past. Not that Amanda had a problem with that, but others did. Her Dalhu was still getting suspicious glances even though he'd proven his dedication and loyalty to the clan in battle. The problem was that only a small group of people had witnessed his heroics. Apparently, hearing about it wasn't the same as seeing it.

Elbowing Kian's door that was slightly open, she pushed it all the way and stepped in. "Good evening." She glanced at her crumb-covered fingers. "I should have brought one for you too."

With a smile, Kian rose to his feet and walked over to the buffet, pulled out a napkin from the dispenser and handed it to her. "I don't know if you've noticed, but everyone is getting fatter around here. Those pastries have to go."

Horrified, Amanda glanced down at her belly. Her pants felt a little snug, but she had thought they'd shrunk because Onidu had laundered them by mistake instead of taking them to the dry cleaners.

Kian burst out laughing. "Just kidding. But that look on your face was priceless. Judging by your expression, an extra pound or two equals the end of the world."

"That was mean, Kian. But I forgive you because I love you."

He narrowed his eyes at her. "What do you want, Amanda? Is it new equipment for the lab?"

"Well yes, that's why I came to see you. But it has nothing to do with me being nice to you."

Kian had never refused any of her requests for lab equipment. He'd refused plenty of others, but not that. Her research was a priority.

"Do you have the paperwork for me?"

She pulled a stack of papers out of her purse and put them on his desk. Given the fact that she was Kian's sister, this was only a formality, but that didn't mean that she could skip preparing a detailed proposal explaining what the new equipment was for and how it would benefit her research.

Kian ran things, but he was doing it with the clan's money and needed proper documentation for all monetary investments.

Kian flipped through the proposal, pausing here and there, probably to glance at the bottom line. "The amounts are reasonable. I'll read it more carefully later."

"Thank you."

"Anything else before I call it a day and go up to have dinner with my wife?"

She was about to say no, when the image of Robert sitting alone in the café popped into her head.

"I saw Robert on my way down here. He is sitting all alone in the empty café. I feel sorry for the guy. He deserves better after what he did for Carol."

Kian put down her proposal. "He isn't lonely. If the rumors are right he found a replacement. Or rather she found him."

Amanda knew all about Ingrid, but the two were not meant for each other. It was a worse match than the one Robert had before. For some reason, she had a feeling her flower girl and Robert would hit it off. The question was how to get him out of the keep.

"Other than Sharon and Tessa, there is another potential female Dormant. A florist I stumbled upon by chance. I would love to take Robert out of here and introduce them. See if sparks fly."

Kian shook his head. "Clan females come first. He is the only unattached and available immortal male, and there are hundreds of single clan females. One of them might find he is her true-love match. And if that florist of yours is a Dormant, then there are a lot of clan males who are ahead of him in line."

"I disagree. Robert deserves more than the short end of

the stick he's gotten. And I have a feeling about him and the florist."

When Kian kept shaking his head, she lifted a palm to stop his rebuttal. "Hear me out. I know that this is highly unscientific and I have no proof, but it seems to me that the Fates reward good deeds. Especially when selfless sacrifice is involved. If I'm right, then Robert should be the next male to get his one true love."

"I hate all that mumbo jumbo, but I get what you're saying. The problem is, I'm still not a hundred percent sure he is who he claims to be, and letting him out of the keep is dangerous."

"You can't keep him locked in here forever, Kian. You're repaying his kindness with cruelty. Besides, this is a perfect opportunity to test him."

Amanda folded her arms over her chest. "I'm going to take him out with me, and as far as Robert is concerned, I'm the one responsible for him. His keeper. But we will have a Guardian trail us in case he tries anything. In fact, I'll make it easy for him to give me the slip."

Kian regarded her for a moment before nodding. "Agreed. I like the test idea. Not that I'll grant him freedom after only one, but we can test him periodically until I'm satisfied that this is not an elaborate hoax to find out our location and deliver it to the Brotherhood."

EVA

"Where is my granddaughter?" Eva asked as Nathalie joined her for lunch at the keep's café. It felt good to say it out loud without worrying about people overhearing and then looking at her as if she was nuts. A twenty-something woman talking about a grandchild.

But that wasn't why she was here. Eva had been hoping to play with Phoenix for a bit. If she couldn't come up to her daughter's apartment because Fernando was there, then Nathalie should've brought the baby with her to the café.

"She's at Andrew's sister's. I don't like bringing her down here. People go crazy, crowding her and wanting to hold her. I thought we could go up to Kian's and Syssi's and you could spend some time with her over there."

Eva shook her head. "We can't keep doing it. Scheduling visits for when Fernando is occupied elsewhere, meeting down here when he is at your apartment. Eventually, I'll have to face him, and vice versa."

Nathalie reached for Eva's hand. "I feel bad about this too.

But I'm afraid of what it would do to him. Imagine the shock."

"Has he been talking about me lately?"

"Not as much as he used to." She sighed. "He forgets more and more things."

Eva leaned back in her chair and pinned Nathalie with a hard stare. Enough was enough. "Let's go upstairs and deal with it once and for all."

"How? How do you explain his wife coming back and looking younger than she did when he met her? He is going to lose the tenuous hold he has on his sanity."

"I'll tell Fernando that I'm Eva's cousin's daughter and just happen to look a lot like her, and that I'm also called Eva after one of the family's matriarchs. I don't want to use a different name and confuse my granddaughter. It's enough that for the time being I have to give up being called Grandma."

Nathalie's expression was pained as she nodded. "I guess there is no other way."

"There isn't."

With a sigh, Nathalie pushed to her feet. "Come on. Let's get it over with." She pointed a finger at Eva. "But if his condition worsens, I'm holding you responsible."

Eva slung the strap of her purse over her shoulder. "No problem. I'm used to taking the blame."

"What's that supposed to mean?" Nathalie cast her a side-long glance.

"Don't tell me you didn't blame me for leaving Fernando. I'm sure you thought I was the one at fault."

They reached the elevators and Nathalie pressed the up button. "I didn't know what to think. You evaded my questions and Fernando said I needed to ask you. But as I told you before, I suspected the truth. I just didn't want to believe it."

The elevator arrived and they stepped in, each leaning against an opposite wall.

Pulling on the bottom of her shirt, a nervous habit Eva hadn't seen Nathalie indulge in since she was a teenager, her daughter looked up at her with guilt in her eyes. "Everyone was so sorry for Fernando. Customers offered their support, and not only the women. The only difference was that the men kept their thoughts to themselves while the women were more vocal about it. They all thought the same thing—that you left him because you found someone younger and more attractive."

Eva grimaced. "Of course they did. Fernando was the one they loved. I was the aloof wife. While offering their sympathies and pretending to be sad for him, I'm sure the ladies were glad to see Fernando back on the marriage market."

The elevator stopped at Nathalie's floor and they stepped out.

Reaching for Eva's hand, Nathalie clasped it. "Life is not fair. People make assumptions based on their own views. It was envy, Mom. Even with the ugly makeup and the baggy clothes you used to wear to hide your youthful appearance, you stood out. You couldn't hide your grace or the perfect symmetry of your features. Every guy entering the café cast you covetous glances, and every woman envious ones."

Eva chuckled and squeezed Nathalie's hand back. "I'm sure you're exaggerating. Every girl thinks her mom is the prettiest."

Nathalie leaned sideways and kissed Eva's cheek. "But mine really is. Suck it up, Mom. You're gorgeous. Own it."

Wrapping her arm around Nathalie's shoulders, Eva pulled her into a hug. "How did I get lucky with a daughter like you?"

"Win the lottery?" Nathalie pushed the door open and took a deep breath. "Ready or not, here we go."

Eva followed her inside. "I'm ready."

Was she though?

As she braced for facing her ex-husband after so long, Eva's heart sped up and the palms of her hands got sweaty. Nevertheless, she kept her expression neutral. Whatever was going on inside her, she had learned to hide it well.

Besides, she was supposed to act as if she was meeting him for the first time. There would be no rehashing of old pains. Just a great performance. Much easier to handle.

As they entered the apartment, Eva was relieved Fernando wasn't in the living room. By the sounds coming from one of the bedrooms down the corridor, he was watching a show.

"Should I call him to come out?" Nathalie asked in a small voice.

"What do you usually do when you have people over and he's home? Do you ask him to come and greet them?" Eva walked over to an armchair and sat down.

"No, I just let him know someone is here. Sometimes he comes to say hello, and sometimes he doesn't. Depends on what's on the television. If it's one of his favorite shows, then he isn't going to leave his room until it's over."

Eva crossed her legs at the ankles. "Do what you always do. Don't show that you're nervous. Act as normally as you can. With his bad memory, he probably takes a lot of cues from you."

Nathalie took a deep breath. "Got it. Act normal. Don't make a big fuss about my new visitor."

Eva smiled and nodded. "Exactly."

As Nathalie headed for Fernando's room, Eva leaned back in the armchair and assumed a relaxed posture. Faking it physically helped to fake it mentally. She was an old pro at that, but Nathalie wasn't. Every emotion was clearly written on that girl's face. Eva could read her like an open book and so could everyone else.

It was interesting that mother and daughter were so different from each other. Nathalie had Eva's looks and Fernando's friendliness, even though he wasn't her biological father. In that particular case, nurture had won over nature.

"Papi, I have a friend over, so don't come out in that old, stained T-shirt, okay?" Eva heard Nathalie deliver her instructions perfectly.

A grunt was her answer.

Nathalie chuckled. "Okay, okay, I'll let you get back to your show, sheesh."

"Will he come out at all?" Eva asked when Nathalie returned to the living room.

"After the show ends, if he remembers what I told him, he will be too curious not to come out." She sat next to Eva and put her head on her shoulder. "Are you nervous?"

"A little."

"I just want to warn you that you're in for a shock. He aged a lot during the years you were gone."

Mentally, Eva was prepared. Emotionally, she wasn't.

When Fernando shuffled into the living room, she barely managed to stifle a gasp, tears brimming in her eyes.

Fernando was a shadow of who he used to be. When she'd left, he'd been severely overweight, but full of vitality and charm and genuine love of life. The man who was staring at her with a confused expression on his face was much thinner, but it wasn't an improvement. He looked wilted, in body and spirit. Only his eyes still held some of the old spark.

"Who is your friend, Nathalie? She is the spitting image of your mother. Are you related to my Eva, Miss?"

Nathalie nudged her. "Go ahead, introduce yourself."

Eva pushed to her feet, plastered a friendly smile on her face, and extended her hand. "It's a pleasure to meet you, sir.

I'm Eva's cousin's daughter. I was told I look a lot like her. In fact, my mother also named me Eva."

Still staring at her face, he shook her hand, and the tears she was holding back almost spilled again. Fernando's handshake had used to be so strong. Now, the bones felt brittle, the grip feeble.

"I'm Fernando, Nathalie's father and Eva's husband. The other Eva, that is." He smiled. "It's a shame you missed her. She would've loved to see you." He winked, some of his old self shining through. "Or maybe not. She might've been a little envious of such a beautiful young lady."

Fernando lifted her hand to his lips and kissed the back of it. "Where have you been hiding for all these years?" His tone got flirtatious.

What a relief.

The old Fernando was still there. A little dimmed and confused, but thank God his personality wasn't all gone yet.

"I just moved to Los Angeles. I used to live in Tampa."

He held on to her hand, covering it with his other one. "Wonderful. That means we will be seeing a lot of you. Right, Nathalie?" He glanced at their daughter.

"She has an open invitation to come visit us anytime."

BHATHIAN

"*A*re you up for a walk?" Eva put her fork down. "I need to walk off all those calories." She patted her flat belly.

"Sure. It's a nice evening, but it's getting cold outside. I suggest you wear something over that tank top." The flimsy thing had a deep plunging neckline that revealed way too much cleavage. It was okay for hanging out around the house, but not out on a walk. He had enough trouble ignoring the looks Eva was getting when fully covered. That much exposed skin would make things worse.

Eva got up. "I'll get a cardigan. Do you want me to bring you a long-sleeved shirt?"

"No. I'm going to be a manly man and brave the cold in a T-shirt."

She chuckled. "You have nothing to prove, big guy."

Bhathian cast her a smile. "I'll clean up here."

While Eva headed upstairs, he collected their paper plates and tossed them in the trash, then wiped the table clean.

As he was finishing putting the leftovers in the refrigerator, Eva came back. "I'm ready."

He glanced at the cardigan she'd thrown over her shoulders. Not a big improvement since her enticing cleavage was still on full display. "You should button that sweater all the way up. It's not much of a protection when it's covering only your shoulders."

A small smirk lifted the corners of her mouth. "Is it about the elements or about this?" She glanced down at her breasts.

He pointed a finger at her. "Those are mine, and mine alone. I don't want horny humans gawking at you."

Eva threaded her arm through his. "I have you to protect me. With you by my side, no one would dare leer at me."

"Not openly. They cast overt leering glances when they think I'm not looking. But forget about them, you'll have me ogling your breasts and leering at you throughout our walk."

She tilted her head. "I'm fine with that. Are you?"

"Come here." He grabbed her around the waist and brought her flush against his body, letting her feel exactly what she was doing to him. "I'm more than fine. In fact, how about we skip the walk and do our physical activity upstairs?"

Eva stretched on her tiptoes and kissed his lips, giving him a few seconds of tongue action before pulling away. "Both. Let's walk first, sex later."

"As my lady wishes." He opened the front door.

The thing was, after all that teasing he was so hard that walking was going to be a problem. He'd manage. A few dark thoughts should take care of his arousal.

Bhathian had a big supply of those. The trick was to take a quick dip into the reservoir and collect a drop or two without getting drenched. Or worse, falling in. The danger of drowning in all that crap was all too real, and climbing out while weighed down by yesterday's horrors was difficult.

"I saw Fernando today." Eva cut through the dark thoughts.

That was big news. Trying to hide Eva from her ex, they had been tiptoeing around the guy for months. "How did he take it?"

She shrugged, but sad shadows clouded her eyes. "I told him that I was Eva's mother's cousin's daughter who was also named Eva."

Bhathian arched a brow. "And he bought it?"

"Yup. Not only that, he started flirting with me."

"Now, that's funny." On second thought, Bhathian wasn't sure she shared his opinion and cast Eva a sidelong glance. Thankfully, she was smiling.

"He'd changed so drastically since the last time I'd seen him, that I was grateful some of the old spark was still there and the Fernando I knew wasn't completely gone. Not yet." Her face got sad again.

Bhathian scratched at his stubble, not sure if he should ask the obvious question; whether Fernando's behavior opened old wounds.

"You're okay? Did his flirting bother you?"

She shook her head. "No. I was relieved. Poor man. You have no idea how sorry I feel for him."

"Sorry enough to forgive him?"

Eva looked up at him with teary eyes. "How can I hold a grudge against a dying man?"

Bhathian snorted. "I hold grudges against men long dead and gone, so that's not a given."

Eva leaned against him, letting him lead the way for a few silent minutes. "The dead you hate had probably been killers who had done horrible things. Fernando's crime was cheating on his wife. There is no comparison."

"He killed your marriage."

"You know what? Maybe it needed killing. Maybe he did me a favor. Imagine if I'd had to run while still married to him and believing I was abandoning not only my daughter but also my loving husband. It would've made me feel even worse."

Bhathian kissed the top of her head. "I'm glad you're ready to forgive him."

"Me too. Anger and resentment have a way of darkening the soul. Letting go of some of the darkness leaves room for more light to come in."

"Good philosophy. I wish I could adopt it."

"One drop at a time. If I can manage it, I think you can too." She wrapped her arms around his neck and pulled him down for a kiss, banishing the dark clouds that had gathered over his head.

When she released his mouth and pushed on his chest, Bhathian didn't let her go. Holding her to him with an arm wrapped around her waist, he cupped her cheek. "With you in my life everything is possible. You make me a better man."

"You're a good man, Bhathian, and it has nothing to do with me." Eva threaded her arm through his and turned them around. "Do you want to go down to the boardwalk? I could use more practice thralling."

"How about we do it some other time? I'm ready to head home and get to the second part of our fitness program for this evening."

Glancing down at the bulge that was once again straining the stitching of his zipper, Eva laughed. "Fine. I've tortured you enough. Let's go home."

14

EVA

"$\mathcal{I}$ believe we have the house to ourselves," Bhathian said.

Standing in the middle of the living room, she listened to the ambient sounds—the hum of the refrigerator, the window shade flapping in the mild breeze, and the cacophony of crickets outside.

The neighbors on one side of the house were watching the evening news, while the Krav Maga instructor on the other was probably out teaching a class in her dojo and had taken her dog with her. Her house was just as quiet as theirs.

With a big grin spreading across her face, Eva turned to Bhathian. "I believe you're right."

He leaned to whisper in her ear. "Let's go up and make some noise."

"Why are you whispering?"

He took her hand and pulled her toward the stairs. "I don't want to jinx our good luck."

"Our luck will run out soon. Nick will be back in time for his reality show. We need to hurry."

Like a couple of teenagers, they rushed upstairs, and

Bhathian even locked the door.

"No one will come up here. There is no need for that."

Bhathian waggled his bushy brows. "I beg to differ. In a few minutes, I'm going to make you scream so loud that the neighbors are going to call the police. I'd rather have the door locked so they can't come in and see my woman naked."

He prowled up to her, grabbing the bottom of her tank top and pulling it over her head. "That's mine." He cupped her breasts. "No other male gets to see that. Ever." He thrummed her nipples over the thin fabric of her bra, sending bolts of desire down to her center.

Arching her back, Eva closed her eyes, when a peculiar thought came out of nowhere, lifting her lips in a smile. "What if the male in question is one day old?"

Bhathian's hands stilled on her breasts. "Don't tell me that you are... that you are..." the poor guy stuttered and choked like an old engine.

"Relax, I'm not pregnant. I just wanted to point out that you need to be more precise with your vows."

Bhathian's huge chest deflated as he let the air out. "Don't shock me like that." He flopped back on the bed.

She lay down beside him, snaking her hand under his T-shirt and stroking smooth skin over hard muscles. "Would it be so bad? To have another child?"

Bhathian turned toward her and gathered her in his arms. "Nothing could make me happier. But is it something that you really want?"

She shook her head. "It's just one of those girly daydreams, like learning how to cook gourmet meals for my family. I can amuse myself with pleasant fantasies, but I know I'm not built for that."

"My love, you forget that time is not an obstacle. You can be one thing today and another tomorrow or twenty years from now."

She sighed and nuzzled his neck. "I'm too old to change."

With a snort, he cupped her buttocks and squeezed. "Oh, really? Dalhu was a mercenary, a ruthless soldier for centuries, and now he is an artist. You're a baby compared to him—change should be easy for you."

"It should, shouldn't it? One would think so, given my many disguises. I'm already used to playing different roles. But real life is not about putting on an act and wearing a disguise. The roles I play are for work, and, I have to admit, a form of amusement."

Another hand joined the first one on her butt, and Bhathian squeezed both cheeks. "What role would you like to play now?" he whispered in her ear, nibbling softly and sending shivers down her spine.

Usually, her moods and wishes dictated the kinds of games they played. Which meant that even when she ceded control to Bhathian, she was still running the show.

It suited her.

Eva loved how easily he adjusted to whatever she had in mind, and she loved knowing that, ultimately, she wasn't really giving up control. But it was a bit selfish.

What if Bhathian had fantasies of his own he wished to fulfill?

Eva was curious what went on in her warrior's brain.

Lucky for him, she could indulge him like no other. Getting into character was effortless for her, and it didn't have to be one that she'd practiced playing before. Eva was good at improvising too. Rubbing a finger over his fleshy lips she asked, "Who would you like me to be?"

He chuckled nervously. "I'm not an imaginative guy. I prefer when you do it."

"Not this time. Think. I'm sure that at one time or another you had a fantasy you wished fulfilled. Maybe as a teenager?"

His brows drawn, he ran his hand up and down her back. "I really can't think of anything. The only woman I ever fantasized about was you."

"Okay. Let's work with that. What did you do with me in your fantasies?"

His lips curved in a smile. "There were many. One was in the club. You came back, and I seduced you on the dance floor again. Another was on the plane, where we first met. I took you in the bathroom, standing up. But none of it requires you to act a part. You are all I ever wanted."

That was incredibly sweet. She couldn't have hoped for a better answer. Except, it didn't sate her curiosity. What made the big guy tick?

"What about when you were a teenager?"

Bhathian snorted. "At that age, a chair looked sexy to me."

"I'm not going to play a chair." She pretended to pout.

He pointed a finger at her forehead. "I know that there are endless plays in there. Much more interesting than anything I could ever come up with."

He was right, of course. Over the years, when she'd been restricting herself to once-a-month hookups, she'd built an arsenal of fantasies to fill the void.

Others might have watched porn or read erotic novels, but Eva didn't like either. Crude language and silly, unrealistic situations were not the stuff her dreams were made of. Her mind was much better at producing erotic scenarios to her liking. True, Bhathian starred in most of them, but in a variety of roles, as did she.

The good thing was that he didn't have any particular sexual preference and could go from sweet and gentle to dominant and even rough, and still be himself. The bad thing was that he had no acting skills whatsoever.

Bhathian could play himself in different moods.

That's all.

She needed to tailor her fantasy to suit him. "Okay. You win. I have one I think you'd like."

His eyes brightened. "I can't wait to hear it."

She pointed a finger at him. "Just so we are clear. It never happened. It's just a fantasy. So don't get all caveman on me."

He affected an indignant huff. "As if I ever."

"Right. Here it goes. I'm on an assignment, breaking into some tycoon's office to gather information for a client. The building is deserted, and there is no one patrolling. The only ones that are there are the security guys at the lobby. Or so I think. I get in through a back delivery door that I bribed someone to leave open and climb the stairs to the twelfth floor. Obviously, I can't use the elevators. With my trusty burglary tools, I open door after door in the tycoon's offices until I reach his. It's dark, but then it's not a problem for me."

Bhathian was hanging on her every word, which prompted her to get more animated.

"The moment I pick the lock, I know I'm in trouble. I can hear someone breathing, but I can't see him. I'm about to back away when I hear a gun cocking. 'Freeze,' he says. 'Hands in the air where I can see them. You move an inch, and I empty a clip into you.'"

Bhathian's eyes started glowing. "Where is he?"

"He is lying on a leather couch that has its back to the door. All I can see is the barrel sticking above it. I'm thinking to make a run for it, but as fast as I am I can't outrun a bullet. So I do as he says."

Bhathian smirked. "I think I can guess the rest. The tycoon wants sex in exchange for your freedom."

"Exactly. But he is into some kinky shit, and he wants to punish me first. I have no choice but to submit to an over-the-knee spanking."

Gleefully, Bhathian rubbed his hands together. "Perfect. After you get me all jealous with a tale of getting it on with a kinky tycoon, I'm more than ready to give you a thorough, bare-bottom spanking."

Eva lifted a brow. "Is there any other kind?"

"Nope. But I just wanted to make it clear that that's how it's gonna go down."

He was so eager to play, to please her in any way he could, that Eva decided to tell him the truth. "One more detail you should know. It was always you. In one fantasy you were the tycoon, in another a pirate, and a tough martial arts instructor in yet another. But it was always you."

His eyes softened. "We've spent so many years dreaming of one another. It's time to bring those dreams to life."

Eva couldn't wait. It was going to be so much fun. Before, their sexual games were about different moods. This was the first time they were going to enact one of the many scenarios she'd created over the years. "Are you ready to play, big guy?"

"There is one detail I need to clarify before we start."

"What is it?"

"Did your tycoon know that you're coming?"

"He didn't. He was working late and decided to take a nap on the couch."

"What about the gun? Why did he have it?"

Eva rolled her eyes. Just like a guy to ask about all the nitty-gritty irrelevant items. "He keeps a gun with him at all times because he has shady enemies who wouldn't hesitate to hire an assassin to take him out. Are we good now?"

It amazed her that Bhathian lacked the little imagination needed to fill in the gaps in her story. She should remember that for their next playtime.

"Yes. I'm going to lie on the couch and pretend I'm sleeping."

Eva grabbed her tank top off the floor and pulled it over her head, not bothering with a bra. After all, in a few moments it was going to come off again.

15

BHATHIAN

*A*s Bhathian stretched out on the couch, he wondered whether he should pull out one of his guns from Eva's fireproof safe in the closet. It would make the game feel more real. Pointing a finger was not going to have the same effect.

Not every detail was important, but some were more important than others. Instead of going out of the room and into the hallway, Eva had gone into the bathroom. But that didn't matter as much as the lack of a gun. A door was a door. A finger wasn't a gun. Damn it. He was sweating the details instead of mentally preparing to become the tycoon in her fantasy.

He was a crappy actor, but he could pull an angry and suspicious guy any day. As to the spanking, it wouldn't be the first time they'd played that particular game.

Whatever got Eva off was fine with him. As long as she found pleasure in whatever they were doing, he had no problem with it getting a little rough.

Like the professional she was, Eva made almost no sound when she opened the bathroom's door. All he could hear was her soft breathing. Her breaths were shallow. She was adjusting her game plan to his immortal senses.

It gave him an idea.

Why stick exactly to the scenario she'd invented? In her fantasy, the only way a man could threaten her was with a gun, but in here, Bhathian had superior strength on his side and much better training.

A gun was not necessary to make this scenario feel real.

He waited a few seconds longer, letting Eva creep up closer before leaping in the air, snatching her by the waist, and slamming her face down on the couch. The impact knocked the breath out of her. She groaned in what sounded like pain, but even if she was hurt, he wasn't stopping the game.

Eva was tough. Besides, she would be mad if he did.

He landed on top of her, pinning her arms behind her back and straddling her hips. She kicked up, trying to dislodge him, but he trapped her legs with his. "Who are you? Who sent you?" he growled in her ear.

"Please, mister, let me go. I'm just the cleaning lady." She did a good job of imitating a Cuban accent, which would've been believable given her looks.

"Right, and I am the Easter Bunny." He yanked her arms back harder. Trapping her wrists in one hand, he caged her neck with the other. "Talk, or I'm going to squeeze." He applied light pressure.

"Really, mister. I come to clean the office." She struggled under him.

Bhathian leaned and nuzzled her ear. "A beautiful woman dressed in a tank top is no cleaning lady. You're a spy, admit it. Who sent you?" His fingers closed around her slim neck with nearly bruising force.

"Please," she whimpered. "Don't kill me."

Damn, she was a fine actress. That whimper had almost

undone him. He had to remind himself that none of it was real.

But just to stay on the safe side, he eased his grip just in case he was indeed squeezing too hard. Perhaps he should move to the second act.

He leaned over her again. "I have ways to make you talk, young lady. Before long you'll be singing, not just talking. You'll do anything to stop the torment."

To his relief, she whimpered again, even more pitifully than before. It was an act. "Please, mister, let me go. I don't know what you're talking about."

He knelt and pulled her up by her wrists, then sat back and flung her over his knees. She fought like a wildcat, trying to get free, but he kept her hands pinned to her back and swung a leg over hers, locking her in place. She still fought, and he was glad it was so damn hard to keep her down. If she was giving a strong immortal male that much trouble, a human male had no chance of subduing her.

With a resounding smack, his hand landed on her still covered butt, and she yelped.

"Ouch, stop that. I told you I know nothing."

As Bhathian delivered an even harder one, the sound was so loud he was glad none of Eva's crew was home.

"Ouch…" she wailed so convincingly, he was tempted to ask her if she was okay.

Except, Bhathian knew Eva well. If she wanted him to stop, she would've used not only different words but a completely different tone. When Eva meant business, there was no mistaking her intentions.

When the next smack didn't come, she turned her head and winked at him, letting him know she was still acting. "Please, mister, let me go," she pleaded, but this time her tone was clearly theatricals.

Damn. He felt like an idiot for letting her down. Sensing

his confusion, she was purposely making her acting more transparent. It was for his benefit, and it was no doubt spoiling some of her fun.

"I'll let you go after you talk." As he yanked her pants and panties down, exposing her glorious behind, Bhathian had to take a moment to caress those magnificent globes. He thought he'd smacked her pretty hard, but they weren't even pinked.

"Mister, if that's how you're going to make me talk, I'll never say a word."

"Cheeky. In the position you're in, sassing me is not the best strategy." He brought his hand down on one cheek and then the other, alternating between the two in a fast volley of smacks that would've made a human female scream murder.

But his Eva moaned, pushing her bottom up for more.

He stopped, caressing the warmed skin and soothing the pain away. "Change of strategy, young lady. Since you seem to be enjoying this so much, I'm renegotiating the terms of your surrender. If you don't talk, I'll stop."

"Ugh. That's sneaky and unfair."

"You give me an honest answer, I give you two smacks."

"Ten."

"Five."

"Deal."

"Who are you?"

"I am a spy."

"I knew it." He smacked her bottom five times and stopped, caressing the ache away. "What's your name?"

"Patricia Evans."

Bhathian smiled. She used the alias he'd known her by before Andrew had discovered her real name. The pink shade of her bottom was getting darker, and the next five he delivered were more taps than smacks.

"Who sent you?"

"Your arch enemy."

"Which one?"

"That's two pieces of information."

"Sassing me again?"

Instead of answering, Eva wiggled her ass as much as her trapped position allowed.

It was time to change tactics again. Instead of a smack, he cupped her center, her copious juices coating his palm. Eva was soaking wet, so aroused that she was ready to detonate. He could use that to his advantage.

When he pushed a finger inside her wet heat, she moaned and let her head loll down to the couch.

He had her.

Pulling the finger out, he rested his palm on her bottom. "If you want more of that, you're going to have to tell me everything."

She groaned. "If I do, what are you going to do to me? I need to know what I'm bargaining for."

He smoothed his palm over her heated flesh. "First, I'm going to finger fuck you until you come, then I'm going to fill you up and fuck you long and hard, and after you're limp and exhausted from your second screaming orgasm, I'm going to make love to you."

She sighed. "That's a deal too good to turn down. But how do I know that you are going to deliver?"

"You'll have to trust me."

"Hmm, should I?"

He slipped a finger inside her again. "I think you should."

Eva moaned. "You're a cruel interrogator. Okay. I was sent by Mr. Boris Kashenko who wanted me to find out how much you were paying for his competitor's widget company."

"Aha, the notorious Boris."

"Yes."

"That information is worth a bonus."

"What do you have in mind?"

He lifted her up and carried her to the bed, divesting her of her pants and panties on the way.

As he laid her on her back, Eva pulled the tank top over her head and tossed it on the floor, then cupped her breasts and pinched her nipples. "Take care of me, big guy, before I self-combust."

"We wouldn't want that, would we?" He spread her legs wide and ducked between them.

Eva's scent was the best possible ambrosia, making him drunk with lust. He speared into her with his tongue, just to get a taste, once, twice, then replaced it with two fingers.

Her inner muscles clamped around his invading digits.

She was close.

As Bhathian lifted his head to take a look at the magnificent woman sprawled before him, he sucked in a breath. Panting, she was pinching and twisting her nipples hard, impatient and hungry for her release, her amber eyes glowing in the darkness like those of a predatory cat.

He pulled out and returned with three, stretching her wide as he extended his tongue and swiped over her clit.

On a mute scream, Eva's sheath spasmed around his pumping fingers, and her back arched off the bed.

Bhathian didn't wait. In a split second, his pants were off and he surged inside her as far as he could go. Setting a punishing tempo, he fucked her hard and fast just as he'd promised.

Eva met him thrust for thrust, her arms holding on tight, her nails digging into his ass, and her bottom lifting to get more of him inside her each time he retracted and pushed back. The bed groaned under the assault, banging against the wall, and once again Bhathian was glad there was no one besides them at the house. Except, with the racket they were making, the humans across the street could probably hear them.

When Eva arched again, opening her mouth on a scream, he caught it inside his own. Her climax hit him like a freight train. Letting go of her mouth, he sank his fangs into her neck and erupted inside her, bringing her to another climax and then another.

16

KIAN

"This is an emergency meeting." Kian addressed the Guardians and Andrew. "Onegus will fill you in."

He'd deliberately kept it secret until more information could be garnered. There was no reason to cause panic before he was sure it wasn't a misunderstanding. Hell, he'd been praying it was.

Regrettably, the worst had been confirmed.

The chief Guardian rose to his feet. "A civilian in the Bay Area was reported missing two days ago. Arwel and I flew in to investigate. We found him in the city morgue."

"Fuck." Bhathian banged his fist on the table. "How?"

"He was found beaten bloody in an alley. The cause of death was determined as brain hemorrhage resulting from a head trauma. But of course we know the real cause."

"But how?" Kri asked. "Andrew as well as Turner are monitoring incoming air traffic and nothing suspicious was reported."

Kian waved a hand. "The fact that nothing was reported is meaningless. If not for the tap at Dalhu's former headquarters, we wouldn't have known about Sharim and his men either."

Kri shook her head. "Still, Turner found their location."

"That's because they bought arms." Kian tapped his fingers on the table. "This time they either bought from a supplier Turner has no inside information about or decided on a different approach. But I have no doubt they are here. The question is how many and where."

"His last known whereabouts was a sex club in San Francisco. I checked it out, and it seems legit. There is a whole chain of them sprouting in various locations around the world, and they are all owned and run by humans. My guess is that he was at the wrong place at the wrong time. The Doomers were there either as guests of the facility or looking for immortal males. In any case, I issued a warning to stay away from that club and others until further notice."

Yamanu flipped his long hair back and tied it with a leather string as if readying for battle. "I'm not aware that the previous warning was rescinded."

"It wasn't." Onegus sighed and sat back down. "But we assumed that expensive, membership type clubs were safe. We were wrong, and we lost a good man."

"They interrogated him," Yamanu said.

"The moment he was reported missing, I ordered every immortal he was in contact with to run. He didn't know the location of the keep, but he could've given the Doomers the addresses of his friends."

Kian thanked the Fates for his insistence on secrecy. The few civilians who'd refused to leave the Bay Area hadn't been given the keep's address, and every clan member who knew it was forbidden to tell others about it. The penalty for revealing it was so severe Kian doubted anyone would do so voluntarily. An irrevocable forfeit of his or her shares in the clan's profits and a public whipping was a strong double deterrent.

Perhaps he should declare the same punishment for those civilians who were still prowling for hookups in clubs. As if those were the only places one could find a willing partner. For the males it was better to resort to call girls than risk their lives by going to clubs. The females had it easier. Males, human as well as immortal, were easy to seduce.

The Guardians were still frequenting clubs. His reasoning for allowing it was that they could take care of themselves and maybe even catch some Doomers in the act.

The thing was, they were setting a bad example.

It needed to stop.

"I want more than a warning. From today, going to clubs is forbidden. And that includes you guys." He waved his hand around.

"Come on, Kian. Where are we going to find any action?" Arwel was semi drunk, his words slurring only slightly. For him, it was as sober as he was going to get.

"Plenty of places. You can go to the beach, hang out in coffee places, college cafeterias… should I go on? There are single women looking for a good time everywhere. And if all else fails, you can afford call girls. I know. I sign your checks."

Thankfully, Kri had Michael because Kian didn't know if there were any call boys. But Kri wasn't the only female he was in charge of. The female population of the clan he was responsible for would face a similar problem. True, it was easier for the females to get a hookup than for the males, but not by much.

"Does anyone know if there are call services catering to women?"

Kri shrugged. "I can check. There should be. We are not living in the Dark Ages anymore. Women have needs just as men do, and finding a partner is not always easy. Sometimes paying for it saves a lot of time, not to mention the whole awkward morning after. I'm so glad I don't have to do it anymore."

"Good. That's your job. See what you can find. I want a report by tomorrow." Kian added the item to his agenda for the next day.

"Who wants to investigate the Allure club?"

Brundar raised his hand. "I'll do it."

Kian pointed the pen at him. "You got it. Choose a partner to watch your back."

"I don't need a partner. I work alone."

Kian narrowed his eyes at the Guardian, but engaging in a staring competition with Brundar was like trying to stare down a statue. Nothing affected him or made him uncomfortable.

Cold and unemotional.

Not for the first time, Kian wondered if it was a well-maintained façade or something that went deeper. He suspected it was the latter. No one could front for centuries, day in and day out. A mere façade would've cracked a long time ago.

The guy was cold to his core.

"You're not going in alone," Anandur said. "As I've learned from experience, you should never go without backup. Right, Onegus?"

The chief Guardian nodded. "The leader of the human team was right, and I'm not too old or full of myself to listen to advice from someone who knows what he's talking about."

Brundar cast his brother a chilling glance. "I know what I'm doing. I don't need you there. You have a tendency to attract attention."

Anandur snorted. "As if you can blend in with that face and that hair."

Brundar shrugged. "True. But I know how to keep my mouth shut. You don't. And I can cast an effective shroud. You can't."

If Anandur was offended by his brother's comments, he didn't show it. "I'm coming whether you like it or not. I'll stay in the car outside. If you're not out by the time we agree on, I'll come after you."

Brundar made a half-assed effort of staring his brother down, but Anandur was immune. After a few moments, Brundar conceded. "You're welcome to stay outside," he said in that flat, emotionless tone of his.

The two had a weird relationship.

Kian suspected that there was a story there, but for all the years they had served as his bodyguards, neither had volunteered any information. Given that they had joined the force at a young age, the big secret they shared must've happened when Brundar was still a kid. Anandur was several decades older.

Kian had never asked.

It wasn't any of his business. Besides, he had a feeling he wouldn't like to be privy to that one. For the brothers to keep it under wraps for hundreds of years, their secret must've been damn ugly.

17

BRUNDAR

"We are done for today." Brundar dropped the baton in his gym bag.

Carol was getting better. Not nearly good enough, but not as pitiful as she'd been at the start of the one-on-one training. The good thing was that she was finally taking it seriously and making an effort. The bad thing was that she still regarded combat training as a chore, a necessary evil.

In her mind, her job was to seduce. Not fight.

Wrong attitude, but he wasn't the right man to change it. He'd already explained that she needed to excel at both, but the lesson hadn't sunk in. Until Carol internalized and accepted it on her own, he would be wasting his breath trying to shove it down her throat.

"Thank you for your mercy, master." She bowed mockingly. "What happened? Do you have a hot date waiting for you?"

He cast her a hard stare, but the chit was one of the few people who were immune to them. He wasn't scaring her. "You're barely standing, and your arms are covered in purple bruises. You need to give those time to heal."

With a wince, Carol glanced at her arms. "Yuk, they look gross. It's a good thing I wasn't planning on going clubbing tonight."

He pointed a finger at her. "No one is going clubbing. Kian's orders."

She shrugged. "Wasn't planning on it anyway. After a session with you, all I can do is crawl into the shower and then straight to bed. You're a cruel and demanding master."

She had no idea. Or maybe she did? It was hard to tell with Carol. She wasn't submissive or conversely dominant, but she didn't strike him as vanilla either. She could be into exhibitionism, or voyeurism, or any number of other kinks. The list was long.

Perhaps she'd even been to the one he needed to investigate. "Have you heard about a sex club called Allure?"

She shook her head, her soft curls bouncing around her doll-like face. "It must be new. I used to know all of them, but ever since the abduction and then Robert, I've been away from the scene. Why?"

"The man we accompanied on his last journey last night visited the San Francisco branch of that club. Those were his last known whereabouts before he was found dead in an alley. I'm going to check out the local one tonight and fly to San Francisco tomorrow. There isn't much information online. It doesn't even say on their website that it's a sex club."

"Maybe it isn't."

"According to Eva, it is. She was there on an investigation. It's a high end, members-only, sex club."

Carol's eyes brightened. "Take me with you. We can pretend to be a kinky couple."

The idea was preposterous. They were closely related, and Brundar regarded Carol as he would a younger sister. If he had one, he sure as hell wouldn't be taking her with him to a kink club. "Not going to happen." He bent and lifted his gym bag.

Carol put her hands on her hips. "Why not? You've got an expert here. You should utilize me."

His lips curved up into an involuntary smile. Whatever expertise Carol believed she had in the lifestyle, it couldn't compare to his. But he wasn't about to share that with her or anyone else for that matter. Even his own brother didn't get to pry into Brundar's sex life.

"First of all, you're family. I'm not going to engage in anything even remotely sexual with you. Secondly, you're training to become a spy. Did you forget your cover story? You're supposed to be a naive runaway girl who gets caught by the big bad wolf. Do you think being seen in a place like that club fits that story?"

Disappointed, Carol dropped her arms to her sides. "No. Damn, I was hoping to find some action with someone other than my mechanical boyfriend."

He almost smiled again. Carol, with her self-deprecating humor and sunny disposition, managed to pierce his darkness like no other. Her Cupid-like appearance matched her personality, but instead of love, the arrows in her quiver were made of pure sunshine.

No wonder men gravitated toward her.

He cast her a parting glance. "Then count yourself lucky that you have tomorrow off. Go to the mall or the nearest college and pick up a young healthy male."

She crinkled her nose. "In a pinch, they would do. But I prefer men who are more seasoned and preferably wealthy."

If those were her preferences, then Allure might be perfect for her. But not while Doomers hunted for immortals in places like that.

"I'll see you the day after tomorrow, Carol. On time."

Hiding a smirk, she nodded.

Punctuality wasn't her strong suit, but she was getting better at that too.

It was a wonder the two of them got along as well as they did. The disciplinarian and the rule-breaker. Anyone else doing the things she did would've gotten under his skin, but not Carol.

It was the guilt. A feeling Brundar was unfamiliar with and was therefore troubled by.

Before her abduction, he hadn't held Carol in high esteem. Like everyone else, he thought of her as the irresponsible, good-for-nothing, lazy airhead.

She'd proven him wrong and had gained his respect. He was ashamed of what he'd thought of her before.

Then she went ahead and accepted the most dangerous mission possible. A lot of imperfection could be forgiven in the face of such bravery and strong will.

ROBERT

*A*s Robert glanced out of the Porsche's window, observing the streets and the shops they were passing by, he couldn't believe he was out of the keep.

It wasn't freedom, not yet, but it was as close as he'd got to it in months. Kian must've started trusting him if he'd let him accompany his sister. Either that or the female had some special tricks up her designer sleeve and was capable of incapacitating a well-trained, strong warrior.

Just like Navuh's sons, Annani's children were no doubt extremely powerful immortals. The closer one was to the source, the more godly abilities one retained.

Then again, she might be carrying on her person the remote control to his cuff, and if he tried anything, she could detonate the explosives embedded in it.

Yeah, it was one or the other. Otherwise, Kian's sudden change of heart didn't make sense. Nothing significant had happened in the week since Kian had told him that it wasn't time yet.

"How does it feel to be out?" Amanda cast him a quick sidelong glance.

"Great. And I'm grateful, but I don't know what prompted it. Kian didn't give me any indication that he was even softening to the idea."

Amanda smirked. "I have a way of changing his mind."

Robert frowned. This was Amanda's doing? But why? Surely she wasn't interested in him. According to Kian, she and Dalhu were true-love mates.

"I don't understand why you would do that for me?"

She shrugged. "You deserve better than what you're getting. Especially since Carol threw you out."

Robert crossed his arms over his chest. "She didn't throw me out. We decided it was time to end it."

Amanda looked doubtful.

He added, "She cried when we parted."

"She did? Then she must've cared for you. Why end things?"

Robert sighed and let his arms drop. "I think Carol cried out of guilt and not because she was sad to see me go. The truth of the matter is that we weren't meant for each other. We got along amiably, most of the time, and I even believed I loved her. But she never loved me back."

"You say you believed you loved her. Does that mean that now you know you didn't?"

"I guess not. It was easy enough to hook up with someone else. Bhathian said that I would've been devastated if I really loved her. The breakup was difficult but not devastating."

Amanda tapped her long-nailed fingers on the steering wheel. "Are you still with that new someone?"

It was kind of ridiculous how both of them pretended as if Amanda didn't know perfectly well who that someone was. There were no secrets in the keep. Rumors spread faster than an electrical current.

"No. I broke it off."

For some reason, Amanda looked relieved. Hell, he really

hoped she wasn't interested in him. Dalhu would have his head.

Literally.

The guy owned a sword.

But as unbelievable as it seemed, it was the only explanation that he could come up with. Otherwise, why would she bother getting him out of the keep?

What was in it for her?

Damn. He was a dead man. To refuse Annani's daughter would mean his certain death by her hand or that of her mother, and to indulge her would mean the same by Dalhu's.

Robert pressed himself against the passenger door, putting as much distance between him and Amanda as the tiny sports car allowed.

"What happened? Why did you break it off?" she asked.

Crap. Think fast. What could he say that would convince her he wasn't worth the effort?

Fortunately, Carol had supplied him with plenty.

"I'm a boring guy. Both Carol and Ingrid thought so. I'm not an exciting lover either. In fact, I'm a sucky lover. No staying power and no finesse. Three minutes and it's over. Bada bing bada boom." He clapped his hands for emphasis.

Amanda's chest started heaving with laughter. "Why are you telling me that? Most guys would do the opposite, boasting how amazing they are in bed."

"It's easier that way. No expectations mean no disappointments."

Amanda frowned. "For whom?"

"The next female who is interested in me. I figured I'd better lay things out on the table, so she'll know what she's getting."

What else could he say that would make him sound like a terrible choice for a lover? He needed to be careful, though, and not overdo it or she would get suspicious.

Aha, got it.

"It's hard to break old habits. In the Brotherhood's camp, showering is communal, and after a long day of training, the guys don't have the energy to trudge all the way over there. I'm used to showering maybe once a week. I tried to do better for Carol, but still, doing it every day is too much. Twice a week is the most I'm willing to do."

Amanda's perfect brows pointed down, creating deep creases in her forehead. "What is this all about, Robert? I've never heard a man trying his damnedest to appear as unappealing as he could."

He bet she hadn't. Males would do everything to impress a gorgeous woman like her. And maybe if she weren't mated, Robert would've done the same. But a hookup, even with a woman like her, wasn't worth his life.

"I'm being honest."

"Are you now? Are people driving you crazy trying to play matchmaker? Is that what's going on? Is everyone trying to hook you up with someone?"

Not sure how to answer her, he shrugged.

"Look. I only want you to take a look at the girl. You don't even have to talk to her. It's a little test I'm running. Nothing more. I'm not trying to hook you up with anyone. I promise."

Thank Mortdh.

Robert sagged in relief. Amanda wasn't interested in him. She wanted him to meet someone. That was strange too, but whatever. As long as it wasn't her, he would look at a hundred women if she wanted him to.

"Sure. I'll take a look. Is she pretty?" He didn't give a fuck, but he was playing along.

Amanda patted his shoulder. "She is. But what I think you'll like most is her personality. She is very peaceful. Now tell me which part of your story was true and which part wasn't."

AMANDA

*L*ooking both relieved and embarrassed, Robert shifted in his seat. "I shower every day."

Amanda chuckled. "I thought so. You smell good. What aftershave is it?" She leaned sideways to take a better sniff.

Robert leaned away, plastering himself against the passenger door as if she was carrying some contagious disease he was afraid of catching.

What was wrong with that guy?

He was behaving so strangely. If she weren't living with an ex-Doomer, Amanda would've thought that it had something to do with the brainwashing those guys were subjected to. But Dalhu was not afraid of females.

Was it her? Was she scaring the guy?

That must've been it. People often found her intimidating. Still, until today, Robert had never acted so weird around her.

"It's nothing fancy. Just Brut," he mumbled.

Maybe the difference in their stations was bothering him. Riding in a Porsche with the daughter of a goddess must be overwhelming for poor Robert. She needed to put him at ease. Let him know that she didn't value wealth and station over merit.

"I love Brut. It's simple and yet very masculine. If you ask me, all those fancy perfumes guys spend a fortune on just make them smell feminine. Real men go with simple stuff."

It wasn't helping. Robert was starting to look like a rabbit caught in a snare.

"Besides, it's what a man does that counts. You're a hero, Robert. That makes you a better man than a prince. Don't forget that."

The sigh that escaped his throat sounded like a whimper. Amanda was at a loss. How the heck was she going to make him relax around her?

"Forget who I am. It doesn't matter that I'm Annani's daughter. In here we are just people, and we should be judged based on our efforts and accomplishments, not our birthright."

Not helping.

Damn. Maybe a change of subject was needed. "What about Ingrid? Why did you break things off with her?"

Robert closed his eyes and sank into his seat with what looked like utter defeat. "If there was one lesson I learned from what happened between Carol and me, it was that dragging out a relationship just because it's convenient was the wrong thing to do. People get used to one another, and instead of searching for the right person, they stay with the one that is there."

"Very true. When you find the one that's meant for you, you know it. No one else would do, no matter what."

"Is that how you feel about Dalhu?" Robert cast her a quick glance, then looked away as if afraid of her answer.

Strange, strange man.

"Yes. From the first moment I met him." She chuckled.

"Even though he kidnapped me and terrified me, I couldn't stop lusting after him. But that was only the start. I didn't want Dalhu to be the one. My brother wanted nothing to do with me because I gave myself to a Doomer. And yet I couldn't imagine life without him. I was willing to take on the entire clan to have Dalhu as my mate."

Robert perked up. He sat up straight and actually looked at her when he asked, "You really love him, don't you?"

"Of course. What kind of a question is that?"

Oh, damn.

Suddenly it all made sense.

Amanda wanted to slap her hand on her forehead. She was such an idiot. The poor guy thought that she was whisking him away from the keep to have her way with him.

And he was terrified by the idea?

What the hell? Was she losing her appeal?

It would've been funny if it wasn't so insulting.

Robert shifted in his seat again, his olive skin turning a shade darker. "I don't know you or Dalhu well. Maybe if I did it would've been more obvious to me."

She turned her head and pinned him with her teacher's stare, the one she used on students who tried to put one over on her. "Tell me the truth, Robert. Did you think I was coming on to you?"

His face turning crimson, he looked away.

"I wasn't. I'm taking you to see a woman I believe is a Dormant because I have a hunch the two of you might be meant for one another."

"I know, you told me so."

He wasn't getting off the hook so easily. "What I don't understand, though, is why the idea repulsed you so. I'm considered a very good-looking woman. Any other man in your situation would've been thrilled to be the object of my desire. Though, let me stress again, I'm happily mated to Dalhu and have absolutely no interest in you."

Robert's face looked even more crestfallen than before. "I'm so sorry. You are a beautiful woman. The most beautiful I've ever seen. And if you weren't Dalhu's, I would've been honored and delighted. But we both know what he would've done to me." Robert slashed his hand across his neck. "And if I refused you, Annani's daughter, I would've been a dead man too. Please tell me you understand."

Patting his shoulder, she laughed. "I do. Poor Robert. I'm so sorry I didn't tell you from the start what this was about. I wanted to see your authentic response to Melissa. Now that you know, it's not going to be the same."

He chuckled. "Maybe we should do it some other time. When at peak state, I can hardly charm a lady, let alone with the amount of adrenaline coursing through my body right now."

"You don't need to charm her. Just be yourself." Amanda eased the Porsche into a parking spot and cut the engine.

Robert unbuckled and got out. "You mean my old boring self?" he asked as she joined him on the sidewalk.

"Exactly. We don't want false advertising, right?"

"Right." He pushed the flower shop's door open and held it for her.

Amanda stepped inside, letting the soothing smells and sounds engulf her. Melissa's shop was like a little piece of paradise.

"Melissa, where are you?" she called.

"I'm back here."

Amanda threaded her arm through Robert's. "Come on. And lose that stiff posture. Act natural."

"Yes, ma'am."

At the back of the shop, they found Melissa with an armload of flowers, collecting more from various buckets.

"Do you need help with that?" Robert asked.

"No, thank you. I'm done."

She turned around. "Amanda, what a nice surprise. Who are you buying flowers for this time?"

"My mate. I mean my boyfriend."

Melissa looked at her askance. "Is that the handsome guy next to you?"

"Oh, no, this is Robert. My cousin. He is helping me choose. Robert, say hello to Melissa."

"Hello. It's nice to meet you." He extended his hand, forgetting Melissa's hands were full, then retracted it.

"Nice to meet you too. Follow me to the front, please. I need to put these down."

As they went through the motions of picking and choosing the right arrangement that was supposed to be for Dalhu, Robert and Melissa exchanged no more than five words.

Obviously, there was no chemistry there. Either that or Robert was still stressed out over his misunderstanding.

"Anything?" she asked as they exited the store.

He shook his head. "She is nice. But I felt nothing special. She seemed like any other human female."

Amanda pressed the remote and unlocked her car. "Okay. So no romantic feelings. Anything else? Would you have liked her as a friend?"

He entered the car and fastened the seatbelt. "I guess. Melissa is nice enough."

Damn, this wasn't what she'd been hoping for. Evidently, her gut feeling was misleading.

20

LOSHAM

"*I* know it's not my place, sir, but why did you order the immortal male killed?"

Losham regarded his assistant fondly. No one else would have dared question Losham's decisions. Not that Rami's intention was to voice doubt or disagreement, the man was well aware of Losham's superior intelligence, but he wanted to understand.

Not a bad quality. Blind obedience had its merits, but it wasn't the same as a worshipful one. Besides, it was a teaching opportunity. Rami should learn to think logically.

"Why do you think we should've kept him alive?"

Rami was familiar with Losham's deduction process and knew he was being led step by step to the right answer. Therefore, he wasn't afraid to speak freely. "Maybe more torture would've eventually made him talk. Or maybe we could've used him as a bargaining chip."

"You can't torture information from someone who doesn't have it. He would've started inventing lies just to stop it."

Rami smoothed his palm over his short beard. "How can you be sure that he really didn't know?"

"Of course he told us everything. He was a civilian with no training. He told us everything else. The clan leaders are smart enough to keep their headquarters secret even from their own people."

"What I don't get is, how did the other immortals whose addresses he gave us know to run? We got there as soon as we could."

"Evidently, not soon enough."

That one was Losham's bad. Shameful. In his quest to avoid suspicion, he'd made the mistake of employing only two immortals per club and shorthanded the operation. Those who'd captured the civilian in the San Francisco club had to get information out of him first and go after his friends later—after they were done interrogating him. With more men in place, they could've split up and done both things at the same time.

The clan must have a system in place for emergency situations like that. Once a member was reported missing, all his clan contacts got evacuated immediately.

After millennia of running and hiding, it was no wonder they were experts at escape routes and organizing evacuations. Everything functioned like a well-oiled machine.

Good for them, but not for Losham. The fact that civilians were kept in the dark about the whereabouts of the clan headquarters presented him with a problem, leaving him with two possible options.

He could continue the hunt just for the sport of it and kill as many clan members as his men could get to. With so few of them out there, he could cripple their operation just by further reducing their numbers.

The other option was to hunt for Guardians.

One or more would no doubt get sent to investigate the

San Francisco club, but the two men he had stationed there would not be enough to capture one of those super warriors. Losham had issued a do-not-engage order.

Until he could secure reinforcements, the operation had been put on hold.

"What about keeping him as a bargaining chip?" Rami asked.

"And court a rescue mission? Not a good idea. A dead man means a Guardian or two sent to investigate. A missing one means every Guardian they can mobilize looking for him, and probably several squadrons of hired human mercenaries. That's why I ordered his body dumped where it would be easily found instead of eliminating the evidence. When there is a body, there is no search party."

Rami nodded. "As always, I'm astounded by your brilliance, sir."

Losham patted his assistant's shoulder. "I too make mistakes, Rami. We need more men for backup."

"It's not going to be easy to get them. It was difficult to secure two per club."

"I know." Some groveling would be required.

21

ANDREW

"You're sure about that martial arts class?" Roni asked as they walked toward Andrew's car with Barty lumbering behind them.

"It will kick your fitness level up a notch. Lifting weights makes you look good, but moving and getting your heart rate up is crucial to your health, not to mention pumping blood into your brain to keep it in top working condition. Right, Barty?" Andrew turned his head back and winked at the handler.

Roni still had no idea what it was all about. Andrew had used his considerable powers of persuasion to sell the kid on the martial arts class, and then convince Barty and his supervisors that it was important. Roni had been sold on the idea once Andrew mentioned that Sylvia was going to be there. Barty and his boss were sold once Andrew explained how critical cardio was to Roni's brain function. Naturally, they couldn't object to something that promised to keep their most valuable asset at top performance.

"That's right, boy. Cardio is just as important as weights, and I don't see you hitting the treadmills."

Roni shrugged. "I'm not a gerbil."

Andrew rolled his eyes. Barty could use some cardio himself. No wonder the only job the agent could get was babysitting Roni. "How about you, Barty, want to learn some new moves?"

Barty hiked his pants up. "I know plenty of moves. Don't let this gut fool you. I can still kick both your skinny asses."

Roni snorted. "Right."

As Andrew clicked the car doors open, the kid rushed to claim the shotgun seat. Barty settled in the back, pushing the baby's car seat aside. "How is the family, Spivak?"

"Fantastic. Thanks for asking. How is yours?"

"Oh, you know. The kids are grown. It's only me and the missus now."

Andrew turned on the ignition. "Empty nesters. Now you can dance naked in the house."

"Yeah, that would be a sight." Barty chuckled.

When they arrived at the dojo. Andrew peeked through the front window. Everything was set up as planned. Anandur had negotiated with the owner a rental agreement for the next month that granted him the use of the dojo twice a week for a couple of hours.

Sylvia and five other immortal females were already there, clad in the requisite white uniforms and practicing moves with each other.

The idea had been Sylvia's. Instead of bringing in Carol, she'd mobilized her friends. All six were hotties. Their mission was again to distract. This time, poor old Barty.

He'd met Ashley, Monica, and Amber before. They'd played the decoy part in the attack on the Doomers' base. The other two were new.

"Is that the instructor?" Roni pointed at Anandur.

"Yes."

"He is not Asian."

Andrew lifted a brow. "That sounds a bit racist. Does it matter?"

Barty snorted. "Our boy Roni is not known for political correctness, or for any social graces. But he is right. I've never seen a martial arts instructor who was six and a half feet tall. This man is a giant."

Andrew pretended affront. "Tsk, tsk. Are you discriminating against tall people now, Barty? Shame on you." He pulled the door open, letting Roni and his handler go ahead of him.

"Look at that," Barty whispered. "Premium pussy bazaar."

Roni cast him a disgusted glance. "You're a dirty old man. They could be your daughters. How old is your daughter? Twenty-seven?"

"Yeah. But these hotties are not mine. I can look. At my age it's the only fun I have left."

Andrew stifled a snort. For all he knew, some of these hotties might be older than Barty. But what bothered Roni the most was that the guy was ogling his girlfriend.

"Just don't look at that one." The kid pointed to Sylvia. "She is mine." He walked over and kissed her cheek. "Hi, baby."

She wrapped her arms around his neck. "Hi, yourself. I'm so glad you decided to join the class. Anandur is a great instructor. You're going to love it."

Anandur walked over with a big grin under his bushy red mustache. "I assume you are Roni." He offered his hand. "I'm Anandur, and I'm the guy who is going to put you in the best shape of your life."

As Sylvia let go of Roni and rejoined her friends, Roni eyed Anandur. "I don't know what you have in mind, but I suggest you dial down your expectations. I'm not training for a gold medal. I only want to look good for the ladies." He tilted his head toward the group of sparring females.

Anandur clapped him on the back. "Naturally, my man." He bent to whisper in Roni's ear. "That's why we all do it. But if I go easy on you, these beauties are going to kick your butt, and it's going to be damn embarrassing. Especially if you lose to your girlfriend. You know what I'm saying?"

Barty snorted and walked over to the row of chairs lined against the wall. Taking a seat, he folded his arms on top of his big belly and crossed his legs at the ankles.

Very smoothly, the women maneuvered so they were right in front of him, blocking his view of the rest of the dojo. Judging by the big smile on his pudgy face, Barty was fine with that.

The show was on.

"Follow me to my office," Anandur said. "There are some forms you need to sign. You know, insurance stuff. And of course there is the matter of payment."

Andrew glanced at Barty, but the handler waved him on. "It's okay. You can keep an eye on him in there. Just make sure he doesn't get near any computers."

Andrew saluted. "Will do."

It couldn't have gone down more perfectly than that.

The dojo's office was the size of a closet. There was a desk, a chair on one side of it and two on its other, and a metal filing cabinet. No computer. Just a phone. Closing the door behind him, Anandur motioned for Roni and Andrew to take a seat, then walked over to the chair on the other side of the desk, squeezing his bulk into the tight space.

The tiny office was on a scale appropriate for the real owner of the dojo, who fit the stereotype Roni and Barty had been alluding to. Din was a five foot four or five Hawaiian of Japanese descent.

Anandur and Andrew exchanged glances. They hadn't agreed ahead of time who would deliver the news to Roni because it depended on who would get to be alone with him.

Although Barty had reacted exactly as they'd predicted, it hadn't been a sure thing.

Anandur leaned forward, bracing his elbows on the desktop. "Damn, I wish Amanda was here. She is so much better at this than either of us."

With a frown, Roni glanced from one to the other. "What's going on, Andrew? This isn't about martial arts, is it?"

"This is a cover so we can talk outside the federal offices which are wired up the wazoo."

Roni nodded. "And he is?" He pointed at Anandur.

"A friend of Sylvia's. In a moment it will all become clear." Andrew rubbed his hand over his nape, thinking where to start. The grandmother seemed like a good opening.

"Your grandmother might still be alive and look exactly the same as she did on that first driver's license photo because she is an immortal."

Roni snorted. "Yeah, right. What is it? Make fun of Roni day?"

"Do I look like I'm joking?" Andrew pointed to his face. "Now shut up and listen." He'd never taken such a sharp tone with the kid before. Not because he hadn't wanted to, Roni was an annoying prick, but because he'd needed his help and couldn't risk alienating him.

Smart guy that he was, Roni shut his yap and nodded.

"Immortals exist and they are hiding among humans. They always did. They are the descendants of the gods, the children those beings had with humans. The special genetics are inherited through the mother. So if your grandmother on your mother's side is an immortal, it means that you carry those genes. There is a way to activate them. You can become an immortal. On top of gaining immortality, you'll become stronger and all of your senses will become sharper. You might even grow a couple of inches."

Roni's sharp eyes regarded Andrew for a long moment. "So that's what happened to you. Why you grew taller and more muscular in the span of a couple of weeks. I've been wondering about that. Now I know."

"Right on. You get an A on the test."

"And him?" He pointed at Anandur again.

"He is an immortal, and so is your girlfriend."

Roni's eyes widened. "Sylvia too?"

Andrew smiled. "Some immortals have special abilities. Sylvia can fritz out electronics at will and with precision. How do you think I was able to sneak her in?"

The kid swallowed. "That's the part I find most difficult to believe. Why did she agree to do it? And why did she stay? I know I'm not a great catch." He lifted his arm and flexed his barely-there muscles.

Andrew lifted his arms. "Beats me. Women are strange creatures. Mortal and immortal alike. She had an option to thrall you and make you believe you had sex with her, or do it for real. For reasons beyond my comprehension, she chose to actually do it."

"What do you mean, thrall? Like in the vampire movies?"

"Exactly. Immortals can get into your head and make you forget things or remember things that didn't happen."

Roni narrowed his eyes at Andrew. "Did you do it to me?"

"No. I'm new, and I don't know how to do it yet. But let's get to the point of this before Barty gets suspicious. Do you want to go for the transition, become an immortal?"

"How?"

"Immortal males have fangs and venom. The venom is what activates the dormant genetics. But the problem is that they can do it only in two situations. With a female during sex, or with a male during a fight. A certain level of aggression is needed for the fangs to elongate and the venom to be produced. If you're lucky, it will happen after one time. If not, you'll need a repeat. I had to go through it twice, and I almost didn't make it. But you're young. Your chances are better."

"What will happen to me during the transition?"

"You'll develop a fever and you might or might not lose consciousness. Everyone is different. It takes weeks for the fangs to reach their full length, and months for the venom glands to become active. Once they are, you'll have the urge to use them every time you have sex. But don't worry about it. The venom contains an aphrodisiac and a euphoric. Sylvia is going to love it."

Roni smoothed a hand over his jaw. "Will I be able to stay where I am and work?"

"No. I can do it because at the end of the day I go home. You don't. Pretending twenty-four-seven is difficult. But why would you want to stay? You're a prisoner. We can get you out. You can be with Sylvia as much as you want and work for the clan. The immortals, I mean."

Roni kept rubbing his chin. "I need to think about it. I'm sitting on top of the best source of information in the world, and as far as I know, it's impossible to hack from the outside. Unless I manage to code a backdoor into it, I can't leave. Not yet." He smiled sheepishly. "I'm kind of addicted to the power."

A knock sounded on the door a split second before Barty opened it and barged in. "Are you guys done yet? How long does it take to fill in a few forms?" He looked around the office. "At least there are no computers here."

"I'm sorry about that. I got carried away telling Roni about all the competitions I won," Anandur said. "You're welcome to join. I have many more tales to tell."

Barty grimaced. "It's much more interesting out there." He waved a hand at Anandur. "Enough with the stories. Finish the paperwork and get down to training the kid. As lovely as those girls are to watch, I want to finish my day and go home at some point."

"You've got it. Five minutes tops."

Barty pointed a finger at Anandur. "No more than that." He closed the door behind him.

Andrew leaned and squeezed Roni's shoulder. "It's not an easy decision, but in the end there is only one thing to do. Immortality is hard to resist. But I get that you need time to think. For the next month, we'll be meeting here twice a week. You can give me your answer then."

"Thank you."

"Needless to say, don't mention any of what we've talked about in the office building. Not even to Sylvia in your own bedroom. You can never be too careful. It's one thing to sneak in a girlfriend, it could be explained away and maybe even forgiven. But talk of immortals and Dormants may put the clan at risk. And that includes your girlfriend."

Roni nodded. "I understand."

22

BHATHIAN

"You can hold her, she is not a newborn anymore." Eva handed Bhathian their granddaughter. "Here, I'll show you how."

Eva put the baby in the cradle she'd made with his arm, so her head was resting on his bicep and her little butt was in the palm of his hand. She kicked with her little legs, her tiny feet dancing on his ribs.

"Please don't go," he told Eva as her hands left the baby's small body. "I'm afraid I'll drop her. Or squeeze her. She is so fragile."

"You won't. But you might feel more comfortable sitting down with her."

"Yeah, I'll do that." He backed to the couch, carefully, as if he was holding a pot overflowing with boiling water and any jarring move would cause it to spill.

Lowering his butt to the couch, he put his thigh muscles to good use, going as slowly as possible. All through that, his granddaughter was regarding him with a curious expression on her little face, wondering who was that strange man holding her.

When he finally relaxed and leaned back, she smiled and lifted a little hand to his cheek, patting him as if to say, good job. Such a little cutie.

"Talk to her." Eva sat down next to him and made funny faces at the baby.

"What should I say? She doesn't understand language yet." He wasn't going to make a fool of himself like her parents.

"How is she supposed to learn if you don't talk to her? Babies need to be talked to a lot. You can tell her she is the most beautiful baby girl in the world, or you can tell her about your day. It doesn't really matter." Eva waved a hand. "As long as you use a gentle loving tone, you can talk about baseball or football or whatever sports you like to watch."

Okay, he could do that. "What sport are you going to play when you're a big girl?"

The baby smiled and cooed.

Bhathian turned to Eva. "Hey, I think she is talking back to me."

"Yes, she does." Eva started with that silly baby talk.

He shushed her with the hand that wasn't holding his precious cargo. "It's my turn to talk to my granddaughter." He turned to the baby and smiled. "I bet you will like basketball. You're going to be a tall girl. A tall, pretty girl that all the boys will chase. But Daddy and Granddaddy are going to chase them all away."

The baby scrunched her nose in protest.

Eva leaned over him and rubbed her tummy. "That's right, little girl. You tell that big old fool that it's none of his business and that you're going to decide which boy you allow to catch you. Right, Phoenix?"

Their granddaughter smiled the sweetest toothless smile and reached for Eva's dangling hair, catching a few strands and giving them a mighty yank.

"Ouch, she is strong." Eva pried the tiny fingers open.

"That's my granddaughter," Bhathian said proudly.

Nathalie entered the room with a baby bottle in one hand and a little blue blanket in the other. "Okay, you guys, play-time is over. Phoenix needs to eat and go nappy." She lifted the baby off his arm.

"Did you have fun with Bhathian, Phoenix? Did you? I bet you did. He is so big and strong. Yes, he is..." Nathalie kept up the baby talk on her way to Phoenix's room.

"You did well." Eva patted his arm.

"I did?" He felt like he'd been pretty pathetic.

"Next time you'll hold her longer. By the way, you don't have to wait for me to come here to visit your daughter and granddaughter. You are here all day. You should stop by, especially when I'm out of town. It's good for the baby to see other people besides her parents. Also, it gives Nathalie a breather when someone else plays with Phoenix."

He hated the days Eva was gone. There had been more of them lately. She was flying out of town almost every week and staying away two or three days at a time. The house in Venice was costing her a fortune and forcing her to take on more and more jobs. Since he was sharing it, he'd dared to offer to share in the expenses as well, but Eva had gotten so mad at him for suggesting it, she hadn't spoken to him for the rest of that day.

Bhathian had gone to see Kian the same evening.

Kian loved the idea of Eva working for the clan. For the first time in forever, they had a few solid leads on immortals who were not part of either camp. It required an investigative effort that could not be done by outsourcing. Eva was perfect for the job, and once her crew was let in on the secret, they could assist her in that too.

The question was whether she would accept the offer and whether she'd send him out to sleep in the dog house for even suggesting that. He had a real hard time predicting her responses.

"What are you thinking about so hard?" Eva touched a finger to the furrows between his brows.

"I spoke to Kian about your need for more local jobs."

"Oh, good. Is he going to ask Andrew's old boss for me?"

"No. He said it was a bad idea. But he would like to offer you a job working for the clan."

Eva leaned back and crossed her arms under her breasts, pushing them up and scrambling his brain. "I'm not accepting charity work, thank you very much."

Point proven. She was mad again for no apparent reason.

"What are you talking about?" he asked.

"Like you don't know. You go talk to Kian, tell him how I accept jobs I shouldn't because finances are tight, and he offers to make up some bogus assignments for me so I can stay in Los Angeles. In short, charity."

"That's total nonsense. Where do you get these crazy ideas from?"

"Okay, smart aleck, what does Kian need me for?"

"Guys, keep it down, you're going to wake up Phoenix," Nathalie whispered.

"Sorry," Eva whispered back.

"To follow the trail of the various immortals we recently came to suspect exist. Like Kalugal, like your ancestress, like Michael's. It's not something we can hire a human detective firm to investigate. But we have you. If you're willing to take it on."

"That's a great idea, Mom. Everyone in the family working for the clan. I love it."

"I don't," Eva said.

"Why? Don't you want to help us find more immortals? And how about your own roots? I'm dying to find out who is the source of our Dormant genes."

"I didn't say I don't want to help. Of course, I do. And if Kian wants to pay me for my efforts, I will not say no. But I value my independence too much to depend on a single client. It's bad business."

Bhathian unwrapped Eva's arms and took her hand. "How much or how little you want to take on is up to you. I'll arrange a meeting with Kian and you can discuss the details of the arrangement with him."

Eva released a long breath and squeezed his hand. "That would be great. Sorry for jumping at you before. I have a problem with anything that threatens my independence. But I should've listened first."

He lifted her hand to his lips and kissed the back of it. "You're forgiven."

She pinned him with a hard stare, but her lips twitched with a suppressed smile. "Do you really want to go down that path again? As I remember, that was how our first big fight started."

"How about I apologize too, and you forgive me?"

"What would you apologize for?"

"Anything you can think of."

23

TESSA

*E*va walked into the office, holding the thick folder Sharon had prepared for her next assignment. "Tessa, what time is my flight tomorrow?"

"Ten thirty-five."

"Thanks." Nose in the file, Eva turned around and went back to the living room.

It was a ritual her boss followed before every assignment. She would settle down in her favorite armchair and read the file, going over it a few times until she was sure she'd memorized all the main points.

Unfortunately, it wasn't the best time for the heart to heart talk Tessa desperately needed. She would have to wait until Eva came back in three days.

Staring at the big pile of receipts accumulated over the past week, Tessa sighed. It was waiting for her to sort out and upload into the accounting software. Regrettably, the accounting department of their agency had only one part-time employee—Tessa—and there was no one she could dump this boring task on. The routine task no longer required any thought, and yet her mind was too scattered to do even that. She just couldn't bring herself to tackle it.

For the past week, she'd barely managed to handle the most immediate items, like making flight and hotel reservations for Eva, or sorting out her emails and other correspondence. The receipts weren't a priority, and Eva didn't care when that was done.

Every day, Tessa checked her forehead for fever, hoping that one bite had done the trick and she would start transitioning, but it appeared that once wasn't going to do it.

The problem was, she couldn't go through another one.

When Jackson had gripped her head and bitten her, holding her immobilized with a powerful, unbreakable grip, Tessa had freaked out. The panic attack had been so powerful, she'd felt like her heart was stuttering and was about to stop. The euphoria that had hit her a split second later had taken care of the panic, inducing a relaxed drug-like effect. The panic had receded, but it hadn't gone away.

Somewhere in the recesses of her mind, she'd remembered another time when she'd been drugged and taken advantage of.

At the time, the drugs had been a curse and a blessing.

They'd made her feel even more helpless than she was without them, but they had also made the nightmare less unbearable. At least until the effects had tapered off.

If she'd been good, her tormentors would give her another dose.

She'd craved the oblivion, the little death, but she'd hated herself for wanting and needing it.

It wasn't Jackson's fault. In fact, she felt incredibly guilty for avoiding him the entire week.

He'd done nothing wrong.

Logically, she understood why he'd had to hold her immobilized; he'd explained it had been necessary so she wouldn't injure her neck by jerking away while his fangs were still embedded in it. He'd even showed her the pictures he'd taken of her sleeping with a blissful expression on her face.

It was impossible for him to comprehend why she'd reacted so differently. Females craved the venom's effects, she was terrified by them.

But the last thing Tessa wanted was to crave it. She'd been there, done that, and had suffered through a hellish detox.

Jackson claimed the venom wasn't addictive in that way, but he'd admitted it was in others. It shouldn't have bothered her. If the venom's only addictive effect was that she would be repulsed by other men, then it would just reinforce what she felt anyway.

Except, Tessa couldn't tolerate any sort of addiction.

To lose control of her mind to chemicals was even worse than losing control of her body. Physically, she was a small woman who was easily overpowered, but mentally she was strong.

Drugs compromised the only strength she had.

Eva came in and dropped the file on Sharon's desk. "Text Sharon and tell her I need the names and financials of all the subsidiaries as well."

With privacy being a thing of the past, they used a special code for texts regarding work. Tessa pulled out the booklet they all used and encoded the message.

When she was done, Eva was still standing there and looking at her with concerned eyes. "What's going on with you and Jackson? You haven't left the house the entire week. Did something happen on that night you fell asleep on his couch?"

Tessa nodded.

"Do I need to beat him up?"

Tessa shook her head.

"Do you want to talk about it?"

Tessa nodded.

Eva closed the door to the office then walked over to Sharon's chair and pulled it from behind her desk.

Straddling it, she faced Tessa. "What happened?"

For some reason, Tessa found it difficult to talk. It felt as if there was a lump lodged in her throat. She pointed to her neck.

"He bit you?"

Tessa nodded.

"I figured that much. Congratulations. So what's the problem?"

Tessa cleared her throat, swallowing the lump. "I panicked."

Eva leaned across, extending her arm over the desk and taking Tessa's hand. "It's perfectly understandable. The fangs are scary, and it hurts for a couple of seconds." She smirked, her tone getting husky as she continued. "But then the fun begins."

"Not for me."

Her boss frowned. "How so?"

Eva probably found the experience highly enjoyable, as would the vast majority of women. But not those who'd been through what Tessa had suffered.

"It felt like drugs. I wasn't relaxed because of me but because of some chemicals, and I wasn't aroused because of me but because of some other chemicals. I don't want to ever feel like that again."

Eva closed her eyes for a moment. "What are you going to do?"

That was so like Eva, going straight to the crux of the problem without any bullshit psychological mumbo jumbo. Tessa loved the woman.

"I don't know. I was hoping once would be enough to

start the transition, but as you can see, it didn't happen. I have to go for another round and I can't."

Eva shook her head. "I thought you had feelings for Jackson."

"I do."

"When I asked what you're going to do, I meant about Jackson, while you responded about the transition. Is that all he is to you? A means to an end?"

"No, of course not." It sounded that way, but only because Eva didn't understand. "Once I transition, I'll be strong. When I'm no longer terrified of my own shadow, I can be with Jackson the way I want to be. Normal."

Eva's sad eyes spoke louder than words. "If you carried a gun or a knife, would you feel less scared?"

"No. Because a weapon can be taken away from me. And I'm not sure I'm capable of pointing a gun at a human being and pulling the trigger."

"What if you had three bodyguards with you at all times. Would you feel safer?"

"I guess."

"Safe enough to be intimate with Jackson?"

Shit. Eva was right. Her fears ran so deep, getting physically stronger wouldn't get rid of them.

But that meant that there was no solution. "What am I going to do?"

"I wish I knew. You need to talk to a professional. You'll remain frozen in place until you learn to manage your fears. Maybe overcoming them completely is impossible."

"We've been over that before. I don't want to talk to anyone. It would be like reopening the old wounds and letting them bleed again. I don't think I can recover from another trip down that rabbit hole. The membrane covering those wounds is so thin it could burst from the slightest prick. I need to be vigilant about protecting it."

Eva squeezed her hand. "Listen to yourself. What you need to change is the imagery you're playing on a loop in your head. No wonder you're terrified if you keep thinking of yourself as fragile and a prick away from bleeding. Change the movie, Tessa. Imagine something else."

"It's not as easy as that."

"I know. And it's not my place to give advice about things I can't even imagine. It didn't happen to me, and I have no professional training in helping people heal. What I said is just common sense. Try to use it. Maybe it can help in some small way. Every little bit counts, right?"

Tessa nodded. At that point, she was willing to try anything.

Except talking to a professional.

24

JACKSON

*P*icking up dirty clothes off the floor and throwing them out into the hallway, Jackson yelled, "Did anyone see my lucky pick?" When there was no response, he kept searching frantically, flinging the couch cushions aside and sticking his hand in the tight crevices between the bottom frame and the arms.

It wasn't there.

He shoved the entire couch forward, but it wasn't under it either.

"Did you look in the laundry basket?" Gordon called.

Good idea. Jackson rushed down the stairs and into the utility room and grabbed the laundry bag. He emptied the contents on the floor and started sifting through his dirty clothes, checking all the pockets and shaking the garments out.

It wasn't there either.

Despondent, he sat on the floor, braced his elbows on his knees, and let his head drop onto his fists.

He was losing his fucking mind.

To say that things were not working out with Tessa was

the understatement of the century. They were back to square one. Worse. She hadn't avoided him at the beginning of their relationship. She was avoiding him now.

He'd been so sure everything was fine, that Tessa had enjoyed the venom bite. What else had he been supposed to think when she'd fallen asleep with a blissful expression on her face?

His illusions had been shattered when she'd woken up and bolted out of his room as if he was the devil himself.

It happened a week ago.

He'd called and texted her numerous times, but all he'd managed to get out of her was that she needed time to process what had happened.

She was breaking his fucking heart.

"I found it." Vlad stood in the hallway outside the utility room, holding the pick between his thumb and forefinger. "It was in the car. You must've left it there after practice.

Jackson exhaled a relieved breath. "I was afraid I left it in the studio at Guitar King. It would've been gone by now."

Vlad crouched next to Jackson, his scrawny arms dangling between his spread knees. "It's not about the pick, is it?"

"Sure it is. You know I can't go on stage without it."

Vlad shook his head, his long black bangs swaying from side to side, obscuring the green eye and then the blue one. "Call her and invite her to the gig."

"I don't think she wants to see me."

"Yes, she does. But you need to man up and make her realize that."

Jackson sighed. "How am I going to do that?"

"You're Jackson the great—the irresistible ladies' magnet. Use your famous charm and don't take no for an answer."

Jackson chuckled. It was a sad day indeed if he needed a relationship pep talk from Vlad. But the dude was right. "I'll do that. And if she says no, I'll tell her you'll be disappointed if she doesn't come."

Vlad shrugged. "Whatever works, man."

"Right."

Vlad pushed to his feet and offered Jackson a hand up.

"Thanks." He took what he was offered.

Back in his room, Jackson closed the door and pulled out his phone, then stared at it for a long time before chickening out and texting Tessa instead of calling. She'd been so sad the last time he'd spoken to her. If he heard that sad tone again, it would floor him, and he wouldn't be worth shit at the gig tonight.

The guys and I are performing at the Screaming Horses tonight. We would love for you to come.

Jackson looked at what he'd typed and shook his head. He erased the last sentence and replaced it with what he should've typed to start with.

I would love for you to come. I miss you. He pressed send before having a chance to chicken out again.

Damn, love was turning him into a wuss. He would've laughed his head off watching another guy get all twitchy and nervous because of a girl.

Running his fingers through his hair, he waited for Tessa's answer.

Sure. But can you guys stop by my place and pick me up? I don't want to drive alone at night.

Jackson let out the breath he was holding in a long stream. She didn't say no. But it seemed that her fears were back full force.

Can you be ready in twenty minutes?

Yes.

Jackson shoved the phone into his back pocket, then headed for the bathroom to spray himself with more of Tessa's favorite cologne.

Later, when Vlad parked in front of Eva's house, Jackson was a little nervous as he got out and knocked.

Tessa opened the door, smiled at him, then turned around and called out goodnight before stepping out.

With Vlad's sage advice still fresh in his mind, Jackson wrapped his arm around her slim shoulders and bent to kiss her cheek.

She didn't pull away. In fact, if he wasn't mistaken, she leaned into him. He tightened his arms and brought her a little closer. "Are you cold?"

"A little," she whispered.

"Let's get you into the car. It's warm inside." He opened the back door for her and then slid in after her.

Vlad turned around and flashed Tessa his best smile. "Glad you could make it. I got so used to you cheering us on that I couldn't think about going on stage without knowing that you're in the audience. Right, Gordon?"

Dutifully, Gordon nodded. "We need you. You're our lucky charm."

His friends the best.

Jackson slid even closer to Tessa and put his arm around her. "How are you holding up?" he whispered, even though they both knew it was futile.

"I'm feeling better, thank you."

Her answer was delivered with a slightly quivering tone, unconvincing, but he detected a note of determination in there as well. His girl was a fighter. She might have gotten knocked down, but she wasn't going to stay there. Tessa was going to pull herself up and try again.

He kissed the top of her head. "I'm proud of you."

She lifted her big eyes to him. "Why on earth would you be proud of me?"

Her expressive eyes filled in the blanks wordlessly. Sadness, shame, regret.

"When knocked down, losers stay down, winners pick themselves up and keep on fighting. You're a winner, my brave Tessa. You don't give up."

His friends proved once again how awesome they were. Vlad turned the radio on and started humming along, while Gordon accompanied him by drumming the beat on his thighs. Between the radio and the two of them, they were making enough noise to keep his conversation with Tessa somewhat private.

She dropped her head, her new blond hair falling in two straight curtains on both sides of her face. "Thank you for giving me another chance. You must be so disappointed."

Hooking a finger under her chin, he made her look at him. "The only way you can ever disappoint me is if you stop trying. You'll never run out of chances with me. Can I count on you to do the same? I don't want you to ever give up on me."

Tessa cupped his cheek. "Never. I couldn't do it even if I tried." She tilted her head and closed her eyes, inviting a kiss.

It could have been lovely if she weren't cringing while waiting for him to do it.

Jackson dipped his head and kissed her lightly, just a gentle brush of his lips against hers, then withdrew and hugged her closer.

Tessa sighed and snuggled up to him. "How did I get so lucky to snag a guy like you?"

He squeezed her shoulder gently. "I'm the lucky one. Fate doesn't smile like this on many immortals. Every day, the first thing I do each morning is to give thanks for you."

25

BRUNDAR

*A*nandur parked his rental a couple of blocks away from the San Francisco branch of the Allure clubs and motioned for Brundar to stop behind him, then got out and walked over.

Brundar lowered the window. "What?"

"Can I change your mind about the wire? I would feel much safer knowing what's going on with you."

"No." He pressed the button to close the window, but Anandur blocked it with his hand.

"Can I for once get an explanation?"

"No."

Anandur's hand didn't leave the glass panel. "Is it a game to you? Because for the life of me I don't get why you need to be so tight-lipped. Not everything is top secret."

Brundar sighed. Anandur should've gotten used to that by now. Most of the time his brother was good about it, not asking questions even though he was curious.

The two of them were the exact opposites.

Anandur was a clown, while Brundar was more of a grim reaper. Anandur loved hanging around people, while

Brundar preferred solitude. Anandur was the worst possible gossip, while Brundar was as good as mute.

"Unlike our secure phones, a tap can be easily hacked. I don't want to worry about it." That wasn't the only reason, but it was good enough for Anandur.

His brother had an inkling as to Brundar's sexual proclivities, but he didn't need to learn more. During the visit, Brundar was going to ask his tour guide questions that would reveal his expertise on the subject. He didn't want Anandur listening in.

"Now, was it that hard?" Anandur shook his head and removed his hand from the glass. As he walked back to his car, Brundar eased back into the street and drove a couple of blocks to the club's valet service.

Eva's advice had been helpful, making his first visit to the Los Angeles branch of the Allure chain go smoothly, but this time he was even better prepared. The only weapons he had on him wouldn't be discovered even if he was subjected to a pat down. A thin blade was hidden inside his long ponytail, and a flexible wire in his belt.

He was rocking the rock star look with leather pants, a muscle shirt, boots, sunglasses, and his Scottish accent.

"Good evening, sir." The receptionist stood up and offered him her hand.

Brundar ignored it. "Bruce MacFaron. I have an appointment." He sprawled on the guest armchair while the receptionist sat back down and flipped open an old-fashioned appointment book.

"Indeed you do, sir." She pushed back to her feet. "There are several forms and a lengthy questionnaire to fill in before you can take the tour, sir." She walked over to a door and opened it. "Everything is on the desk. If you have any questions or need help filling in the questionnaire, you can call me on the intercom." She pointed to the device. "And, of course, please let me know once you're done, and I'll send your guide over."

"Thank you." He stepped inside, ignoring her expectant expression. If she was waiting for a smile or a come-on line from him, she'd be standing in that doorway for a long time.

Getting comfortable on the large chair, Brundar lifted a brow. She dipped her head and closed the door.

The forms were identical to the ones he'd filled in at the Los Angeles club, as were his answers except for his name. In Allure Los Angeles he'd presented himself as Brad Reynolds.

The clubs were impressive by anyone's standards. Brundar had played in enough of them to appreciate the level of finesse and sophistication that went into the chain. Whoever came up with the concept and its execution was brilliant.

He or she should write a manual on how a place like that should be run. Every last detail was carefully thought out, like the uniforms that were meticulously pressed and starched, and clearly identified each club employee's responsibility.

The guide showed up promptly after Brundar had informed the receptionist that he was done. The timing, like everything else in the clubs, was calculated perfectly for her to go through the paperwork and ensure that everything was properly filled in and signed before the guide opened the door. Especially the nondisclosure form.

"Hello, I'm David, and I will be your guide this evening." The guy didn't offer his hand, which meant the receptionist had communicated Brundar's dislike of skin to skin contact.

Another point for Allure's management.

David kept up a steady drone of explanations Brundar wasn't listening to as he followed the guy through the main areas and into the more secluded ones.

Brundar had already seen all of that in the other club. He

cut into the guide's chatter. "Could you show me a private room?"

"Naturally, sir. This way."

Brundar followed David into a side corridor lined with doors on both sides. "It's very quiet in here. You have good soundproofing." It was unusual, and a security concern, which Brundar had gotten an answer to in the other club, but hoped this guy would volunteer more information.

David smiled, glad to finally have a question to answer. "Yes, we do. We offer our guests complete privacy when they require it, or conversely complete exposure, as you have seen in the open areas."

"What about security? How do you ensure your guests' safety?"

"Everything is explained in the membership contract. The paperwork you signed today was just the appetizer."

Brundar cocked a brow. "There is another questionnaire?"

"Once you decide to purchase a membership, you need to sign more forms before being allowed the use of the club beyond the main public areas. One of those forms states that all the private rooms are monitored, and you need to sign it as an acknowledgment that you've been told about it and agree to the terms."

"That's unusual. Private rooms are supposed to be private."

"No human is actually looking at the feed. It goes to a computer that runs the audio through a program designed to pick up on certain trigger words. Like the word gag. Gags are not allowed in the private rooms. So if the computer detects the word gag, that room is flagged and a human looks at the feed to make sure rules are being obeyed. That's just one example. Besides, knowing that everything is recorded and can be retrieved in case someone complains is a strong deterrent."

That was a much more thorough explanation than the one Brundar had gotten in Los Angeles. "Excellent. I applaud the management."

David immediately switched to salesman mode. "Allure is the best club of its kind, by far surpassing the next best one. The membership is pricey, but it's worth every penny. It ensures a classy clientele."

"What about paid services? Do you provide those?"

David scanned Brundar's muscular body from top to bottom and back up. "With your looks, you don't need to pay. You'll have plenty of takers."

As the guy leaned closer, Brundar fought the instinct to pull away or kill his guide on the spot. "Regardless of your preference, you'll have a waiting line. There will be plenty of takers from both sides."

"What if I prefer paid service?"

"Then I'm sure something could be arranged."

Brundar managed a curve of his lips. "That's what I wanted to hear."

In fact, he had all the information he needed. After thanking the guide, Brundar stopped at a couple of spots for appearances' sake, then made his exit as promptly as possible.

He called Anandur as soon as he drove away.

"You're out?"

Wasn't that obvious? "Everything that's going on in the private rooms gets recorded and stored. We need William or Eva's guy to hack into their computers and check out everything from the day of the murder."

"Good job, little brother."

"Fuck you."

"I love you too."

TESSA

"*Y*ou look nice." Gordon gave Tessa the once-over.

"Thank you."

The remark had Jackson give her one too. "I was wondering why you seemed taller. Sexy shoes."

"Thanks." She chuckled. "They are killing my feet, but I like the added height."

Jackson walked her over to a table. "You'd better sit down. We need to put the equipment backstage, and there is no reason for you to follow in those shoes. You can relax here."

"Okay."

Another band was going first, and she watched them setting up their stuff on the stage. The club wasn't officially open yet, and there was no one there aside from the staff and the two bands, including whoever they'd brought with them. She was the only one who'd come with Jackson and his friends, but it seemed the other band members had each brought their girlfriends along. The four were sitting one table over, and casting her curious looks.

Normally, she would've been intimidated by them. Especially the tall buxom one. The girl had a swimsuit model's body, with enviable curves in all the right places.

But not today.

Jackson hadn't given Tessa much time to prepare, but she still managed quite a getup, including the four-inch heels Eva had bought for her. Paired with skinny white jeans, they made her legs look amazing. Walking was another matter. She'd had to hold on to Jackson to avoid twisting her ankles.

Thanks to the Brazilian blowout, her fancy hairdo required no maintenance, looking just as good today as it did fresh from the salon. And thanks to Eva, her makeup was expertly done in less than five minutes. The woman was a pro.

Tessa had never looked better. For the first time in forever, she actually wanted to look good.

Her talk with Eva had accomplished two things.

One was good. She'd made up a new positive mantra and was playing it on repeat in her head, sending herself a message that she was strong, and her wounds were not only healed but reinforced with steel plates.

The other was bad. A new fear had settled in the pit of her stomach. What if Jackson was fed up with her and was going to leave her, or relegate her to the friend zone? After all, that was what she'd asked of him at the start of their relationship.

He'd been so patient with her. But what if he got tired of waiting?

In spite of his assurances, at some point Jackson would realize she wasn't worth all the misery she was causing him and dump her. Especially when she'd been avoiding him for an entire week.

While Tessa had been deep in thought, another girl joined the four at the other table, eclipsing the buxom beauty by at least another cup size.

For some reason, Tessa disliked her on sight.

The disproportionate frontage was either the result of a super pushup bra or an unscrupulous plastic surgeon. Her face was pretty, but her expression wasn't. Her only redeeming feature was her long blond hair. It was thick and flowed in a shimmering curtain down her back. The color even looked natural.

Tessa ran her fingers through her own short hairdo, wondering if hers looked natural or not. Probably not. The blond didn't match her skin tone.

As the girl kept glancing her way, Tessa angled her chair away from the other group, turning her back to them.

The bimbo could stare at her back.

"Hi, who are you with?"

Reluctantly, Tessa turned around. Of course it had to be the one she disliked the most. "I'm with the other band."

The blonde rolled her eyes. "I know that. I meant whose sister or girlfriend are you?"

"Jackson's."

The blonde gave her a dismissive once-over. "You don't look like him."

"I'm not his sister."

"Oh yeah? So who are you? A cousin?"

Tessa had never been a violent person. With her size and lack of muscle, she couldn't afford to be. But at that moment she wanted to slap the condescending bimbette.

"Jackson is my boyfriend."

The blonde dropped her jaw dramatically and let it hang for a couple of moments. "Get out of here. You're joking. Right?"

Tessa lifted a brow.

"I'm sorry, where are my manners. I didn't introduce myself. I'm Daphne." She offered her hand.

Tessa had no choice but to shake it. "Tessa."

Daphne put a hand on her hip and moved her leg

forward, striking a pose. "Kinky. Jackson is dating school-girls. How old are you? Sixteen?"

Tessa narrowed her eyes. "None of your business."

"Oh, come on, no need to be rude. I'm not going to tell anyone Jackson is screwing an underage girl. Right, girls?" She turned to her friends.

One of the four lifted her drink. "It's a free country."

Daphne's smile reminded Tessa of a piranha. "This must be the attraction. A young, untrained pussy." She leaned toward Tessa. "Are you a virgin, dear? Is that what he sees in you? Because that's the only way a guy like him would choose someone like you when he could have me." She ran her hands down the sides of her huge breasts.

Tessa rose to her feet, turned around, and walked away without giving the slut the satisfaction of a response. For a moment, she contemplated hiding in the bathroom until Jackson and the guys came back, but there was a chance Daphne would follow her there. God only knew what that bimbo was capable of. Tessa wouldn't put it past her to get physical.

Daphne was a bully.

The sad truth was that Tessa would probably lose in a physical confrontation with Daphne. The girl was about half a foot taller and outweighed Tessa by at least thirty pounds.

She really needed to join her neighbor's self-defense class. Tessa was sick of feeling like a victim. Evidently, a sophisticated hairdo and high-heeled shoes were not the answer.

Changing directions, she headed toward the bar.

"What can I get you?" the barman asked.

Tessa wanted a coke, but that would only reinforce Daphne's assumptions. She shouldn't have cared, and yet what left her mouth was, "A screwdriver." She wasn't even sure what it was.

"Can I see an ID?"

"Sure." She reached into her purse and pulled out her license. It was fake for reasons that had nothing to do with age. Tessa wasn't worried, though. It had been done by Eva's guy who was supposedly the best in the business.

The barman looked at it and then back at her. "You look different."

Damn. It was the hair. The last thing she needed was for him to refuse her a drink, or worse, kick her out of the club.

"New hairdo." She lifted the bangs off her forehead and tucked the sides behind her ears. "See? It's me."

He looked at her license again. "Yeah, it's you. Nice. You look better as a blonde."

"Thank you." She paid for her drink.

It tasted pretty good, and Tessa took small sips while watching the five girls from the corner of her eye. It seemed that they'd lost interest in her. Daphne was busy tormenting someone else.

Hopefully, Jackson didn't have a history with that one. She was so far beneath him, he should've been disgusted by her. But then he most likely hadn't gotten to see her ugly side.

Daphne oozed sex appeal and probably rendered most guys blind and stupid with those huge boobs of hers. Had Jackson been one of her conquests?

Tessa shivered at the thought. For some reason she'd imagined his past girlfriends differently. But who knew?

The altercation made one thing abundantly clear, though. If she didn't secure her hold on him soon, someone else would. Jackson was handsome and charming and was the leader of a freaking rock band. It had been naive of her to think he'd stick around, waiting patiently while she battled her demons.

27

EVA

*B*hathian opened the car door for Eva and offered her a hand up.

She took it but didn't use it to pull herself out. Stubborn woman. He could understand her need to appear strong, and, naturally, she didn't need his help getting out of a car, but she could've humored him, allowed him to feel chivalrous. And to think that she complained about the younger generation of men and their lack of gentlemanly manners.

"Are we meeting Kian in his office or his penthouse?"

"His office. The same place we met him with Tessa and Jackson."

"I don't like the underground. Why doesn't he make an office for himself in one of the upper floors? I know some of the clan members do."

Bhathian shrugged. "Maybe he prefers it there. The older ones and those closer to the source prefer dark places. Their eyes are very sensitive to sunlight."

She didn't know that. The elevator arrived and they stepped in. "Someone should write a manual for newcomers with all those bits and pieces of information. I feel like I learn a new thing every day."

"That's good, isn't it? Makes things more interesting.'

She chuckled. "Trust me, things are interesting enough. I'm sure I would've appreciated a guide book. And when Sharon and Nick's time comes, it would make life easier for them to have one too."

They arrived at their floor and exited.

Bhathian shook his head. "What if it falls into the wrong hands? We make sure that our written records are secure. For instance, none of the clan members has a copy of the clan law. If anyone wants to read it, they have to get permission from Edna—our legal expert and judge—and a key to the records vault. Everyone can get in and read as much as they want, but nothing leaves that room. Even note-taking is not allowed. You have to memorize it."

"Hmm…" Eva tapped a finger on her lips. "That's actually very smart. You can never be too careful about things like that. But then there are people like me with a shitty memory who could use something written. What about writing the clan's history as fiction? You know, like *Lord of the Rings*, a fantasy, or a romance. It's too fantastic for anyone to take seriously."

"Could work. You should suggest it to Kian."

"I just might," she said as Bhathian opened Kian's office door and held it for her.

"Suggest what?" Kian asked.

Eva took the seat Kian pointed to at the conference table, and Bhathian sat on Kian's other side. "An instruction manual for Dormants and clueless immortals like me in the form of a fantasy novel or a romance. That way even if it falls into the wrong hands no one would suspect what it is."

Kian regarded her for a moment, making her uncomfortable. Not something that happened to Eva often. But the guy had the most intense stare of anyone she'd ever met.

"I'll think about it. We have several writers in our midst who could tackle a project like that. Obviously, I have to run it by Annani first."

The goddess.

It was on the tip of Eva's tongue to ask Kian if he could arrange an audience. If she had to wait to meet the mysterious and probably awesome Annani until someone got married, Eva would be waiting a very long time.

But a request like that was highly inappropriate. The clan had welcomed her into the fold as if she was one of them, but she wasn't. Annani wasn't the matriarch of Eva's line.

Eva didn't have the right to ask for anything.

She could offer her services, though. Not exclusively, she couldn't and wouldn't do that, but she was willing to give up the smaller less profitable jobs to clear time and investigate whatever the clan needed her to.

"I understand that you have a work proposition for me."

Kian nodded. "I do, and I would be grateful if you'd accept it."

"I will do whatever you need me to, but I can't promise you exclusivity. I have a few long term clients that are a great asset to my firm. I owe them priority."

"I understand. Though with time, I hope your priorities will shift in our favor. I have more work for you than you can handle even if you dedicate all your time to it. And even then I would need to hire human detectives to cover some of the assignments. Once we are done here, I would appreciate it if you could recommend a few."

"I will gladly provide you with names once I know what you need done. Every agency has its own niche expertise."

Eva's curiosity had been whetted. What could Kian want done that required such intensive investigative work?

"There are two separate matters. One that I can't assign to anyone but you, and the other that can be handled by humans."

Kian got up and walked over to the buffet, pulled out three glasses and a tall bottle of sparkling water, then brought them back to the conference table. "Help yourselves." He handed out the glasses and opened the bottle.

It was a little disconcerting having the clan's regent serve her like that. After all, he was like a prince, or even a king, and serving commoners like her and Bhathian should be beneath him.

But apparently not.

Bhathian seemed perfectly fine to be served by his leader.

Kian waited until their glasses were filled. "I want you to investigate your and Michael's ancestors. Your family trees. Somewhere down the line there could be an immortal female who's an ancient. The reason I suspect that is the ease with which you and Nathalie and Michael transitioned. You must be very close to the source, with only a few generations separating you from the gods. I also want Bridget to check if the three of you are of the same matrilineal descent. I suspect that you are, but if not, it means that we are dealing with two ancients, not one."

Wow. Talk about mission impossible. But it was also the most thrilling hunt imaginable.

The Holy Grail.

She chuckled and shook her head.

"What's funny?" Bhathian asked.

"This is like the quest for the Holy Grail."

Kian's baffled expression made it clear he had no idea what she was talking about.

"There are many theories surrounding the Holy Grail. One says that it refers to royal blood while another says it holds the secret to eternal youth. An ancient immortal female embodies both. She is of godly blood, and she carries the genes of eternal youth."

With a wave of his hand, Kian dismissed her musings. "I don't care about all that mystical nonsense. Do you want the job or not?"

"Of course I want the job. It's the most fascinating investigation I have ever undertaken. But I have to warn you that the chances of me actually finding the female or females are ridiculously small."

"I know that. But I have to try, and for obvious reasons, I can't assign the task to an outsider."

"Naturally. Let's start with the good doctor. It will help to know if I'm looking for one or more females. One would obviously be better. More cross reference between the two family trees."

Kian tapped his fingers on the table. "Good. Then that's settled. Let's move to the other investigation, which I think is even more complicated than the first."

Eva arched a brow. "I can't wait to hear it."

"Our enemies, the Brotherhood of the Devout order of Mortdh, or Doomers as we call them, have an island somewhere in the Pacific. The island serves two purposes: one as a base for tens of thousands of mercenary warriors, and the other an internationally renowned brothel."

Eva pursed her lips. "Interesting combination."

"Actually, it makes perfect sense. Navuh, their leader, needs to provide his army with females. As long as they have an easy supply of sex, they are content. So that's one purpose. But the despot is an enterprising SOB. He figured he could make tons of money by offering sex services to the rich and powerful from all over the world. Not only that, but he could use it to both bribe and extort those clients as well."

"Where does he get all those women?"

"He buys them from slavers. We believe he has several

suppliers who pick young runaways and junkies off the streets and bring them to the island. The main areas they harvest are here in the United States and the former Soviet Union. According to Dalhu, fair-skinned, blue-eyed blonds and redheads are in high demand in Navuh's brothel."

That was so disgusting. Eva felt bile rise in her throat. Too close to home for one who'd heard Tessa's story. "How does he get them to perform? Drugs? Beatings?"

Kian must've realized what was going through her head, and reached for her hand. "I'm sorry. I know this is a disturbing subject for you."

She wasn't a softy who needed coddling. Eva pulled her hand away. "It's okay. Please continue."

He nodded. "A combination of several methods of coercion works better than crude beatings and addiction. If they don't want to work in prostitution, they are given the option to work as maids and cooks and laundresses and the like. But the working and living conditions of the service staff are miserable. The prostitutes get nicer rooms, shorter work days, and they can use their patrons' gifts to buy mild drugs, alcohol, and other luxuries."

"But basically all of them are slaves."

"Exactly. It's a life sentence. They never leave the island."

"What do you want me to do?"

"Not you, the other detective firms. I need to find who the suppliers are."

"What are you going to do with that information? Try to stop them?"

"No. It's futile. If we eliminate one organization, another will take its place. I just need to find out who they are in case I want to use that knowledge to infiltrate the island."

The cogs in Eva's brain began spinning faster and faster as she tried to branch out and find an angle that would serve her particular interests. Finding the suppliers wasn't enough.

She wanted them eliminated. And how the hell did Kian intend to infiltrate the island through the slavers? Plant a woman they would kidnap? Was he insane?

Eva crossed her arms over her chest and narrowed her eyes at the clan's regent. "If you plan to send a woman in as a spy, I'm not helping you. I will not contribute to the slaughter of a sacrificial lamb."

28

KIAN

Stifling a curse, Kian raked his fingers through his hair. Eva's angry words echoed his own thoughts. Sending Carol in was a suicide mission.

"I get what you're saying, and it's not different from what's buzzing in my own head. But that's the only in we have. Those fuckers have been messing not only with us but with humanity at large throughout history. They outnumber us in order of magnitude. We can't defeat them in a military attack. And even if we could, we would be destroying what's left of our kind. I hate to bundle us with them, but, unfortunately, we share the same genetics. Our only chance is to start unrest from within. A revolution. We need someone to plant the seeds."

Eva looked into his eyes for such a long time that Kian started to think she was trying to stare him down. Wasn't going to happen, but he appreciated the balls on the woman.

She dropped her arms by her sides. "Should the good of the many outweigh the good of the individual? Always a difficult choice. I get the moral dilemma. But do you truly believe that one woman, who these mercenaries are going to think of as a whore, can achieve such a lofty objective?"

"Frankly, I don't know. If anyone can pull it off it's her. But if you ask me if I am confident in the chances of her success? I am not. And the idea of sending her into the lions' den without backup and without the ability to communicate is abhorrent to me. I'm not going to do it if we can't figure out a way for her to communicate with us, and if we don't have a solid plan for extracting her if needed."

Again, Eva's gaze focused on his eyes, but this time he realized that her intention wasn't starting a battle. She was trying to ascertain the truth of his words.

"I believe you mean what you say."

"Good. When you get to know me better, you'll realize that I always do."

Bhathian spoke up for the first time. "He does. Whether you like it or not, Kian always tells it as it is. No sugarcoating."

She nodded. "I have some experience on the subject of human traffickers, which I'll gladly share with you. On one condition."

"What is it?"

"You share yours with me once the other detectives supply the information. I reserve the right to sabotage any of the organizations that are not suppliers for the island. I'm sure you'll get a lot of info on those."

"Deal. But how do you propose to sabotage them?"

Her smile was chillingly cold. "In any way I can."

Kian glanced at Bhathian who shifted in his chair and looked away. The guy knew exactly what his mate was going to do with the information, but he wasn't going to spill.

It was an interesting development. One that Kian hadn't foreseen. For the first time a Guardian faced a conflict of interests. Loyalty to his mate versus loyalty to his clan and his clan leader. If Eva weren't an outsider, it wouldn't have been an issue.

Unfortunately, staying out was her choice.

If he managed to bring her into the fold, she might share her plans and not put Bhathian in an awkward position.

"Whatever your plans are, I'm not going to try to stop you or try to dissuade you from pursuing the destruction of the worst scum possible. The opposite is true. You can count on my help. I don't know if I can spare any manpower, but I can finance outside resources."

Bhathian sucked in a breath and glanced at Eva.

Kian was well familiar with that response. "What's the matter? Did I detonate some kind of a bomb? Trigger something?"

Eva shook her head and patted Bhathian's arm. "No. You didn't. Bhathian knows I hate offers of support. But that is for me personally. I'm perfectly capable of supporting myself and running my business profitably. This is different. You're offering to help with a cause that is dear to me. I'm willing to accept it."

Bhathian snorted. "You never react the way I think you will. And don't say that I don't know you because I do."

Eva's eyes softened as she looked at her mate. "You know big parts of me, but you still have a lot to learn. As I'm sure I have a lot to learn about you."

"Nope. I think you've already learned all there is to learn about me. I'm a simple guy."

Kian didn't want to butt in, but Bhathian could use advice from someone more experienced on the subject. "Women are much more complicated than we are. You can spend a lifetime with Eva, and I'm talking in immortal terms, and still not discover all there is to discover. But that's the beauty of it. This will keep you on your toes."

Eva smiled broadly. "You're a wise man, Kian."

"Not really. But I'm fortunate enough to have three sisters and a wife whom I love dearly but who keep baffling me on a daily basis. Not to mention my mother. I think she considers logic a bad word. Annani is all about the heart."

"Is there any chance I might meet the goddess? I'm just dying of curiosity."

"I don't know that she has plans to visit anytime soon, but we all know what she always comes for. Right, Bhathian?" He winked at the Guardian.

"That was what I said."

Eva rolled her eyes. "Tsk, tsk, tsk. Shame on you boys. You behave like a couple of yentas."

No one called Kian a boy other than his mother, but he was too amused to get angry. He lifted his hands in the air. "As I said before, I tell it as it is."

Eva laughed. She was a striking woman. Especially when not scowling because of this or that.

Kian glanced at Bhathian who was gazing adoringly at his beautiful mate. Two scowlers in love. How the hell had these two grouches produced a happy, good-natured person like Nathalie?

Genes were a funny thing, a Russian roulette, as the late Robin Williams had said. One could never predict the specific mix a kid would inherit and from whom.

29

AMANDA

*H*annah knocked on Amanda's open door. "Do you have a minute?"

"Always. Come on in."

Yesterday, the postdoc had returned from a two-week vacation, looking troubled and emitting wave after wave of guilty scent. Amanda had been wondering what all that was about.

Sitting down, Hannah crossed her legs and threaded the fingers of her hands together, holding on to her elevated knee. "I've been offered an assistant professor job at the University of Montana."

The traitor.

Amanda pinned her with a hard stare. "That's where you were on your vacation? Not visiting your ailing grandmother like you told me?"

"I did both. My grandmother lives nearby, and she is suffering from the early stages of Alzheimer's. That's one of the reasons I accepted the position. Their neuroscience department focuses on memory research. I went into the field because I wanted to research memory loss."

With a sigh, Amanda leaned back in her chair. Hannah had been saying that she wanted to work on memory from the beginning, and Amanda had been promising her that at some point they would. But with the current project dragging on and not producing the results they'd been hoping for, she wasn't ready to switch to something new.

Maybe she should. Extrasensory perception was real, but the test results weren't consistent enough to publish in a scientific paper. Hannah needed to be named on one, or her career path would stall.

Poor William. He would be so disappointed.

Thank the merciful Fates, Syssi hadn't had the talk with him yet.

Damn, she was losing more than a competent researcher. The clan was losing a potential Dormant.

"I understand. I hate to see you go, but you need to do what's right for you."

Hannah let out a relieved breath. "Thank you. Telling you was the hardest part. I love working here, but I need to think about the future."

"Naturally. How soon do you need to leave?"

"They want me as soon as possible, but I told them I have to give you at least two weeks' notice. But if you think you'll need me for a little longer, I will ask for more time."

Amanda shook her head. "I'll try to find a replacement as soon as I can. I don't want to hold you a day longer than I must."

"Thank you. Frankly, I didn't expect you to be so understanding."

"What can I say? I'm awesome." As if she had a choice. Better appear gracious and supportive than throw a hissy fit.

Besides, she was more concerned with the loss of a potential Dormant than a research assistant.

For the next two weeks, she'd have Hannah work closely

with the immortal volunteers and collect as much data as possible. If the girl proved to be a good prospect, maybe William could pay her a visit in Montana.

Amanda pulled out an index card from her drawer. "I have two volunteers coming in today." She scribbled the names on the card. "Bridget and Charlie. I want you to show them how to operate everything. They need to watch you run a couple of tests. When they are ready, I want you to have each subject tested by each volunteer. It doesn't matter who administers what test, just that the subjects are exposed to each of the volunteers."

"No problem. But may I ask what the purpose is?"

Amanda had an explanation prepared. "Certainly. One thing I want to test is if people perform better when the tester is of the same sex or the opposite. The other thing I want to test is whether switching testers has a positive or negative impact on the diminishing results phenomenon. We always believed that mental fatigue is mainly the result of boredom. Switching testers may provide the stimulation needed to keep the test subjects going."

Hannah took the card. "No last names?"

"I have them, but you don't need them. Both Charlie and Bridget filled out all the paperwork."

Hannah cast her a suspicious glance but said nothing. By now she was used to what she thought of as Amanda's odd work habits.

A few minutes after the postdoc had left Amanda's office, Syssi came in and closed the door.

"I'm so glad I didn't tell William anything. The poor guy is going to be devastated enough by her leaving, without piling on the loss of a potential Dormant."

Amanda folded her arms over her chest. "Maybe we should tell him. We have her for the next two weeks. It's enough time to induce a transition and see it through."

Syssi's lips twisted in a grimace. "But what if she isn't? Out of everyone we have, she is the least likely. We would be subjecting both her and William to misery for nothing. Besides, I don't think our guy is the sort that can jump on an opportunity. He is more about the slow buildup."

"Agreed. Before we do anything, let's see what our volunteers have to say after spending some time with Hannah. I'm of a mind to call the two who are scheduled for tomorrow and have them stop by. I want to throw everything at this last-ditch effort to assess her Dormant potential."

"Thank you for coming." Amanda closed the door behind Bridget and Charlie. Syssi was already there, perched on a corner of Amanda's desk, leaving the two guest chairs for the volunteers.

Bridget sat down and crossed her jeans-clad legs. "I needed a change of scenery. Not that it's such a stretch from my clinic to your lab. But still."

Charlie didn't seem as happy. "It's boring. And none of the test subjects were hot."

"Anyone caught your attention?" Syssi asked.

He shrugged. "Hannah is pretty. But she works here."

Syssi perked up. "Did you feel anything for her? Did you like her?"

"If you're asking if I felt like shagging her, then yeah. Definitely."

The boy wasn't the sharpest tool in the shed. "What Syssi means is, did you feel an affinity for her. Was her vibe different than that of other humans?"

Charlie gave it about a minute of thought, which was better than Amanda had expected of him. "Can't say that I felt anything different about her. She is smarter than most of the chicks I hook up with, and she seems nice, but that's about it."

Amanda turned to Bridget. "How about you, anything different?"

The doctor uncrossed her legs and planted her elbows on her knees. "I have to agree with Charlie. Hannah is intelligent and charming, but if you ask me whether I want to invite her to dinner or introduce her to my son, then the answer is no."

That was disappointing. But at the same time, it was a relief. There was no need to tell William anything, and saying goodbye to Hannah would be heart-wrenching only because Amanda liked the girl, but not because she was letting a Dormant slip through her fingers.

"What about your test subjects, Charlie, anything?"

He shook his head. "The first guy was a prick, the second one was okay but nothing special. Same for the two girls."

"How about you, Bridget?"

"Again, I have to agree with Charlie. I filled out my report so you can read exactly what my impressions were."

Syssi sighed, echoing Amanda's sentiments.

Today wasn't a good day.

30

SYSSI

O ut on the terrace, drink in hand, Syssi lay sprawling on a lounger and stared at the sunset.

This evening the beauty of it failed to lift her spirits.

She'd had such high hopes for the shrooms, but even the larger dose she'd taken last night had failed to bring about visions. It had no effect other than making her a little dizzy.

So that was that. Another door closed. Hallucinogenic substances had no effect on true visions. At least not in her case.

She heard Kian step outside, the scent of his aftershave mingling with his own masculine one a balm for her soul.

"I have a surprise for you." He sat down next to her on the lounger.

"Am I going to like it?" Hopefully, her loving husband hadn't gone and bought her another extravagant piece of jewelry as a consolation for last night's failure.

"I'm not sure. But if you don't like it, I can always cancel the appointment. The fee is nonrefundable, though."

Ugh, he knew her so well. She hated to waste money.

"You think you're so clever. What if I don't care about money anymore? After all, I have a rich husband," she teased.

Kian smirked, a playfully evil expression on his handsome face. "Even better. I could finally buy you all the diamonds I want you to have. But I think you're going to be excited about this one. I got us an appointment with Madame Salinka—the famous medium."

"Why? She talks to ghosts. If anyone should go see her it's Nathalie. Other than that one time during her transition, she hasn't had any visits from her friendly ghost. She misses talking to Mark."

"Aye, but Madame Salinka also predicts the future." Kian used his Scottish accent that was known to have a dual effect on her. Make her smile and make her horny. Not that she didn't smile or get horny just from being near him, but usually not at the same time. More than his sexy accent, it was her husband's stern gaze that melted her panties.

Syssi laughed. "She's probably a quack."

"Not from what I heard. But even if she is, what do we have to lose? Worst case scenario we will be pleasantly entertained by a very convincing theatrical performance."

"You must've paid a fortune to get an appointment with her. Her waiting list is a year long."

"Aha. So you checked her out."

Syssi crossed her arms over her chest and lifted her chin. "I did not. I heard it on the radio on some talk show I listened to on the drive to work."

Kian leaned and kissed her pouting lips. "For a lofty sum, she agreed to see us after hours. The appointment is at eight."

Syssi glanced at her watch. "Is it far? Because we don't have much time."

"Around the corner. She rents an office in one of the nearby high-rises. Not one of ours, though."

"Fancy. I was imagining a storefront with a glowing neon hand."

He chuckled. "I did too. But given her fees and the length of her waiting list, I'm sure she can afford the entire top floor of a fancy office building."

Rising to her feet, Syssi stretched, knowing Kian couldn't resist a chance to grab her for a kiss. She wasn't wrong. His powerful arm encircling her waist, he tugged her into his solid body and kissed her long and hard.

She melted into him, holding onto his neck and prolonging the kiss. By the time he let go of her, her legs had turned into noodles.

"Are you going to put on a bra, or are you going like this?" He gazed at her puckered nipples poking through the thin fabric of her loose T-shirt.

"Stop ogling me or we are never going to leave this apartment."

He lifted a brow. "And that's bad because?"

She put her hands on her hips. "I'll be mad at you for wasting good money on a no-show appointment."

"We wouldn't want that. Now hurry up and get on with it, woman." He slapped her ass none too gently.

She turned and pointed a finger at him. "You're not playing fair."

"Just evening the score for those." His eyes roved over her breasts.

"I'd better go."

"You should," he said with that stern expression that had her thinking of hot, rough sex.

Damn it. Maybe they could have a quickie and be a little late to see Madam Salinka. Nah, if Kian said her fee was lofty, every minute of that appointment was probably worth hundreds. The quickie would have to wait for later when they had time for several in a row.

Yeah, a much better plan.

*T*he woman who opened the office door wasn't wearing a turban, or heavy eye makeup, or a long gown. And she wasn't ancient either.

Madame Salinka, who seemed to be in her mid-forties, was short and pleasantly plump. Instead of a caftan, she wore a Chanel suit paired with four-inch spiky heels. A string of pearls adorned her neck, and a pair of stylish spectacles perched midway down her nose.

She smiled and offered her hand. "Kian, Syssi, please come in." She opened the door wide and motioned for them to go ahead. "My receptionist had to go home, so I'm doing the honors. May I offer you something to drink?"

"No, thank you." Syssi didn't want to inconvenience the woman.

"As you wish. I have water bottles in my office if you change your mind."

Her office, as she called it, was arranged like a living room. A couch, two armchairs, a coffee table, an entire wall of bookcases and a thick rug. No desk, and no pictures on the walls.

"I understand you want to hone your ability to see the future, Syssi." Madame Salinka sat on one of the armchairs, her feet crossed at her ankles.

As Kian and Syssi got comfortable on the couch, he took her hand and brought it over to rest on his thigh.

"It's not about honing it, Madame Salinka, it's about harnessing it. I have no way to control the visions or summon them. I'm completely at their mercy."

The woman nodded and smiled. "Very common for the untrained. But, please, call me Olga. Madame Salinka sounds good on a talk show. In here everyone calls me Olga."

Syssi couldn't help but warm to the woman. Fake or not, she was pleasant and not full of herself.

"Did you train?"

"Of course. Even those born with an incredible talent must get guidance. Tell me everything about your visions. How frequently they come, what time of day, what do you feel before and after. Every little detail is important."

For the next hour, Syssi did a lot of talking, answering Olga's numerous questions. It was clear the woman knew what she was talking about, and after a while Syssi no longer doubted that Olga was the real thing. One had to experience visions to know what to ask.

"That's all. I don't think there is a single thing we didn't cover," she said after answering the last question.

"I can help you, Syssi, but it will take time and a lot of practice."

"I'm not afraid of putting in the work."

Olga clapped her hands. "Good. We have a little time left, so let's start with the basics. After today, I want to see you once a week to check on your progress."

Thinking about the expense, Syssi cringed.

"Don't worry. Now that I know you're for real, I'm not going to charge you as much. I'll give you a professional discount. How does five hundred per hour sound?"

Even though it was a fraction of what Olga had charged for the first visit, it was still an outrageous amount. But then again, when one had a year-long waiting list of clients, one could charge as much as one saw fit.

"Sounds expensive, but I guess you can't go lower than that."

Olga shook her head. "As it is, to make time for you, I will be turning away clients who are willing to pay ten times as much. But I feel it's my obligation to train the next generation, and I hope you'll do the same when the time comes for you to train the one that comes after you. It's how it's always been done. The only way to preserve the craft."

31

RONI

*R*oni pulled out a towel from his bag and wiped the sweat off his face.

Sparring with a bunch of immortal females was a lesson in humiliation. Sparring against one's girlfriend and taking a beating was fucking emasculating.

And if that wasn't pathetic enough, Roni was almost certain that they were holding back.

Getting obliterated by that giant of a man pretending to be the sensei was no big deal—anyone would lose to Anandur, but to keep up appearances, Roni had to take part in the fake class.

As it was, Barty was getting suspicious.

Contrary to what his outward appearance implied, the guy wasn't an idiot.

"Come on, Roni. We are not done." Sylvia assumed the stance.

He winked at her. "How about sparring with me somewhere private? Just you and me."

Barty laughed. "As if a hottie like her would give a scrawny piece of nothing like you the time of day."

Roni flipped the jerk. "Screw you, Barty. If you can find anyone who would, that is." The guy knew Sylvia was his girlfriend. Roni had told him that his previous handler had taken him to meet her in cafés and restaurants, which was true, partially.

Most of their time together was spent at night in his room with Andrew sitting on the other side of the wall and waiting for them to be done.

The truth was that Roni didn't understand it himself. Sylvia was hot and could get any guy she wanted. Why would she settle for a geek who was several years younger, had a bad attitude, and lived like a bug under a microscope?

It didn't make sense.

Was it his super brain that attracted her?

Nah. If that was the case, Sylvia would have spent more time talking to him than screwing him. But she seemed to prefer the latter. Must have been his amazing lovemaking.

Right. As full of himself as Roni was, he found that as hard to believe as all the rest.

Sylvia rolled her eyes. "Shut up, Roni. Don't antagonize him," she whispered.

Roni assumed a defensive pose. "Anything else would make him suspicious," he whispered back. "That's me being me."

She smirked. "Let's give him a show."

The girl moved like a blur, and before Roni knew what hit him, he was sprawled on his back on the mat with Sylvia on top of him. "How about a kiss? Would you like that?"

Roni let his arms flop by his sides. "I surrender. Do with me as you please."

Sylvia dipped her head and kissed him, her tongue entwining with his for an erotic dance that had him harden in no time.

Barty whistled and then made a howling wolf sound. "Give it to him, girl."

"I intend to," she answered before kissing Roni again.

He wondered what her game plan was, but it became clear when she rose to her feet and offered him a hand up. "Come on, Roni. Let me give you some private tutoring."

Barty almost fell off his chair. "I'll be damned. Can you give me some lessons too? Any of you, girls?"

Sylvia's friends giggled as Barty was expecting them to, while Sylvia dragged Roni behind her into Anandur's office, or whomever the place belonged to. There was a picture of a buff Asian dude on one of the walls. That guy was probably the real sensei.

Closing the door behind her, Sylvia moaned loudly, then added in an even louder voice, "Oh, Roni, what are you doing to me? You make me so hot."

Roni sat on the desk and spread his legs, beckoning her to him. "I want a real kiss. Not one for show," he whispered.

Sylvia sauntered over and got between his outstretched legs. As she kissed him, her hand traveled down his chest all the way to his stiff cock and cupped him. "Is this for me?"

"Do we have time?"

Her face fell. "I wish, but we need to talk."

"Then let's talk fast, and then go for a quickie. I miss you."

She touched her forehead to his. "I miss you too. But we can't risk me coming at nights in addition to this. Once we get you out, we can be together as much as we want. No more sneaking around."

Fuck, it was tempting. But he couldn't. Not yet.

"I can't leave until I build a backdoor into the system."

"How long is it going to take?"

"I don't know. Days. Maybe weeks. We are talking about the best-protected system in the world. I want my backdoor to be completely undetectable. Because if they find it and close it, I could never get back in."

Her eyes were sad. "Is it really that important, Roni? More important than us?"

"Please don't do this. What we have is special and I would give up anything to be with you. But this just means waiting a little longer while securing our future as well as your people's. Access to all that information and computing power is priceless. I would have to be a total moron to give it up just because we are impatient and want to be together."

She nodded. "I hope that by the time you're ready it's not going to be too late. Barty is watching everything. He is not stupid."

A wicked grin spread over Roni's face. "Then let's give him one hell of a show, or a broadcast as it may be."

"What do you have in mind?"

"Something we haven't done yet. Sex on a desk." He hopped down. "Lean over it."

He guided Sylvia to bend over the desk, then pulled her uniform pants down and knelt behind her.

She turned her head and glanced at him. "What are you doing?"

He cupped her ass cheeks, then slid lower to part her already moist folds. "What does it look like I'm doing? Homework."

Her latest sex lessons had been about how he should pleasure her orally.

Sylvia laughed, but as his tongue made contact with her bare slit, her laughter died out and turned into a soft moan. He'd been meaning to ask her whether she waxed, or were all immortal females hairless down there, but until now there had been no opportunity. Not that now was a good time while he was busy showing her what a quick study he was.

It was truly amazing how uninhibited she was.

Her friends, plus Anandur, plus Barty were all on the other side of that flimsy office door, and yet Sylvia made no effort to silence her needy moans. On the contrary. Her "Oh, dear Fates, I'm coming," was probably loud enough to be heard next door.

Roni pulled down his own pants and speared into Sylvia's wet heat from behind, sending the old desk skidding forward a few inches. That too was no doubt heard by everyone in the vicinity. But Sylvia didn't care, and as his climax neared, neither did Roni.

After they had cleaned up as well as they could with a bunch of tissues, Sylvia pulled Roni into a crushing hug. "Think about it. We can have this every day. Hell, we can have it several times a day. When you turn immortal, you'll have even more stamina."

He pulled back. "Any complaints?" He doubted many guys could go three and sometimes four times in a row.

"No, baby. You're a stud. But after your transition you'll become a thoroughbred stallion."

Damn, way to make him feel inadequate and jealous. No wonder she was so experienced. She must've been shagging immortal studs left and right.

But if that was the case, why had she settled on a geeky human with acne on his face?

Was this some kind of a ruse to have him agree to work for her and Andrew, or whoever they were working for?

That was exactly what was going on.

Fuck. He'd been so naive. What was he thinking? That a beautiful, sensual woman like Sylvia could fall for someone like him?'

A conspiracy to steal him and his unparalleled talent made much more sense than the fantastic tale they had told him about immortals and Dormants and all that shit.

Fuck. What an elaborate setup.

Whoever had planned it must've really wanted him to go to such lengths. Or maybe they had been afraid that Roni was too smart to fall for something simple. To fool him, they had to invent one hell of a hoax. Like the stunt they had pulled with his dear departed grandmother.

Roni had been wondering about Andrew bringing in an outside program for him to use. It was much more dangerous than anything he'd asked Roni to do before. But it had been all a smokescreen. The real purpose was for Roni to see the two driver's licenses with his grandmother's picture on both.

"Roni? Are you okay?" Sylvia nudged him.

He looked at her, then followed her eyes back to his state of dishevelment. His pants were still down around his ankles.

As he yanked them up, the small office suddenly felt suffocating and he couldn't wait to get out.

"Let's go." He opened the door, went straight for his gym bag, and lifted it off the floor.

"Get up, Barty, we're going home."

32

EVA

*B*hathian opened the door to Kian's office and flipped the lights on. "It looks like we are the first ones here."

Eva walked over to the oblong conference table and pulled out a chair. "It's strange meeting here without Kian. I feel as if we are intruding."

"He is meeting with Turner at the guy's offices."

"Is it about the murder?"

Bhathian nodded.

"I wish he would let me help with that."

Kian had refused her offer, saying there was nothing she could do. Eva begged to differ. If he were willing to pay for a membership for her, she could sit there evening after evening and listen. One could learn a lot that way. True, it wasn't the fastest way to gather information, but it was safe and paid off in the long run.

She wondered if his refusal had had something to do with Bhathian, who would have argued vehemently against it. Members of this particular old-boys club gave each other's mates a wide berth.

Bhathian clasped her hand. "Turner has people everywhere. He is better suited for the job. Besides, you're the only one that can lead the investigation into the mysterious immortal females."

"Or one female. Bridget said she'd have the results of the test ready for us today."

Bhathian lifted her hand to his lips and kissed the back of it. "Have you met Michael already?"

She'd encountered so many immortals since her first visit to the keep, it was hard to remember who was who. Especially with her shitty memory. "I don't think I have. But you know how I am with names. It doesn't mean anything."

"I was just thinking that if Bridget's test reveals you have a common ancestor, you guys should get to know each other."

It would be nice to have another person to call family. Aside from Nathalie and Phoenix, Eva had no other blood relatives.

"Is Michael a nice guy?"

Bhathian shrugged. "He is a kid. Only twenty-one. I like him. He works his butt off to qualify for the Guardian force."

"Is he any good?"

"He will be. It takes years of training. He is mated to Kri, our one and only female Guardian."

Eva lifted a brow. "Twenty-one and married? Isn't it too young?"

"They are not married. But it's obvious to everyone that they are a mated pair. When you find your one and only, age doesn't matter. I think he is extremely lucky to have found his true-love match so early in his life. It's going to save him many years of loneliness."

The pain and longing in Bhathian's tone squeezed at Eva's heart. He deserved his happily-ever-after.

The big question was whether such a thing existed.

Bhathian obviously believed it, as did the rest of these immortals, but the truth was that their fairy tale had never been put to the test. The few committed clan relationships were new. No one knew whether they would withstand the test of time.

The myth of the true-love match had only one source—the goddess, who might have romanticized her love for the young husband she'd lost.

Perhaps Eva should ask permission to examine the vault Bhathian had mentioned and read through the clan history books. Maybe there was mention of other couples who'd had such a strong bond. But then again, the history books might have been based on Annani's memories.

Not a very reliable source.

Come to think of it, neither were history books in general. There was no such thing as objectivity. Historians had their biases, and even if they sought to provide an objective report, they were forced to align with the version their current ruler or regime favored.

One person's truth was another's lie.

"Sorry that I kept you waiting." Bridget pushed through the doors. "I had a little emergency to take care of first."

"Is everybody alright?" Eva asked.

"Yeah. Just a twisted ankle. But my patient was sure it was broken. I had to take X-rays to prove to him it wasn't."

Bridget pulled a printout from her briefcase. "I have good news." She smiled at Eva. "You and Michael have a common ancestress."

Bhathian slapped his hand on the table. "I knew it!"

"Certainly makes the investigation easier. Only one lead to follow and two intersecting threads leading to it. Now, all we have to do is research the family trees."

"We need Andrew to mine through the data," Bhathian said.

Bridget stuffed the report back in her briefcase without anyone actually looking through it. The doctor had forgotten that not everyone could read and understand her lab results. "Wasn't he supposed to be here?" she asked.

Eva apologized for her son-in-law. "He asked if we can come up to their place. Phoenix wants her daddy and starts crying every time he tries to leave."

"That child is getting spoiled rotten."

Eva cast Bhathian an amused glance. "As if you can refuse her anything."

"I'm the granddaddy. It's my job to spoil her. Her parents need to establish boundaries."

She rolled her eyes. "What boundaries? Phoenix is still an infant."

Bridget pushed to her feet. "I'll let you guys argue about parenting styles without me."

Eva followed Bridget's example and got up. "Thanks for your help."

"Sure. It's my job." The doctor turned on her heel and walked out.

"Come on, Bhathian, we can keep arguing on the way."

He stood, but instead of following her out he pulled her into his arms. "I'd rather make love than argue." He dipped his head and kissed her.

As she opened for him, his tongue swept into her mouth, finding hers, and Eva forgot what they'd been arguing about.

"Now I know what to do when you get in one of your moods."

She narrowed her eyes at him. "Are you saying that I'm moody?"

"No, of course not. I wouldn't dare." He wrapped his arm around her waist and walked her out.

As they headed for the elevators, Eva wondered whether he was right. Had she been more moody than usual lately?

Not really, but her fuse had gotten shorter. She was too ready to explode at the most insignificant provocation.

Was it stress?

Probably. Too many changes in a short period of time would do it. Even the good ones. Reuniting with Nathalie was wonderful, and becoming a grandmother was wonderful as well. But the move from Florida had been stressful, and she was still feeling the impact. Less income from jobs and higher living expenses were causing her stress, as was Tessa's relationship with Jackson. The girl's road to recovery was full of obstacles the size of mountains, and success was in no way guaranteed.

And then there was Bhathian, pressuring her into a relationship she wasn't ready for.

But that was a lie.

She was the one who'd invited him to move in because it had been the right thing to do. He hadn't pressured her into it. Aside from the huge hints about a wedding, he'd been waiting patiently for her to take the next step and then the one after that.

"I'm not usually like that," she murmured as they waited for the doors to open.

"Like what?"

She stepped into the cab. "Quick to anger. I don't want you to get the wrong impression. It must be the stress of the move. You can ask my crew. I've never exploded at them like I do at you."

He lifted a brow. "Are you saying that I'm annoying?"

She shook her head. "Not at all. You're wonderful. That's why my responses are so out of whack."

The grin that split his face was precious. "You think I'm wonderful?"

"I do."

"Then nothing else matters. If you need to yell at me from time to time to release pressure, it's fine with me." He banged his fist on his massive chest. "I can take it."

33

BHATHIAN

For the next hour, Eva kept their granddaughter busy while Andrew sat at the dining room table and worked on his laptop. Phoenix was satisfied with seeing her daddy was there, while the three other adults in the room provided the entertainment.

Mostly Nathalie and Eva. Bhathian helped as much as he could.

Holding Phoenix still scared the crap out of him. Despite what everyone claimed to the contrary, she was tiny. Maybe compared to other babies her age she was big, but to him she looked too small and fragile to handle with his big hands.

Andrew used his laptop to investigate the two family trees. Apparently, birth and death records weren't considered highly classified information, therefore allowing him access to the databases from home.

"I think she is getting tired," Nathalie whispered.

Eva rocked the baby gently. "Her eyes are closing. Do you want to give her a bottle and put her to sleep?"

"I'll warm it up."

Eva nodded and kept rocking gently, planting small kisses

on one sweet little cheek and then the other. "I can't get enough," she whispered. "It's intoxicating."

He had to agree. Eva, for lack of a better term, looked high on endorphins. Maybe if he wasn't stressing as much whenever he held the baby, he could've experienced the same kind of high.

Perhaps when she got a little older and looked less breakable. Babies were so fragile. Even older kids. Until they transitioned they were just as vulnerable as human children.

"Nathalie should take her to Annani," he said.

Eva cast him a questioning glance. "Why?"

"All our new mothers travel to Annani's sanctuary. In fact, most choose to go when their time nears so they can deliver their babies there. Our children are safe there, and for the girls it's the only way they can turn. The earlier they gain immortality, the better." He hadn't discussed it yet with Nathalie and Andrew. But it seemed they were in no hurry.

"I wonder how Annani does it. Angel dust?"

Bhathian chuckled. "No. She glows, but no glittery dust."

"Okay, Mom. Hand her over." Nathalie stuffed the bottle in her pocket and took the baby from Eva. "Ten minutes tops." She smiled as Phoenix let out a big yawn.

Adorable.

A few minutes later, Andrew closed his laptop and came over to where they were sitting on the couch, the yellow pad he'd been scribbling on in hand.

"Here is what I got. Michael's family has been living in Minnesota for generations. Yours, Eva, has been all over the place. It seems like every new generation got up and left to settle somewhere else. Maybe you have some gypsy blood in you?"

Eva shrugged. "I have a face that can belong to any nationality. Who knows?"

"I was joking. Though like most Americans, your ancestors came from all over the world."

Eva looked thoughtful for a moment. "I heard of a new genetic test that can tell you what percentage of your genes come from where. It's all done through the mail."

Bhathian patted her hand. "Not a good idea. For many reasons."

Eva nodded. "You're right. The last thing I need is for some depository to have my genetic information."

"Exactly. Besides, one day, science may advance enough to break the code on our unique genes."

"She is sleeping. What did I miss?" Nathalie plopped down in her favorite armchair and lifted her legs onto the ottoman.

"I was just starting, baby." Andrew cast her a loving glance. "Two whole generations separate Eva from Michael, meaning that his grandmother is your age. Naturally, I made sure to compare the female ancestors who were contemporaries. I'll refer to yours, Eva, because it's easier than saying great-great- grandmother, etc."

She nodded. "Makes sense. And also makes me feel old, but I digress."

Nathalie snorted. "You look younger than me, Mom. So stop complaining."

Bhathian looked from mother to daughter and back. In their appearance, the two looked the same age, but Eva's expression was more mature. As it should be. "You're both beautiful and look no older than twenty-five."

Nathalie waved a hand. "You're biased."

He shrugged. "We can put it to the test. Ask random people on the street."

Andrew snapped his fingers. "People, can I have your attention, please?"

Eva dipped her head in a perfunctory bow. "I'm sorry for the interruption. Please continue."

"I found the birth and death certificates of your grandmother and her mother before her, but the woman who was named as your great-grandmother's mother has neither. No birth and no death certificate. Now, this wasn't unusual in the late 1800s, especially in rural communities. But, the same is true of Michael's ancestress who was her contemporary. The reason may be the same, there was no law mandating birth certificates, but it's worth investigating."

"How?"

"Michael's great-grandmother is still alive. She might have some family memorabilia, maybe some stories that were passed on from generation to generation. You can start by interviewing her. I suggest taking Michael with you."

"What about my side?"

Andrew shook his head. "No one on your mother's side, and your father's side is irrelevant."

"Do I have any living relatives at all?"

"Some second cousins and their families. Do you want me to make you a list?"

Eva's shoulders slumped. "No. There is no point. They wouldn't even know who my mother was. I've been resigned to the fact that I have no family for a long time."

Bhathian clasped her hand. "You have a family. You have me and Nathalie and Phoenix and Andrew, and an entire clan of busybodies who want to know everything there is to know about you and gossip endlessly behind your back like every big family does."

That got a smile out of her. "Gee, I'm such a lucky girl," she said with a note of sarcasm.

"Yes, you are. They might be nosy and gossipy, but they got your back. When push comes to shove, every clan member will stand by your side."

Nathalie nodded. "After a lifetime of no one to depend on other than myself, it was hard for me to internalize that I have a huge family that cares about me and is not only willing but eager to help. It's a good feeling." She crossed her arms over her chest. "Well worth the inconvenience of having everyone in your business. Nothing is sacred to them. My sex life was the most discussed topic of conversation for months."

The tips of Andrew's ears got red. "I'm sure you're exaggerating."

"I'm not. Ask him." She pointed at Bhathian.

"Is it true?"

Bhathian had no choice but to nod. He'd been no better than the others, going to Bridget and asking her to intervene. "Everyone was worried, that's why they talked. It wasn't malicious."

"I know. Still, it was embarrassing. But whatever, as I said before, the safety net and support are worth the sacrifice of privacy."

Andrew sighed. "In this day and age there is no real privacy to be had. Everything we do can be easily traced."

Eva leaned forward. "That's why I don't use electronic devices when I want to keep something secret. I use old fashioned pen and paper."

Andrew lifted his yellow pad. "Same here." He tore out the page and handed it to her. "By the way, we have another investigation coming up. Roni's grandmother. We know she is an immortal and we know her last whereabouts, but after that nothing. She seems as clever as Eva at hiding her tracks, and this time there is no government pension to follow."

Eva crossed her legs and rearranged her long skirt. "I doubt we would find Michael's ancestress either. We need to find a way to lure those immortals to us. If I had the slightest clue that there were others like me, I would've searched for them."

For a few moments no one said anything. Eva was probably right. If someone didn't want to be found and was smart about it, he or she could stay hidden. At least for a few more years. Already, there were surveillance cameras everywhere and more were installed every day. Soon, it would become impossible to go to the supermarket without getting detected.

Especially when all those camera feeds connected to some central super computer that analyzed the data. That day wasn't in some distant future. It was around the corner.

Those who needed to hide would have to wear the kind of disguises Eva used on assignment every time they left their homes.

For the first time in history, the clan's existence was in peril not because of their ancient enemy but because hiding would become impossible.

"But, Mom, how can we attract those immortals without giving the Doomers clues as to our whereabouts? And what if those immortals are not good guys? Like that Kalugal fellow and his group. We might bring another enemy to our doorstep."

"I don't know, sweetheart. Something to brainstorm, I guess."

34

EVA

*B*hathian sprawled on the hotel bed. "Paid vacation, all expenses covered. I love it."

Eva kicked off her shoes and sat down next to him. "We are on assignment. It's work."

"If I'm not sweating, then it's not work."

She punched his bulging bicep. "Are you going to survive not lifting weights for three days?"

"I'm going to sneak out at night and lift some cars."

He winked, but she wasn't sure he was kidding. "Can you do that? Lift cars?"

"Of course. One in each hand. But it's going to be difficult to get a good grip."

She punched him again. "Stop joking around and answer me."

"Yes, I can lift a car. Impressed?"

"Very."

"But so can Michael."

"No way is he as strong as you."

"He can lift your Prius. I can lift my Tahoe."

"That's a big difference. Still, I was surprised to see his dad was buff too. The guy is an accountant."

"His folks are nice. Good people, as Sharon would say."

Eva lay on her side, propping her head on her elbow. "Who did she say it about?"

"Jackson and me. She called us menschen."

It warmed Eva's heart. Sharon was never wrong about things like that. She called it after the first minute of meeting someone. "You are good people."

"Thank you."

"Michael's mom has a different opinion. She was suspicious of us. That's why she insisted that both she and her husband accompany us to visit her grandmother."

"Or, it might have to do with her feeling guilty about not visiting the old lady in over a year."

"Do you think she bought our story?"

"Why not? Michael was pretty convincing."

"That's because he was really excited to discover you guys were related through a common ancestor."

Eva smiled. "He was. And we weren't lying. We really are investigating my family tree."

"Just not for the reason we gave them."

She shrugged. "I'm going to take a shower, want to join me?"

His eyes brightened. "That's an invitation I'm never going to turn down."

Kian's budget for expenses was more than generous, and the hotel room they'd reserved was luxurious, with a large shower and an adjoining whirlpool tub. But even though the shower was big enough for two, it had only one shower head, which wasn't necessarily a bad thing.

Eva had an idea. "Let's play out another one of my fantasies."

Bhathian cupped her ass. "I'm listening."

"You're a warrior on a distant planet who's been captured and put on the slave market. I bought you with one thing in mind—sex. You have to pleasure me. You hate me because I own you, but you can't resist me. You want me."

"I like it except for the hating you part."

"Okay. So let's change it a bit. You hated me at the beginning, but you fell in love with me and decided to stay mine forever."

"That's better. What would you have me do, mistress?" He bowed his head.

"You can start by shampooing my hair and soaping me all over."

"With pleasure, mistress." Bhathian squirted some of the shampoo she'd brought with her into the palm of his hand and started working it into her scalp.

His strong fingers were pure heaven as he massaged and lathered, rinsed and repeated, then worked the conditioner into her hair.

"I'm done with your hair, mistress. May I soap your magnificent body now?"

"You may."

Standing behind her, he squirted liquid soap into his hands and started at her shoulders, then moved around to her collarbone.

Melting, Eva leaned against his solid body.

One of his hands moved up, encircling her throat, while his other cupped a breast. "Is that good, mistress?" he whispered in her ear then tweaked her nipple hard. Instinctively, she pushed away from him, but his hand on her throat anchored her in place.

He moved his hand to her other breast and repeated the same harsh treatment. This time she anticipated it and didn't jerk forward.

"You're quite bold for a slave."

"Would you prefer me timid?" he said softly, then nuzzled her neck.

Eva was turning into a puddle of need. "No."

"I didn't think so." He nibbled on the sensitive spot where shoulder met neck, his fangs scraping her skin. Still holding her immobilized with his hand on her throat, he alternated little nibbles with licks and kisses, turning her legs to jelly.

His fingers loose, applying no pressure at all, he only sought to cage her. Her head falling back on his shoulder, Eva relaxed further into his body, letting her slave dominate the scene.

"That's a good girl." His hand left her throat to join the other one on her breasts, alternating between gentle caresses and tweaks, the line between pleasure and pain blurred.

"Make love to me, Bhathian."

"Are we done playing, mistress?" One hand glided south to cup her hot center, the heel of his palm pressing on the seat of her pleasure.

Unable to articulate a response, she moaned.

"First, you're going to come for me, my mistress." Bhathian penetrated her with two thick fingers, the palm of his hands rubbing harder and faster.

His erection at her back felt enormous, and yet he was in no hurry to take his pleasure. No matter what game they played, Eva always came first.

"Come for me, mistress." He closed his fingers around her nipple and pinched lightly, the fingers of his other hand working her into a frenzy. When he pinched harder, the coil sprung and she erupted, her channel spasming around his digits.

"Beautiful." He held her up as he rinsed the soap and conditioner off, then lifted her into his strong arms and carried her out of the shower and set her down on the vanity.

She felt loose, boneless, letting Bhathian do everything

for her. From wrapping a towel around her wet body and toweling her hair with another, and even rubbing lotion into her legs and arms the way she always did after a shower. When he was done, he lifted her again and carried her to bed.

"You're spoiling me," Eva murmured.

He smirked. "That's my job, mistress. I have to work off what you paid for me. Was it a lot?"

"A fortune. But you're worth it."

"Good to know."

35

SYSSI

*I*t had been an intense week. Every day after work, Syssi practiced what Olga had taught her. But like the time she'd tried meditation, she couldn't empty her mind enough to enter the state of calm needed for either.

Exasperated, she walked into Kian's home office and plopped onto a chair. "It's not working. I'm doing everything exactly the way she taught me but it's no use. Every minute I'm awake, there is a raging storm of thoughts in my head. How am I supposed to quiet that down?"

Kian got to his feet, came over to her side of the desk and lifted her in his arms, then sat in the chair with her on his lap. "I know a few ways to help you relax."

"*Pfft*, you think? The storm still rages, just with a different kind of thoughts."

"Tell me about them. I want to know."

"I bet you do."

"Why not? Are you still embarrassed after all this time?" Yeah, she was. But Syssi wasn't going to admit it. "I want you to keep guessing. If you know everything, you'll get bored."

He tapped her nose. "Never."

"I think you should cancel the next appointment. It's a waste of money."

Kian shook his head. "No, it's not. This is important to you. Keep trying. Or perhaps the opposite. It's possible that you are trying too hard. I remember you telling me about the diminishing results of repeated tests. The brain gets tired or bored doing the same thing over and over. Do one exercise a day, no more."

"I wish I could. But once I set my mind to something, I want to achieve it as soon as I can. I believe in the total immersion method. You want to learn something quickly, you need to feed your brain with everything that has to do with the subject and exclude everything else."

"Sounds good in theory, but impractical. You have work to do, and a husband to keep satisfied..."

She lifted a brow. "Do I hear any complaints?"

"On the contrary. I'm the luckiest bastard on the planet to have a sexy, passionate wife like you."

"You forgot smart."

"It goes without saying. You're fucking brilliant."

Syssi rested her head on Kian's shoulder. "I promised Nathalie to babysit Phoenix and Fernando for a couple of hours. She and Andrew want to go down to the movie theater and pretend they are on a date."

"When?"

"She said whenever, but no later than ten."

Kian glanced at his watch. "Plenty of time, sweet girl. It's only five after seven."

Hell, why not. She needed some real relaxation, not enforced emptying of the mind that only added to her stress instead of alleviating it. There was nothing that left her boneless and blissfully content like sex with her Superman. "Take me to bed."

"You sure?" He waggled his brows. "I was thinking to make use of this very sturdy desk." To demonstrate, he kicked the side panel. "See? It didn't move an inch."

Syssi's vivid imagination immediately painted a picture of her bent over the desk, her pants and panties around her ankles, and Kian thrusting into her from behind. She got moist in an instant. "I like how you think, my kinky Superman."

Kian's evil smirk held the promise of something deliciously wicked. "Bend over the desk, Syssi, and bare your beautiful behind for me."

"Yes, sir."

Their sexcapades only started at the office. They continued in bed, then in the shower, and by the time Kian was done with her, Syssi couldn't keep her eyes open.

"Wake me up at nine," she mumbled as he tucked her in bed.

"I will. Sweet dreams, sweet girl." He kissed her cheek.

---

*I*t was a beautiful day. The grass was the most vivid of greens, the sky was pure light blue, clear of clouds, and the sun was shining through the canopies of trees, casting a warm glow on the scene unfolding before Syssi's eyes.

"Phoenix, please be careful, he is too little for that. Go slow," Eva called out. Sitting on a bench in the same park Syssi had seen Andrew play with his yet unborn daughter, Eva watched an older version of Phoenix push a younger boy on the swing.

The dream was extremely vivid. Syssi felt as if she was watching a movie, aware of being an outside observer and not a participant.

Who was the little boy?

Could he be hers?

Please, God, make it so.

Squinting her eyes against the sun's glare, she tried to see his features. Maybe the boy looked like her? Or like Kian? Though if he was Andrew's son, the boy could look like her too.

Phoenix got tired of pushing and sat on the next swing over. "Auntie Eva, could you please push us?"

"Of course, sweetheart." Eva put down the magazine she was flipping through and walked over to the two children. "How high do you want to go?" she teased.

"All the way up!" Phoenix lifted her arm pointing to the sky.

"How about you, sweetie? How high do you want to go?"

"That high." The boy extended his arm parallel to the ground.

"Okay, munchkins, get ready!" Eva shoved Phoenix's swing, sending her flying up high.

"Yay!" the girl squealed happily.

Eva pushed the little boy gently. "Is that okay, sweetie?"

He nodded.

Damn. Syssi was waiting for Eva to say something that would indicate who the boy was, but it seemed her vision was meant to leave this most important detail vague.

Just as the picture began to blur, the boy looked her way as if he could see her, smiled and waved.

Her eyes popping open, Syssi gasped. She needed to memorize every detail of that prophetic dream before it faded the way dreams tended to do. Staring at the ceiling, she replayed the entire scene in her head from beginning to end before it had the chance to sink below the barrier of her consciousness.

When she was sure everything was securely stored in her prefrontal cortex, Syssi glanced at the time display on the bedside phone. She'd been asleep for less than an hour.

There was still plenty of time until she was needed at Nathalie's.

Good. Maybe if she fell asleep again, she would dream more about the little boy and find out if he was hers. Closing her eyes, she drifted away effortlessly.

"Syssi, wake up. It's nine." She heard Kian after what seemed like no more than a minute later.

"Already? I just fell asleep."

Kian's smile was pure male satisfaction. "Poor baby, I tired you out. You want me to call Nathalie and tell her that you need to reschedule?"

With a sigh, Syssi sat up, letting the comforter slide down and expose her breasts. "No, it's okay."

Kian couldn't resist and cupped one gently. "You look tired. You should go back to sleep."

"No, I'm fine. A little disappointed. That's all."

Kian's smile vanished. "Whatever was missing from the previous round, I'll rectify immediately. Tell me what you need."

Syssi rolled her eyes. "It's not the sex I'm disappointed about, silly boy." She cupped his cheek and leaned to kiss him. "You're my Superman. Everything I could've ever wanted and more."

The smile was back. "Phew." Kian wiped imaginary sweat from his brow. "For a moment there I was afraid I was losing my touch."

She shook her head. Joking aside, apparently even an overconfident man like Kian could succumb to insecurities—a huge ego but a fragile one.

"I dreamt about Phoenix playing with a little boy in the

same park I'd seen her in before she was born. She was about five and the boy looked to be a year younger, maybe more. Eva was watching both of them. It was like a movie—full color and sound, but I couldn't figure out who the boy was. Obviously I hoped he was ours."

"Oh, sweet girl." Kian pulled her into his arms. "Don't worry. We will have a boy and a girl, at least one, preferably more. I want a couple of little princesses. Spread over time, naturally, so we can enjoy each one individually."

Syssi put her head on Kian's chest. "I hope so. After I woke up from the dream, I went back to sleep, hoping to dream again and get some more clues. But I ended up not dreaming at all."

Kian smoothed his hand down her back. "If that was a true vision, it means a new baby boy is coming soon to our family. Which is great news even if he isn't ours. Right?"

She nodded. "If he's Andrew's, I'm going to be really jealous."

"What if he is Kri's and Michael's?"

"I'm going to be jealous too."

"Amanda and Dalhu's?"

Syssi paused to think, then shook her head. Amanda's situation was complicated. "I don't know if Amanda could handle having another child. She would freak out over every little thing. Not that I could blame her. I would be the same."

Soothing, Kian's hand kept stroking her back. "The boy couldn't have been Amanda's. If she conceives again, Amanda will travel to Annani's sanctuary when her time comes. She is not going to take any chances next time. She'll stay there until it's time for her son's transition. Even her research wouldn't keep her here."

That would be a disaster.

Syssi was glad Amanda didn't want children. Otherwise,

she would've felt extremely guilty for wishing her sister-in-law wouldn't get pregnant anytime soon.

Kian was right, though. The boy couldn't have been Amanda's. "In the dream, Eva was babysitting him together with Phoenix in a local park. Not the sanctuary."

36

EVA

*T*he back windows of the limousine had been tinted black, with a mirror finish on the other side, so at a casual glance they looked reflective rather than completely opaque. The partition between the passengers and the driver had received similar treatment.

Eva felt it as the automobile made turns, or when it went up or down, so presumably she could've made an effort to memorize the route by those little clues. But there was no point. It wasn't as if she really needed to know.

Kian was guarding the location of the new compound fanatically.

She turned to Bhathian. "How come it's okay for the butler to know the way to the new compound and not for you? Or is it just me Kian is worried about?"

"I don't know where it is either. And the driver is special in ways you wouldn't believe."

"Try me."

"Didn't you notice that Okidu is a little strange?"

"So?"

"That's because he is a robot."

She'd never heard about robots that advanced, but then Eva didn't follow the latest news in technology unless it had to do with surveillance.

Science was supposedly reaching the singularity point, where new technology and other advances would grow at an exponential pace. Perhaps prototypes of super advanced robots were already available. Knowing Kian, he'd probably acquired the first manufacturing facility of its kind.

"You can make a machine that is that realistic?"

Bhathian shook his head. "No. Okidu and his brothers, for lack of a better term, were a present to Annani from her groom. They were considered an ancient relic even then. No one knows who created them and how. William tried to figure it out for years. But it's not like we could cut them open to see how they work. We don't want to do anything that might harm them. Besides, trying to do so may trigger a booby trap. The Odus are indestructible."

Eva leaned back and folded her arms over her chest. "Fascinating. And no one knows who made them? Even the goddess?"

"No. Annani was very young when the nuclear disaster destroyed her people, and she didn't know all that much. The only reason we have any advanced technology at all is that she stole her uncle's tablet before running away. The thing has immense stores of information, but unfortunately in only a few limited fields. Annani's uncle wasn't interested in medicine. Her aunt was the one in charge of that."

"I want to visit that vault you were talking about and see what I can find there."

Bhathian chuckled. "Nothing there is written in English, and what there is are laws and customs. Annani believes in oral transmission of our history. We have no written record of it."

"You guys need to write it down and translate it into English."

"You're probably right."

The limousine came to a stop, and a moment later the butler opened the door. "We have arrived."

Bhathian got out first and offered Eva his hand.

The parking lot they were in looked like a replica of the one in the keep, just twice as big, and instead of three elevators, there were six.

Okidu pressed the button up. There was no button for down. Another thing that was different from the keep.

"No lower levels?" Eva asked.

"No. The other underground levels are built above the garage and the tunnel leading to it. Both the garage and the tunnel are booby-trapped in case of an invasion. Obviously, we couldn't have levels below it that would get cut off from the rest of the complex if the traps were triggered." The elevator arrived, and the three of them entered.

Eva watched the display with fascination. They passed ten underground levels until the elevator stopped, and unless the lift was incredibly slow, there was a lot of earth between one level and the next.

They exited into a sizable pavilion, and then out through one of the sliding glass doors that currently stood open. It seemed like the automatic closing mechanism wasn't engaged yet.

For some reason, Eva had expected the place to be tranquil. After all, no one was living there yet. Instead, she was surprised to find a lot of bustling activity and the place not nearly done.

"What about all these people? Do you have Okidu drive them to work too?"

"No, they stay on the premises until the job is done. The supply trucks are driven by Okidu and Onidu. It's good that the Odus don't need rest because it's a twenty-hours-a-day job."

"Are all the workers Chinese?"

"Yes, and they don't speak any English. The chief contractor, who is one of ours, hired several Chinese construction firms to do the job. As long as they are paid well, they don't ask questions. Once the project is completed, Yamanu will rearrange their memories. He is incredibly powerful. We use him only when mass thralling is needed."

"Which reminds me. I haven't practiced thralling in a while." Eva threaded her arm through Bhathian's. "It's going to be beautiful here when it's done."

The mature trees hiding the structures must've cost as much as the building project. It was a forest, planted in strategic places to provide cover. The development sprawled over what Eva estimated to be around a hundred acres. Most were small family homes, between eight hundred and two thousand square feet each, but in the center there were larger buildings too.

The place was built like a village, with a big central square that was designed like a mini park, with ponds, and walkways, and benches, and a playground for kids.

The larger buildings were probably meant to serve communal functions like offices, a clinic for Bridget, and a gym. But in that case, what was the extensive underground for?

"Is Kian moving everyone out of the keep once this is ready?"

"Not all at once. It will be done in stages, and he still hasn't decided whether this will be just residential and work will be done in the keep, or if everything will be moved here. There are still some logistics that need to be worked out."

"I'm sure. It's an impressive undertaking. I don't think I internalized how wealthy the clan is until now. I can't imagine how much money went into all this." She turned in a circle, waving her hand at all she saw.

One of the workers looked at her askance. She dismissed it. But when another cast her the same evil eye, she turned to Bhathian. "Why are they looking at me like that?"

"Superstition. They believe women bring bad luck to a construction site. They asked for no female visitors during the building process."

Eva bristled. "What a barbaric attitude. Kian shouldn't have hired them. If enough people turned their services down because of that, I bet you good money that they would have forgotten all about their stupid superstition very quickly."

"You're absolutely right. But these people are experts at digging tunnels. The best in the world. I think that having a solid underground that wouldn't collapse on us is more important than teaching these people a lesson. Besides, nothing is going to make them abandon their irrational beliefs. They will take the job because they need it, and then work while expecting a catastrophe, resigned to their impending demise. It would be cruel to force them to work like that."

Bhathian leaned and kissed her cheek. "Ignore them. Let's go check out the houses and pick out the one we want before anyone else has a chance to call dibs on the best ones. Andrew and Nathalie are coming over tomorrow, and I want them to pick one that is next to ours."

Eva halted. "I told you I have no plans for moving in here, and you said you understood. This was supposed to be just a tour."

He wrapped his arm around her and propelled her forward. "Don't get your panties in a wad. I know that you're not ready to move anytime soon. But I want to pick a house nonetheless. If we wait, we'll get the crappiest location. Like near the incinerators or something like that. As a Guardian I get priority, and I intend to use it."

"Fine. As long as we are clear that this is not for now."

"How about after Sharon and Nick transition and join the clan? Would you be willing to move in then? Think about all the money you'd be saving. You wouldn't have to work as hard, and you'd have more time to spend with Nathalie and Phoenix."

He was making a very compelling case in favor of moving into the village, as she thought of the place. The word 'compound' had a military connotation that didn't fit the relaxed beauty of the clan's new keep.

The only thing she would be giving up was a small measure of independence and a big measure of privacy. Eva wasn't sure she wanted to live with a bunch of busybodies who gossiped about everyone and everything. Then again, as Nathalie had pointed out, it was a small price to pay for the safety net they provided.

"I have to admit that it's tempting. Once everyone in my crew transitions, I might consider moving our agency here. But are you willing to share your house with them?"

"First of all, it's our house. Second, they wouldn't want to live with us after their transition. They would much prefer to move in with their new mates."

The thought brought tears to the back of her eyes. Eva had imagined she had years until her adopted hatchlings flew the coop. Now it seemed like it was around the corner.

Too much was changing too fast.

"What happened? You look sad."

"I thought I had more time. The house will feel lonely without them."

"First of all, you have me. Secondly Nathalie and her family would most likely visit every day. And third, you'd be seeing your crew at work. You'll get a nice office overlooking the square. It's going to be great."

Taking a deep breath, Eva leaned into her man. "Since when did you become so positive and optimistic?"

"Since you walked back into my life."

37

TESSA

*T*essa looked down at the three-inch pumps she had on her feet, then lifted her head to look up at Jackson. The shoes didn't have much impact on the height difference. He still towered over her.

"I'm not going to last long in these." As good an excuse as any to cut short their trip to the mall. For someone who hated crowds and thought everyone was out to get her, Sunday was not a good day to push her limits. They didn't have a choice, though. It was Jackson's only free day.

"When you get tired, or when your feet start hurting, we can stop for coffee, or lunch. And if that is not enough, we can buy you flats and drop the heels into the bag." He lifted his hand and pretended to drop a pair of shoes. "Problem solved."

He wasn't going to let her off the hook.

She took his hand. "Or you can carry me piggyback."

"You've got yourself a deal. Now let's go shopping, girlfriend." Jackson affected a snotty valley-girl tone and snapped his fingers.

"You're funny."

"Thank you. Thank you very much." He did an Elvis impression.

Her guy was the total package. Handsome, smart, ambitious, and an entertainer at heart.

As they weaved their way in between the crowds of Sunday shoppers, Tessa clasped Jackson's hand with both of hers, walking as close to him as was physically possible.

He stopped, pulled out his hand from her grip and wrapped his arm around her, bringing her flush against his side. "Better?" he asked.

"Yes. But how are we going to walk without tripping each other up?"

"Easy. You move your left foot, and I move mine at the same time. We need to synchronize."

"Your legs are longer."

"Don't worry about it. We are going to walk at your pace. Ready?"

She nodded.

"Left, right, left, right, left…"

"I got it. You can stop."

Jackson halted.

"I meant the left right thing."

"I know. I like that outfit." He pointed at the display.

A stretchy red and white skirt with a matching top that left the mannequin's midriff exposed. Tessa was much shorter than the doll, but that top wouldn't cover her belly either.

"I don't like shirts that show the belly."

"Why not? This is made for skinny girls."

"It's too daring for me."

"You're going to look so hot in that. At least try it on."

She could do that. Model the outfit for him in the store and walk away without buying it.

"Can you help us? My girlfriend wants to try on that

outfit." Jackson showed the attendant the red and white combo.

The salesgirl, who was about Tessa's age, looked her over. "Size extra-extra-small, right?"

She wasn't that skinny. "I think a regular extra-small would fit me better."

The girl gave her the once-over again. "I'll bring both sizes. Try them on and see which one looks better. You want the skirt to hug your curves, not skim them."

"Okay."

"I'll be right back."

As they waited, Tessa sifted through the sale rack, but nothing caught her eye.

The salesgirl returned a few minutes later with two identical sets and a shoe box. "Let me show you to a fitting room."

She pointed to a chair. "You can sit here," she told Jackson.

"Can't I go inside?"

The girl winked. "Sorry, no monkey business in the dressing rooms." She ushered Tessa into one. "I also brought a pair of white pumps to go with that outfit. Size six, right? You're going to look amazing in that. Are you shopping for a special occasion?"

The girl was so nice and friendly that Tessa felt comfortable talking to her even though she was a stranger. Which didn't happen often. "My boyfriend wants me to wear that." She looked down at what she had on. "As you can see, that's not my usual style."

"You never know. Try it on. Maybe you'll change your mind once you see yourself in the mirror. My name is Sophie. Call me if you need anything." The girl closed the curtain behind her, leaving Tessa alone.

First, she tried the larger size, but Sophie had been right, the fit was all wrong. The smaller size fit her like it was made for her, and the tiny top somehow managed to make her small breasts look bigger.

Tessa had to admit that she looked awesome. The stretchy fabric accentuated the little curves she had, and the contemporary red and white print went well with her new sophisticated hairdo. All she was missing were a pair of white shoes. Or red.

Lifting the lid off the shoebox, Tessa snorted. The shoes had a monster six-inch heel and a three-inch thick platform. Just for the heck of it she tried them on.

Holy moly. She looked like a runway model... or a miniature version of one. She was never going to wear an outfit like that in public, but Jackson had to see her in it.

Surprisingly, the platform made the shoes just as comfortable as the three-inch heel she'd had on coming in. Still, her new vantage point was weird. Tessa had never felt so tall. Getting out of the dressing room area, she sauntered like a runway model.

Jackson's jaw dropped. Tessa giggled, hiding her mouth with the palm of her hand.

Sophie put a hand on her hip. "What did I tell you? Stunning. You've got to take it."

Tessa shook her head. "It's very pretty. But I don't wear things like this."

"Now you do," Jackson said. "Sophie, please pack Tessa's other things and ring this up."

"Jackson. Don't be silly. I'm never going to wear it."

He pressed his palms together and made a pleading puppy face. "Please, for me."

She couldn't refuse him when he begged. "Fine, let me just get my purse and collect my things."

When she came out, Sophie was waiting for her with an empty shopping bag and a pair of scissors. Tessa dropped her other clothes and shoes into the bag.

"Enjoy your new outfit," Sophie said after snipping the tags off and dropping them into the shopping bag.

"Wait, don't you need that tag to ring it up?"

"Your boyfriend already paid. You're good to go."

She needed to have a word with Jackson. The outfit was pricey, but she could afford it. Eva paid her a decent salary, and provided lodging and a car, so Tessa had almost no expenses.

"You shouldn't have done it," she told him.

"I had to. I practically begged you to buy it, and you're probably never going to wear it again. It's only fair for me to pay for something I wanted."

She pointed a finger at him. "Just don't do it again."

"I won't." He took the shopping bag from her and wrapped his arm loosely around her bare midriff. "Now let me show off my gorgeous girlfriend."

38

JACKSON

*T*he eyes of every man, from a twelve-year-old kid to an over-seventy-year-old grandpa, followed Tessa. And not just quick glances. She was turning heads.

His arm around her tightened.

"Jackson, your fingers are hurting me."

He followed her eyes as she turned her head sideways to look at his hand on her shoulder. His fingers were digging into her upper arm.

Damn it. Jackson loosened his grip immediately. There were faint bruises where his fingers had gripped her. "I'm sorry, does it hurt?" He rubbed the spot gently.

"A little. You need to be more mindful of your strength." She lifted her head to whisper in his ear, "I'm still a fragile human."

"I know, baby, I'm so sorry. Usually I am. I was preoccupied imagining beating up all the men ogling you. I'm the only one allowed to do that. But it's my fault. I was the one who insisted you wear this knockout outfit."

"I agree. But you're imagining things. No one is looking at me."

Jackson laughed. "Trust me, they are. It is you who are not looking. That's why you don't see what I see."

She shrugged, but a small smile was tugging at her lips. "It's the outfit. They are probably thinking I'm a show-off or a slut."

Jackson stopped in front of a window display. "Look at yourself." He pointed to their reflection. "What do you see?"

"A woman who isn't me."

"Who is she then?"

"Someone who is overdressed for the mall?"

"Would that be the first thing to cross your mind if you saw a girl looking like that?"

Tessa tilted her head and made a face at her reflection, then struck a pose, one leg forward and a hand on her hip. "If she were a foot taller, I would've thought she was a model hired by that store to advertise their clothing line."

"What if the store specialized in petite sizes?"

"There is no store like that in the mall. If there were, I would've been a loyal customer. Provided their prices were reasonable, that is."

Jackson moved his hand down to her waist. "Another advantage of this outfit is that I get to touch your skin no matter where I hold you." He started walking again.

Tessa might've protested a lot, but her posture and the way she walked told another story—of confidence that wasn't there before. If all it took was a flattering outfit and sky-high shoes, he'd buy her ten more outfits like that even if it meant setting his savings goals back a month. Tessa was worth it.

There were only two problems with that plan. One was that he'd need to constantly push her to dress like that, and the other was that he would have to accompany her everywhere she went to guard what was his. By herself, men would swarm to her like flies to a tasty treat.

The first one he was okay with. Apparently, Tessa needed a little pushing to break out of her shell. But the second was impractical and had a creepy feel to it.

There was no way he would tell Tessa she couldn't go anywhere without him.

Her steps got slower. "My feet are starting to hurt. Can we sit down somewhere?"

"How about lunch?"

"Where do you want to eat?"

Normally, he would've suggested the food court, but Tessa looked too good for that. "How about the Factory?" He pointed to the restaurant.

"Is it any good? I've never eaten there."

"Me neither, but I heard good things. The portions are big." Also that it was pricey, but whatever. Tessa deserved a little spoiling. "At least you don't need to walk far. It's right here."

"Very true."

The place was packed, which was a good indicator of the quality of their food, but it meant a thirty-minute waiting time.

"We can wait at the bar," Tessa offered.

He bent to whisper in her ear, "I didn't bring my fake ID."

She giggled. "I keep forgetting that I'm a cradle robber. If we order a nonalcoholic drink, no one will ask to see your ID."

"Cradle robber, my ass." He marched them into the bar area and found them a table.

"What can I get you?" The waiter put two menus in front of them.

"I'll have a coke," Tessa said and opened the menu. "Can we order food here?"

"Certainly." The guy's eyes stayed a second too long on Tessa.

Oblivious, she smiled. "That's great. We don't need to wait for a table, Jackson. We can eat here."

"Fine by me. I'll have a coke too." He glared at the waiter.

"Right away. I'll be back to take your orders."

"Thank you," Tessa said.

Jackson flipped the menu open. "Let's see what we can eat here."

The selection was huge, but he ended up going for a simple burger with fries. Tessa ordered Asian lettuce wraps. "That's an appetizer, not a full meal," he told her after the waiter left.

"The portions here are really big." She glanced at the table next to them. "You know I can't eat that much."

He took a piece of bread from the basket, smeared it with a liberal helping of butter and handed it to her. "I'm working on changing that."

"You're going to make me fat." Tessa took a bite from the bread. "It's good. I don't mind having another." She reached for the basket.

Jackson stayed her hand. "Please, let me."

"No more," she said after the third piece. "I need to leave room for the actual meal."

Jackson decided to follow her lead. He put back the piece he was about to coat with butter, not because he couldn't handle the entire bread basket and a hamburger or two, but because it wasn't polite to talk while chewing.

"Bhathian and Eva stopped by yesterday for lunch."

"I know. They brought us takeout."

"Did they tell you that they went to look at houses?"

Tessa frowned. "No, they didn't. Why would they go looking at houses? Do they want to buy one together?"

"Remember I told you about the new place my family is getting?" They were in public. It had been drilled into every clan member's head that talking about anything pertaining to the clan was prohibited outside their homes or the keep.

Tessa caught up, as he knew she would. "They went looking around there?"

"Yes."

"Does it mean Eva is going to leave us?" Tessa's expression turned panicked. "She can't do it. I need her. I know it's selfish of me, but when she and Bhathian are in the house at night it makes me feel safe."

Tessa was like a little bird. Every little gust of wind ruffled her feathers.

Jackson reached across the table and clasped her trembling hand. "Nothing is happening now or in the near future. First of all the house is not ready. And second, she said she was going to wait until the three of you were all mated. I mean married," he corrected himself. "She is not going to leave you alone. You know she thinks of you as her kids."

Tessa nodded. Closing her eyes, she inhaled deeply through her nose and exhaled slowly through her mouth, then inhaled deeply again. After five cycles of breathing, her hand stopped trembling.

"You gave me one hell of a scare."

It became obvious to him why Eva hadn't told Tessa about the house, and frankly, he should've known better and phrased it differently.

"The reason I'm telling you about it is that I can get a place for us as well. For the future, of course. Not for now," he added quickly before she had a chance to panic again. "Bhathian made a valid point. Now, we have many options to choose from. Later, who knows what will be left over. Though I'm sure I will not get priority choosing like Bhathian. Police officers and other officials get first dibs. Young guys like me are probably at the end of the list."

"Did you ask your cousin? I would be surprised if any houses have been allocated to people your age."

"My mom did. Everyone has a place. There are more units than takers because they took into account future needs."

Tessa's expression had gotten more relaxed, which was a good sign. She was not rejecting the idea of them moving in together at some point. Maybe the prospect would make her more confident, helping her get over the current hurdle. They'd been making great progress until it had all come to a screeching halt, with the air whooshing out of the wheels that had been propelling them forward.

Jackson felt as if he was blowing the air back into them, one tiny puff at a time.

"I'd like to see the place," Tessa said. "Even if we don't get to choose yet. I'm curious."

"I'll talk to my cousin and see if he can arrange for us to see it."

39

ANDREW

*S*omething had crawled up the kid's ass. It must've happened during the last excursion to the dojo, the one Andrew hadn't escorted him to.

It would've looked suspicious if he accompanied the kid to each class. Besides, it had been one of those days at the office. Andrew had had no choice but to stay late, finishing a case that needed to be done as soon as possible.

On the drive over, Roni had been tight-lipped, sitting in the back and staring out the window while Barty was telling Andrew about his glory days as a field agent.

"Where is Sylvia?" Roni asked as they entered the dojo.

"She's running late," one of Sylvia's friends told him.

Barty clapped him on the back. "Anxious for another round? Not that I wouldn't be if I were you. A hot piece of ass like her comes along once in a lifetime. Especially for a nerd like you. Enjoy her while you can, and don't ask yourself why. It doesn't matter. If you can get it, take it."

After imparting those words of wisdom, Barty strolled over to his usual chair—the one with the best view of the attractive females sparring with each other with such sensual grace that it looked more like dancing.

No wonder the old agent was enthralled.

"Girls, keep practicing the new moves I showed you. Roni, Andrew, take positions." When they did, Anandur walked over to Roni's side. "Look at the sequence of this kata. I'm going to repeat it twice, and then you're going to follow. It's a simple one you can practice at home."

"Yes, sensei."

"Follow closely. One—the long forward stance. Bring your foot forward and bend your knee like this. Then move your other leg straight behind you as you move forward. Like so."

He demonstrated, repeating it twice. "You need to keep your center of gravity constant to remain stable."

Anandur waited for them to follow his instructions. "Second move. Raise the fist of the arm on the same side as your forward foot over to your shoulder and then sweep it downward, protecting your groin and hitting your opponent's arm. Like so. Then finish with your blocking arm pointing straight down over your forward leg. Like so."

Again, he waited for them to follow before moving to the third. "Square your hips and shoulders as you face your opponent and strike from the same side as your forward foot, aiming right there." He pointed at Andrew's solar plexus.

Moving a couple of steps away, Anandur blocked Barty's line of view with his massive body. "Your turn."

"Did you decide what you want to do?" Andrew asked in a low voice. The girls practicing in front of Barty were purposefully making a lot of noise, shouting with every move.

Roni started another repetition of the kata. "I need proof that the story you told me is true."

"What kind of proof?"

"That you're really an immortal. That immortals exist. How do I know you don't work for the Russians or something and want to kidnap me for my talent?"

Andrew chuckled. "If that were the case, the Russians would've had you a long time ago. They don't ask permission. They would've taken poor Barty out and hauled your scrawny ass to some secret location."

That gave Roni pause, and he messed up his moves. Anandur clapped his hands. "Look over here." He repeated the kata. "Now do it again."

The Guardian was giving Barty a perfect show.

"Whatever. I want proof."

Damn kid. When retracted, Andrew's fangs were not long enough to be considered anything other than slightly longer canines, and he'd never tried working himself up into an aggressive enough mode to produce venom in a fight.

Thralling was also something he hadn't learned how to do yet. "I'm new. And there isn't a lot I can do yet. But he can." Andrew pointed his chin at Anandur.

"I don't care who shows me proof as long as I see it. And it has to be damn convincing or no deal."

Anandur clapped his hands again. "Okay, men, that was good. But before we continue, I need you to fill out new insurance forms. Apparently, the ones I had you sign before are no longer good. I really should get a computer in here and print the bloody forms on demand. They keep changing things on me." He shook his head dramatically.

"No problem," Andrew said.

Roni glanced at Barty. The agent nodded and waved him on toward Anandur's office.

As the three of them crammed into the tiny space, Andrew closed the door behind them.

"A quick demonstration." Anandur smirked. "But I need

to warn you that it's going to be scary as hell. I don't want you to scream like a girl when you see a terrifying demon in front of you."

Roni rolled his eyes. "Bring it on."

"He's not bluffing, Roni. Grown men shit their pants when he does it."

"Right." A bored expression on his face, Roni leaned against the desk and folded his arms over his chest.

"Brace yourself. Here it comes."

Naturally, Andrew could no longer see the illusions produced by his fellow immortals, but given Roni's wide-eyed expression and slack jaw, Anandur was putting up a good show.

As Roni scooted back on the desk, his eyes about to pop out of their sockets, Anandur dropped the illusion.

"Cool, eh?"

Regaining his composure with surprising speed, Roni nodded several times, his head bobbing up and down. "Incredible. Can you do it again?"

Anandur shrugged. "Why not."

This time Roni was ready, and he even poked a finger at Anandur's chest. "Unbelievable. I can feel the fabric of your shirt, but what I see is a scaled red chest. How do you do it?"

Anandur pointed to his head. "It's all a mind trick. We have that power over humans. I'm not even that good at it. My brother could make you feel what you see as well."

Roni turned to Andrew. "How come you can't do it?"

"Didn't learn how to yet. But enough chitchat. Barty is getting suspicious."

"Right." Anandur handed them both insurance forms. "If he comes in, pretend you are reading them over."

"I need an answer, kid. Time is running out. We can't keep this charade going on indefinitely."

Roni scratched his head. "I'm not ready yet. I can't leave

before I have a backdoor in. It's in your best interest that I stay until it's done. You guys need access to all that data as much as I do."

40

NATHALIE

"I have a strong sense of déjà vu." Nathalie cuddled closer to Andrew as the limo lumbered uphill. "It reminds me of the drive up to Sari's castle."

Andrew hugged her closer and kissed the top of her head. "You were asleep for the entire drive from the airport to the clan's Scottish keep. I'm surprised you remember anything at all."

"I remember that it was night and that there were no lights so I couldn't see anything out the windows. Same as now but for a different reason. Syssi and Kian, you guys were there as well, and the limo was climbing up and up and up. Almost as it does now."

Syssi closed the magazine she'd been reading and put it over her knees. "It's kind of symbolic. The first limousine ride was on the way to your wedding, and the second is on the way to your new house. Chapter one and chapter two in the story of Nathalie and Andrew. I'm glad to be part of both."

That statement deserved a hug.

Leaving the comfort of Andrew's embrace, Nathalie

moved across to sit on Syssi's other side. "Come here." She opened her arms.

Reluctantly, Kian let go, so Syssi could accept the offer.

"You're the best sister-in-law ever." Nathalie kissed her cheek.

Syssi blushed as she always did at the slightest compliment. "You're just saying that because I babysit for free."

Glancing at Kian's grouchy expression, Nathalie let go of Syssi and moved back to sit next to Andrew. "There is that, true, but you're great all around."

As Syssi returned to Kian's embrace, his grouchy expression morphed into one of content and calm, the way it did only when he had his wife in his arms.

Nathalie wondered how Kian would handle having kids who would compete with him for Syssi's attention. Would he be even more grouchy than usual?

She had a feeling he would.

"I hope Eva and Bhathian are okay. You've never left them alone with Phoenix for more than a few minutes," Syssi said.

Nathalie waved a dismissive hand. "They'll manage. Phoenix adores them both. If they don't, they'll call me."

As the limousine stopped, Okidu lowered the partition. "We have arrived, master."

Kian pushed open the door, got out, and offered his hand to Syssi who took it with an indulgent smile for her man.

They were a cute couple, if one could call Kian cute. The guy was too intense.

Natalie giggled as Andrew practically lifted her out of the limo, straight into his arms. "Andrew, what are you doing?"

"I won't be outdone by my brother-in-law," he whispered right into her ear, his hot breath tickling. "I saw how you were looking at them."

"They are a cute couple," she whispered back.

"My sister is cute. Him? Not so much. But yeah, they are very much in love. I'm happy for them."

They followed Kian and Syssi to the elevators.

"This looks exactly like the garage at the keep," Nathalie remarked.

"Three times as big," Kian corrected her. "It wraps around. The elevators' hub is in the center."

As they entered the hub, which was also much larger than the one in the keep, one of the elevators was waiting with its doors open and they stepped in.

Kian resumed his tour-guide presentation. "There are ten additional underground levels above the garage, with fifty feet of earth separating each level. If we are ever under siege, we can collapse the tunnel at several strategic places. Even if the Doomers somehow manage to get to one of the upper levels, we can block off access to each one independently. The safety features incorporated into this compound are too numerous to list. We are even protected from an aerial attack. The underground levels will keep us safe. Large areas are dedicated to the storage of canned and dried foods, and our water supply is independent, limitless, and well protected. We pump it directly from the ocean and then desalinate it."

Nathalie shuddered. Either Kian was extremely paranoid, or they were in real danger.

When they arrived at the surface, Nathalie looked around, taking in the views of the clan's new super-duper secure compound. The place was messy, with building materials and debris strewn about, but it wasn't difficult to imagine how amazing it would all look when completed.

Following Eva's warning, she avoided looking at the Chinese workers. It wasn't that she felt offended by their superstitions or bothered by them. As one believer to another, she understood that at the core of it lay fears, and that it wasn't personal. Still, it wasn't pleasant to be considered a bad luck omen either.

"You did an amazing job here, Kian." Andrew clapped his brother-in-law on his back. "When you told me the place is invisible from the air, I thought you were exaggerating. But it really is. Whoever designed it did a brilliant job."

"We had a team working on the project. And yet there were some features we'd overlooked. I authorized some major modifications. Let me show you."

The guys walked away with Kian explaining something about the process of water desalination, and Andrew asking to see the trash incinerators.

Syssi put her hand on her hip. "You think we're going to see them back anytime soon?"

"Not likely. Your hubby seemed very excited about having an eager ear for all the technical details."

Syssi waved a hand. "I know. I got the whole tour a week ago. Kian is going crazy with this project. Do you want to check out the houses in the meantime? I can show you ours and Amanda's."

"Lead the way."

Surprisingly, Syssi and Kian's house seemed smaller than their penthouse. "Is it an optical illusion, or is this place not as big as your penthouse?"

"Not by much. The living room is not as huge and there is one bedroom suite less. Okidu has his own little cottage in the back."

"Finally some privacy, eh?"

"You've got it. I don't care that he is supposedly a machine with no feelings. He feels real to me and I don't want him seeing me strutting naked around the house."

"Do you?" Nathalie lifted a brow.

A blush painted Syssi's cheeks red. "Sometimes I just want

to grab a glass of water from the kitchen and I don't want to get dressed for it."

Nathalie suspected that there was more to the story, but it seemed that Syssi would appreciate a change of subject. "Do you know which house is Bhathian's and Eva's?"

"I'll show you."

It wasn't much different than Syssi and Kian's, which surprised her. In the keep, their accommodation reflected Kian's status. They should've done the same here.

Not only was the guy the clan's leader, but he was also the most hard-working of them all. He deserved luxury.

Never one to shy away from asking a question, Nathalie put her hands on her hips and turned to Syssi. "Why is your house so modest? You should have something that is much fancier than the rest of us plebs."

Syssi shrugged. "I'm a pleb too. Besides, we still may. It's all in the finishes. We also have a large private yard with a lap pool. I think that's luxury enough."

"What about the rest of us? No pool?"

Syssi pointed a finger at her. "You see? That's what I wanted to avoid, people asking why we have things that they don't. But to answer your question, there is a huge pool in the underground. There isn't one on the surface because it's impossible to hide it from the air. You can screen a Jacuzzi tub or a small lap pool, but not a big-ass Olympic-sized one."

Nathalie lifted her hands. "Sorry. It was just a question, it wasn't meant as an accusation."

"I know. But others may mean it that way."

It was time to change the subject. "Let's go to the one over there." She pointed. "Do you know if it's taken?"

"It's not. Kian is letting the couples choose first."

They crossed the short distance and entered a house that was almost identical to the one they'd left.

"I need to check out the kitchen." Nathalie walked over

and examined the appliances. "Good quality. No complaints here. Do you know if the water is working?"

"It should. Try the faucet."

The thing made the bursting sound a faucet makes when it hasn't been used in a while, and what came out didn't look pretty, but after a minute or so, the water ran clear.

"Good. I need to use the bathroom."

Syssi grimaced. "There is no toilet paper."

Nathalie reached into her handbag and pulled out a pack of tissues. "I always come prepared."

Syssi laughed. "Do you have soap in there too?"

Nathalie reached into the bag again and pulled out a hand sanitizer. "Ta-da!"

"You are prepared for anything. I wonder what else is in there."

"I'll tell you after I'm done."

Nathalie rushed into the nearest bathroom. Ever since the pregnancy, her bladder needed emptying more often. When she was done, she washed her hands with water and then with the sanitizer. She checked her hair in the mirror above the vanity and pulled out a brush to smooth a few runaway strands.

You're gorgeous, girl. Being a mother suits you.

"Mark. Where have you been?"

I didn't want to freak you out again and make you think you were dead.

"I only thought so because you came to me in a dream. You don't freak me out when you talk to me while I'm awake."

So you don't mind if I pop in for a chat once in a while?

"Not at all. Just try to do it when I'm alone, like now. And not while I'm sitting on the toilet. Not around Phoenix either. Who knows what babies can sense?"

I know. That's why I left you alone during the pregnancy. But I was there. Guarding your mind against evil spirits.

"You're kidding, right? There are no evil spirits."

I wish I were. But no. Just like there are nasties in life there are nasties on the other side.

"In heaven?

Not in heaven. It's not where I am. I'm here—in the in between.

She narrowed her eyes at the mirror where she knew he could see her. "Why are you still here, Mark? Weren't you supposed to cross over after Amanda accepted your forgiveness?"

I'm not sure. Just to remind you, time moves differently over here. While you went through pregnancy and delivery, I spent a few days thinking about things and arrived at the conclusion that my work here isn't done. I need to stay around and keep you safe.

She blew him a kiss at the mirror. "I'm sorry you're stuck here, but I'm happy to have you back. How long were you here? Did you see this place through my eyes?"

I did. It's going to be fabulous, but it needs a café. Like the one you had at the keep.

A sad reminder that the place she thought of as her own was now managed by someone else, and that she was probably never going back to run it again. "I don't see how, Mark. I'm a mother now, and finding an immortal babysitter is difficult. Syssi works, as does my mother. They can do it for a couple of hours but not an entire work day. Besides, I would miss my baby too much."

You'll figure something out. You always do.

"Thanks for the compliment. I doubt I'll find a solution for this one, though."

I have faith in you.

"Thanks. It was great chatting with you, but I need to get back before Syssi comes looking for me."

See you in the mirror, gorgeous. He faded from her mind.

As Nathalie put the hand sanitizer back in her handbag, she realized she hadn't asked Mark about the evil spirits he'd mentioned.

Were they of people she'd known?

Or strangers that for some reason wanted to enter her mind?

41

CAROL

*P*anting, Carol bent at the waist and braced her hands on her knees. "No more, please," she implored her ruthless, heartless, merciless teacher.

As usual, Brundar didn't reply, didn't shake his head in disapproval, didn't respond in any way that would have made him seem flesh and blood and not a machine. He just stared at her with those cold blue eyes of his, his face an expressionless mask.

No doubt others would've felt intimidated by that glare, or at least unnerved, but all Carol felt was annoyance mixed with pity. Something terrible must have happened to Brundar to make him the way he was.

People didn't shut themselves off from others on a whim.

But even though curiosity was eating at her, she wasn't going to ask. Not out of politeness or respect, but because she wasn't going to get an answer.

Brundar didn't talk, let alone share.

"Stop glaring at me and give me a minute to catch my breath. You're killing me." She could've sworn that one corner of Brundar's thin lips twitched in a parody of a smile.

"I'm not killing you. It's the other way around. I'm teaching you to survive."

"It's not going to do me any good if I die from overexertion before the mission."

Again, she got no response. Brundar was probably as fed up with her whining as she was with his ruthless style of training.

He surprised her. "I'm going to give you a break. Let's move to the shooting range."

Carol dropped to her knees and pressed her palms together in mock worship. "Thank you, merciful master. Your slave is eternally grateful."

Brundar wasn't amused. "Get up, Carol," he barked.

"Sheesh, would it kill you to laugh at a joke from time to time?"

"I'm your teacher, not your friend." He walked out, not waiting for her to follow.

Grunting, Carol lifted her gym bag off the floor and ran after him. "You could be both," she told him once she caught up.

Brundar halted, cast her one of his stern glares, and then kept going.

Carol had no problem carrying on a one-sided conversation. "Aren't you tired of that silent act? It must be hard to keep it up when everyone is trying to get you to talk. I bet living with Anandur isn't easy. He is your exact opposite. If you let him talk he never stops. And don't get me started on how funny he is. He loves making people laugh. How can he stand living with you?"

She wasn't expecting an answer.

"We are brothers."

"I know, so what?"

"He has my back, and I have his."

"Naturally. But I'm not talking about going into battle.

I'm talking about everyday living. You guys are roommates, so you have to get along, and I can't see it happening with two people who are so different."

They reached the shooting range and Brundar pulled up the target. "Shoot. Don't talk."

She rolled her eyes and grabbed her gun out of her bag, put in a magazine, and got in position. This was easy. Carol was an excellent shooter. Emptying the chamber, she made a circular bullet hole pattern at the target's center.

"Good. Now let's try the sniper rifle."

She was equally good with that.

"I need to take you hunting," he said out of the blue.

"What? Why?" The thought of killing innocent animals was repugnant to her.

Brundar leaned against the counter and crossed his arms over his chest. "Shooting a cardboard target, even a moving one, is not the same as shooting a living thing. I'm not teaching you a fun sport, I'm teaching you to become a killer." His delivery was calm, cold, and toneless.

His words chilled her to the bone.

In her excitement, Carol had only imagined the aspect that was easy for her, seduction and manipulation; killing wasn't supposed to be part of her mission.

"That wasn't in the job description."

Brundar let his head drop forward, staying like that for a long moment, his stick-straight almost white hair falling in two long curtains at the sides of his austere face.

When he looked up, Carol was shocked to glimpse an echo of fleeting emotion in Brundar's eyes.

"You're a survivor, Carol, and that's the only reason I suggested you for the job. Your other talents are helpful, but on their own they will not keep you alive. If you want to survive this, you need to become a killer. This job is not for the soft of heart. You need to deaden your emotions and become ruthless, killing without a moment's hesitation. Because that moment will cost you your life."

This was the most Carol had ever heard Brundar say, and she wished she'd never encouraged him to talk.

"I don't think I can become that person you're describing. Besides, I'm an immortal who will be facing other immortals. All that talk about death and killing is irrelevant to us."

Brundar's gaze was deadly. "That's not true and you know it. You just don't want to think it through. A bullet to a vital organ, and an immortal goes down as easily as a human. The only difference is our rapid regeneration. You need to deliver final death while he is still out. Swift and efficient." He demonstrated, pretending to pull his heart out of his ribcage.

"I can't do that. Even if I could stomach it, I don't have the strength. You need to break the ribcage apart to reach the heart."

He nodded. "That's right, and I'll teach you how to do it. But you need to work to strengthen your muscles."

Carol put her hands on her hips and shook her head. "I can't. There must be some other way. Poison maybe? Something extra potent?"

"There isn't."

"Then it's a no go. I'm not going to pull anyone's heart out or chop off his head. Forget it."

He glared at her. "Then you can forget about the mission. I'm not authorizing you until you are willing and able to do it."

She chuckled without mirth. "And how the hell would you know if I can or can't? It's not like we are going to practice it?"

"Yes, we are. On animals."

Bile rose in Carol's throat. "No."

"Then your lessons end now. There is no point in continuing."

She shook her head. "How come you are so heartless? How can you talk about pulling out hearts and severing heads with such indifference?"

For a moment, she thought she saw pity in his eyes. But it was gone between one blink and the next.

"In this world, there are predators and prey, and those who straddle the fence unsure who they are, until life forces them into the role they were born to play. Survivors, like you, those who fell victim to predators but escaped by the sheer power of their will, become predators themselves to guarantee it never happens to them again."

"I'm neither. Not prey and not predator."

Brundar shook his head. "When push comes to shove, there is no in between."

42

LOSHAM

"*W*alk with me." Losham waited for his assistant to log out from his computer and join him.

His upcoming audience with Navuh required a clear mind, and Rami was an excellent sounding board for the simple reason that he wasn't afraid to speak his mind. Losham had cultivated that trust in the guy since the day he'd chosen him as his assistant.

It went both ways.

Rami was the only one who knew Losham's true agenda and the reasons behind his actions. Not even Sharim, who he'd adopted as a son, had been privy to his inner motives. Sharim had been too ambitious to be trusted.

As they reached the boardwalk along the beach, Losham slowed down his strides to match those of the strolling humans vacationing on the island. "I need to convince our leader to let me stay abroad for longer periods of time. And I need more men. What do you think is the best way to go about it?"

Rami smirked. "Profits. Don't even mention the failure with the civilian. It's crucial that you uphold your infallible reputation. Talk about how profitable the clubs are, and how you can make them even more profitable by tweaking the operation, then explain that you need to be there to see what needs tweaking."

Losham nodded. He'd been thinking along the same lines. But profits aside, the clubs were not going to help him find the clan's stronghold if civilians had no idea where the stronghold was. Killing them for the sake of reducing the clan numbers could work, but only in the short run until someone connected the dots and followed the trail back to his clubs.

He needed to catch a Guardian.

"How do we go about capturing a Guardian?"

Rami chuckled. "By sending a large contingent of men."

"Obviously. But send them where?"

Rami shrugged. "Maybe we will get lucky and a Guardian will join one of the clubs. But we need more than two warriors assigned to each one if we want to actually capture him."

That was a problem. Even though the Brotherhood numbered many thousands of warriors, Navuh was reluctant to provide Losham with the manpower he needed as if his resources were as limited as the clan's.

"How do we lure them? What would make them come out and investigate?"

"We can kill more of their civilians."

"That's an option. Lead them to a location of our choosing and set a trap."

"Sounds good."

It did, but it wasn't enough. Waiting around for another civilian to show up could take months. It was okay as long as Losham had needed only a few soldiers to maintain that side of the operation, but if Navuh authorized more manpower, he would expect immediate results. "What else can we dangle as bait?"

"Maybe we could start killing off their pets. They care about their humans."

True. The clan was all about helping humanity. Perhaps it could be their Achilles heel. "It's tricky. We need to stage it so it's obvious to other immortals that we are behind it, but not to the human authorities. The last thing we need is another witch hunt."

Rami's brows clenched in concentration. "I have nothing. Do you? Have we done anything like that in the past?" He looked at Losham hopefully.

"Not intentionally." Rami was on to something. "Here and there one of our less than brilliant brothers left the puncture wounds unsealed, and the females bled to death while under the euphoric influence of the venom. That's how the vampire stories started."

Rami's eyes widened. "So we do it again, this time intentionally. The clan will know it was done by immortals, the humans will think a weird new cult is responsible for the deaths."

Losham nodded. "We can help the misconception by spreading rumors about one."

"Or we can start a real cult. Assemble a bunch of idiot humans and thrall them into believing in some nonsense. We could even make them take responsibility for the murders. Ritual killings or something of that nature."

Losham clapped Rami on the back. "Brilliant, my boy. You make me proud."

Rami bowed his head. "I have the best teacher."

"Yes, you do."

Later, when Losham sat in his father's antechamber, waiting to be admitted, he contemplated his new plan. Selling Navuh on it shouldn't be too difficult.

But as always, a new success in one area demanded a sacrifice in another. If Navuh agreed to let Losham stay away from the island for extended periods of time, it would benefit the clubs and help drive their objectives forward. But at the same time, being away from the seat of power was risky.

Navuh was fickle, and Losham could lose his position as his father's top advisor. Not only that, in his absence Navuh might make decisions without consulting with Losham, which could be disastrous.

The servant emerged from the side door, his robes flying behind him as he pretended to be rushed. "Lord Navuh will see you now."

Losham bowed his head. "Thank you."

43

EVA

*T*he stroll on the boardwalk had become a ritual, one Eva was very fond of. Every evening after dinner, she and Bhathian would leave her crew at home and go for a nice walk and a private talk. Just the fact that her house was walking distance from it was worth the costly rent.

Whether she wanted to admit it or not, they were a couple, and it had even stopped freaking her out. Bhathian was everything she could've ever wanted in a man. Not an easy accomplishment since her demands seemed to contradict each other. She wanted a passionate, patient and understanding partner who at the same time was sexually dominant. She used to believe it was like wishing for a unicorn.

But then Bhathian was real enough, and he was hers.

Her arm threaded through his, and her cheek resting on a bulging bicep, it didn't get better than that.

"Are we going to practice thralling today?" Eva asked as they reached the boardwalk.

She'd been tempted to try it on her own, but then reason

prevailed, and Eva decided to wait until she got better at it. If she messed up, Bhathian needed to be there to fix it. She didn't want to leave some innocent person with a messed-up brain.

"What do you want to try today?"

"I don't know. What do you suggest?"

"Let's try something a little more ambitious, like planting a story in someone's head."

"What do you mean by a story?"

"You go up to a random stranger and say hi, how have you been? He has no idea who you are and tries to remember where he met you. You plant a story in his head that you met him at a concert or a movie or a mutual friend's house. It's more complicated than what you did before because you'll need to collect the information from his head."

"What if I can't?"

Bhathian shrugged. "Then you apologize and say that you were mistaken. He is not who you thought he was."

"Sounds easy enough."

It wasn't.

Eva tried it with two different guys, and in both cases she was unable to get into their heads. She wanted to try again, but Bhathian shook his head.

"That's enough for today. We will practice digging into people's brains tomorrow."

"It feels worse than the other stuff, an invasion of privacy."

"True. But you need to practice on someone."

She wondered how the other Dormants turned immortal were doing. "Are you teaching Andrew and Nathalie to thrall?"

"No, but I should. Especially Andrew. He could use it on the job."

Which reminded her about the topic of their conversation from the evening before. "How is the investigation into the face recognition matches going?"

Their own trip to Minnesota had been a waste of time. Michael's great-grandmother had only remembered that the woman in question had died young. Hopefully, Andrew and William were having better luck.

Bhathian chuckled. "Splendidly. Most of our matches are of clan members. Kian is freaking out."

Eva stopped. "Really? That's funny."

"Not at all. It's a huge hole in our security. Kian is having everyone's driver's license picture reworked by an artist and paying a hacker a fortune to upload the new pictures into the system."

"You mean a hacker other than Roni?"

"Yeah. Andrew says that Roni shouldn't do anything for us. He suspects the kid is being watched even more than he was before."

"What about his grandmother?"

"That's the only real one we got. There were a few that were simply fraudulent, and a few of clan members, but interestingly not all. It seems that either the software is not foolproof, or the government's database is incomplete."

Eva wrapped her arm around Bhathian's midriff. "Isn't it amazing that the only real one happens to be Roni's grandma? It's as statistically impossible as my encounter with Kalugal and then you."

Bhathian kissed the top of her head. "It's fate. We already agreed that we are at her mercy."

"It would seem that way."

They reached the bench that was their turning point. "Do you want to sit for a little bit before we go back?" Eva asked.

"Sure."

"I keep thinking that we are missing something. I just

can't accept that there is no way to find these other immortals."

Bhathian patted her thigh. "It's not like we can put an ad in Craig's List. Hey, if you are an immortal please call this number."

She chuckled. "Maybe you should. Call it the immortal hotline."

"You know how many crazies would call that number?"

"Yeah, but maybe not only them."

Several minutes passed as they sat in silent companionship, watching the waves crashing gently to shore. It was so soothing, the smells, the sounds, and yet that beautiful and peaceful ocean could be so deadly.

"A movie," she said after a while.

"You want to go to the movies?"

"No. A movie about my story. It probably happened the same way to the other Dormants. The story would resonate with them."

"And then what?"

She lifted one shoulder in a shrug. "I don't know. It's just the beginning of an idea."

Bhathian frowned. "If it were a book, we could arrange a book signing. The author would have to be human of course, but we could have one of us with her or him."

Eva crossed her legs at the ankles. "It would have to be a very popular book."

"Maybe a book and a movie?"

"With a huge promotional budget."

"Obviously," Bhathian agreed.

A few more moments passed before he spoke again. "The problem is that it might also attract Doomers."

"We can minimize the risk by making it into a sappy romance—a chick flick no self-respecting man would watch unless his woman drags him there against his will."

Bhathian's lips quirked in a smile. "You're good at making up fantasies. Why don't you write it?"

She waved a hand. "Pfft, I can imagine it. Doesn't mean I can write it."

"We can hire a ghost writer to write the story for you."

The idea was intriguing. Eva had spent her life doing one kind or another of undercover detective work. She was good at it, and a small portion of it was interesting and exciting, but most of it wasn't.

Detective work was not as glamorous as people thought it was.

Most of it involved endless hours of background checks, long days of watching and listening, often not learning anything useful, and long hours of typing up reports.

It could be nice to do something different. To let her imagination soar. Bhathian was right. She was good at creating fantasies, had been making them up on the spot during her numerous lonely nights.

Instead of typing up reports about cheating spouses and dishonest business associates, she could be typing up stories about love.

Turning her face to Bhathian, she smiled sheepishly. "I can try my hand at it. Maybe a short story. Just one fantasy to see if I have the knack for it."

He wrapped his arm around her shoulder and brought her in for a hot kiss that couldn't have been mistaken for anything other than a prelude to wild sex.

"What was that about?" Eva asked after he released her lips.

"I was reminded of the two fantasies we'd already enacted and it got me in the mood for a third." He tapped a finger on her temple. "What else do you have for me in that brain of yours?"

Eva smirked. "Let's go home and I'll show you."

44

BHATHIAN

*S*tanding between Bhathian's spread thighs, Eva asked, "Are you ready for your fantasy, big guy?"

He cupped her buttocks, massaging gently. "If I get more ready than this, my zipper will give up."

She caressed his cheek. "But I haven't told you the story yet."

"I know it's going to be hot."

"Hmm, which one do I want to play out tonight... any special requests?'

"Nope. I'm not going to mess with your creative juices." Though he was certainly going to mess with the other kind. Bhathian ran a finger down the apex of Eva's thighs. The fabric of her skirt was so sheer that the panties underneath it were the only real barrier between his digit and her hot center.

"This one is along the theme of our previous talk. I'm a world renowned best-selling romance writer, and my life is threatened by an obsessed fan. You're the bodyguard sent to protect me. The thing is, I like writing while wearing sexy floor-length silk nightgowns with nothing underneath. My only concession to modesty is the matching robe I throw on, but it does nothing to hide my body. You're going crazy, but you don't dare to approach because I'm a celebrity and it can get you fired."

Eva owned several such sexy nightgown and robe sets. Bhathian's eyes started glowing, casting gray pools of light on Eva's shirt. "Are you going to wear it for me?"

"Of course." She cupped his cheek and he leaned into the palm of her hand. "I want you too, but I'm shy. I'm only brave on the pages of my novels. So I ask you to read a passage from the one I'm working on. It describes you and how hot I think you are. The details are unmistakable. You know what I want."

Bhathian swallowed. "Go get changed. I'll be sitting on the couch and pretending to read your novel."

Eva smirked. "No need to pretend." She walked over to her side of the bed and pulled out a book from the night-stand's drawer. She handed it to him. "Open it at the book-mark, and start reading from there."

As Eva ducked into the closet to get into her costume, Bhathian sat on the couch, crossed his leg over his knee and opened the book where she'd told him to.

A few minutes later, he was ready to forget about the play, throw Eva on the bed and fuck her into oblivion. That book was hotter than any porn flick he'd ever watched. The reason being that he was casting Eva and himself in the starring roles.

Bhathian chuckled. And here he'd thought he had no imagination.

"I see that you like it." Eva glided into the bedroom, the thin robe billowing behind her doing nothing to cover the clinging white nightgown that was practically see through. Not only was the outline of her breasts and nipples visible, but the shade variations as well.

Five minutes. That was all the time he was willing to spend enacting the scene. After that, he was going to be inside her regardless of her script.

Bhathian affected a stern look. "Ms. Vega, this is highly inappropriate. Please go back and cover yourself." He looked away.

"But, Mr. Smith, this is the only way I can write. Each writer has her own rituals. This one is mine. If you're uncomfortable, you can avert your eyes." She glided by him and sat behind the small writing desk no one ever used, pulled out a few sheets of paper from the drawer, and started scribbling furiously.

Bhathian pushed to his feet and walked over to her desk. "It's unwise to taunt me, Ms. Vega. You just might get what you wish for."

Eva put a hand over her heart and batted her eyelashes. "I don't know what you're talking about, Mr. Smith." In real life, he knew Eva was a much better actress than that, but the over-dramatization worked for him.

No second guessing.

"I think you do." He lifted her off her chair and slung her over his shoulder.

"Mr. Smith! What in the world are you doing?"

"Taking you to bed just the way you want me to."

"You're mistaken. I want no such thing!" She playfully banged her fists on his back. "Put me down this instant!"

Bhathian was struggling to stifle a laugh. Eva must've been in a playful mood because she was making a parody of her fantasy.

Worked for him.

Hell, anything did. Just a glimpse of Eva's magnificent body beneath that flimsy nightgown had been enough to send him into overdrive. The playacting was like adding a sprinkle of spice to what was already a very hot dish.

He dropped her on the bed unceremoniously, then pounced on top of her. "Would you mind terribly if I tear this off your body?"

She made an angry face. "Yes, I would. It's one of my favorites." The real Eva made herself perfectly clear.

"What a shame." He pretended to rip it while sliding the straps off her shoulders. Leaving her precious night clothing unmolested, Bhathian had her naked in five seconds flat nonetheless.

Eva draped one arm over her breasts, hiding her nipples, and covered her mound with the palm of the other. "Mr. Smith, you mustn't."

"Oh, but I must." He moved her arms away. "A beauty like you should not be ashamed to bare herself to the hungry eyes of her lover," he quoted from the book she'd given him.

"Well, if you insist." Eva let her arms drop to her sides.

"I do." He spread her legs with his hands. "Pull up your knees. I want to see all of you."

Chewing on her lower lip, she turned her head sideways to avoid looking at him as she obeyed.

He ran a finger down her pink, moist folds. "Ms. Vega, you're very wet for me."

"Uh-huh."

"What shall we do about that?" He scooped some of the moisture with his finger and rubbed it over the center of her pleasure. "Is that it?"

Eva nodded enthusiastically.

"Or maybe this." He pushed the finger inside her.

She moaned.

"Or maybe this." He dipped his head and extended his tongue, flicking it over that tight bundle of nerves while adding another finger, pumping both into her deep and hard.

Eva's hands found their way to his scalp, her fingers digging in. "Yes, that's it." She was slick on his fingers, a light sheen of perspiration glistening in the valley between her breasts.

He didn't let up, driving her crazy with arousal until he pushed her over. Her spine went taut, her bottom lifting off the mattress as her pleasure spiked, cresting at the peak of a carnal tidal wave.

His shaft pulsing with the need to be inside of her, Bhathian kicked off his jeans and yanked his shirt off, then splayed her legs even wider and thrust inside her.

They both groaned.

Once he was all the way inside her, he stilled, her tight sheath clenching around him as she rode out the aftershocks of her climax.

Eva's arms and legs wrapped around him in a tight grip. "Fuck me, Bhathian." Using his name meant that play time was over.

It was a command he gladly obeyed.

45

TESSA

"You look beautiful." Jackson kissed Tessa's cheek. "Thank you for wearing this outfit for me."

"You look not too shabby yourself." She lifted her face up to him, but even with her six-inch monster heels, he had to bend his neck for her to reach him.

He offered her his cheek.

That was not what Tessa wanted.

Grabbing his chin, she turned his head toward her and planted a kiss on his lips. His hands on her midriff, he made a slight move to push her away, but she held on and licked at the seam of his lips, prompting him to grant her entry.

With a pained groan, he pulled her into his body, lifting her up as he took over the kiss the way she'd hoped he would.

God, it felt good to finally break the ice between them. Or at least melt a sliver of it. It seemed that her freak-out the last time they'd been intimate had had more of a lasting effect on Jackson than it had on her.

Tessa was anxious to give it another go, while Jackson was doing everything to avoid being alone with her. Yesterday, it had been a movie, the night before that had been the observatory in Griffith Park, and the one before that had been a stroll down Hollywood Boulevard, then a tour bus to Beverly Hills for a peek at the estates of various movie stars.

Tonight he was taking her to a popular restaurant in Santa Monica. Hopefully, the daring outfit he'd bought for her would make her irresistible, and he'd finally take her home for some heavy necking.

She shook her head. It was so weird how the tables had turned. Jackson was acting like the skittish virgin, while she was playing the seductress.

"What was that head shake for?" Jackson asked as he opened the car door for her.

They needed to talk, but she wasn't ready yet. "Nothing. I'm just shaking out my hairdo." She did it again. "I like how my hair falls into place without tangles. That Brazilian blowout was worth every penny." She slid into the passenger seat and buckled up.

What the hell was she going to tell him? It wasn't as if she could promise Jackson no more freak-outs. Tessa was going to do her damnedest not to, but there were no guarantees it would end up differently this time. She had a feeling that a conditional promise wouldn't be enough for Jackson.

The place was huge, with a large bar taking up its center. They got seated in a small booth overlooking the ocean, perfect for a couple on a romantic date.

Tessa opened the menu, scanning for something inexpensive to eat. The main dishes were all in the forty-dollar range. She decided to order a salad.

Jackson, unsurprisingly, went for a fifty-two dollar steak.

"What happened to saving for your future business empire?" Tessa asked when the waiter left with their order.

"I put it on hold for now."

"At least let me pay half."

"No."

"Really? I'm going to report you to the PC police. Equality between the sexes demands I pay half the bill."

"Nice try. Not when you order a miserly salad, and I order the most expensive entrée on the menu."

Tessa leaned back and folded her arms under her chest, which pushed her breasts up and got Jackson's attention. Good, she needed him to notice her assets. Not that she had much to show, but the low neckline combined with the pushup bra she'd ordered specifically for this outfit displayed what little she had to the best advantage.

"Next time then."

Jackson smirked. "Sure."

Seeing right through him, she rolled her eyes. "Eating at your café or ordering a burger in a fast food joint doesn't count."

When her salad turned out to be really small, Jackson tried to feed her his steak. "Just one bite." He dangled the fork in front of her mouth.

"I don't like beef. But I'll take some of your mashed potatoes."

Jackson scooped a hefty portion into his bread plate, topped it with all the asparagus spears that came with his steak and slid it over to her. "Here you go. Enjoy."

"Don't you want any of the asparagus?"

He made a face. "I don't know how people eat that. It tastes disgusting."

"I like it."

"That's why I said enjoy. I knew you would."

Jackson was done with his steak long before she pushed her plate away. "It was delicious, but I can't eat another bite. There was more butter than potatoes in this." She pointed at what was left on the small plate.

Jackson looked crestfallen. "What about dessert?"

Where he packed it all was a mystery. "I can't. But go ahead and order us coffees and something sweet for you."

He reached for her hand. "I have something sweet right here."

Tessa smiled. Whether Jackson was loosening up around her, or just reacting to the endorphins from the food, she was glad to see him flirting again. This was the Jackson she knew and loved. Not the overly cautious guy who treated her as if she was made from eggshells.

"I need to use the bathroom." Reluctantly, Tessa pulled her hand out. Nature was calling, and she couldn't put it off any longer.

Jackson pushed to his feet. "I'll come with you."

She pressed down on his shoulder. "Don't be silly, I don't need you to stand guard outside the ladies' room."

"I don't want to leave you alone for a moment. I made you a promise that I'll guard you whenever we go out, and I'm going to keep it."

She bent and kissed his cheek. "You can see the entrance from here." Turning toward the sign, she pointed. "It's right there. You can see anyone going in or out of that opening."

Jackson looked very displeased but didn't make another attempt to follow her.

After holding it in for so long, Tessa almost didn't make it to the stall on time. The relief was profound. When she was done, she washed her hands and examined her reflection in the mirror.

Her hair was still fabulous, thanks to Francine and her amazing blowout. But the lipstick was gone and she looked pale. One disadvantage of going blonde was the lack of color. Tessa found herself applying eyeliner and mascara every morning now, just not to look like the walking dead. The bright red lipstick was only for going out. She pulled it out of her purse and reapplied it carefully. It changed her face completely, making her look older and more sophisticated.

Taking one last glance at her profile, she dropped the tube of lipstick back into her purse and pushed the bathroom door open.

Come to think of it, she should refresh her perfume as well. Digging into her purse, she didn't watch where she was going as she searched for the sample she carried around for just that purpose, and bumped into a guy coming out of the men's room.

"I'm so sorry," she said, backing up.

The guy glared at her. "Watch where you're going, missy."

Panic surged up to the surface. It wasn't just the rude way he'd responded, or his baleful expression as he stared at her; the man looked familiar even though she was sure she'd never met him before.

Martin. That was it. He looked a lot like Martin.

Tessa looked down at the floor and rushed out, leaving the angry, menacing guy behind.

Jackson got up. "What happened? You look like you've seen a ghost."

"I did. Can we get out of here?"

"I need to pay."

She didn't want to wait for the waiter to process Jackson's credit card. Pulling out her wallet she pulled out the two twenties she knew she had there. "How much cash do you have on you? I want to leave the money and go."

Jackson pulled out three more twenties. "That's all I have."

"It's enough." Tessa combined their money and put it on the table. "Let's go."

"You want to tell me what this is all about?" Jackson asked as they waited for the valet to bring his car.

"Not here."

She might have seemed paranoid, but after years of

working with Eva, Tessa had learned that talking where anyone could hear her wasn't a good idea.

Martin had a brother. The two had had a fallout long before Martin had bought her. She'd never met the guy or even seen a picture, but the resemblance was uncanny. Not so much in their appearance, but in the ruthless cruelty of their vibe.

Was that the man Eva had overheard planning Tessa's search and capture?"

Impossible. It was too much of a coincidence. It was probably a different man.

But the way he'd looked at her... It hadn't been sexual, just pure hate. Did he recognize her?

Tessa glanced behind her, checking if anyone had followed her and Jackson out of the restaurant. No one had.

Her fear was irrational.

There was no way anyone who'd seen her photographs from five years ago would make the connection. There hadn't been that many. Maybe one or two. It wasn't like Martin took her picture or anything.

Thanks to Eva's insistence on precaution, Tessa looked like a different woman. Besides, the man was probably not Martin's brother. Just another angry, violent piece of shit.

Still, that angry glare was etched in her memory, causing shivers to run down her spine.

God, she was so tired of living in fear.

46

JACKSON

*S*omething had spooked Tessa big time. Or rather someone.

He'd seen the rude jerk who'd followed her out of the bathrooms. A bruiser and a low life Jackson would've gladly taught a lesson in proper manners. But Tessa had been so shaken by the encounter, he'd had to let the guy get away unscathed and take his girl home.

Once in the car, he brought it up. "I heard the jerk and how he talked to you, but that's no reason to get so worked up."

"It's not that he was rude. He reminded me of Martin, the guy Eva saved me from."

That explained it. Jackson reached for her hand and brought it to rest in his lap. "Are you okay?"

She smiled feebly. "I don't know. My first thought was that it must be his brother and that he was the same guy Eva overheard talking about me in Tampa. But it's too much of a coincidence. It was just another hateful jerk. That's all."

Tessa was using too mild language to describe the one who'd kept her as his slave when she was practically a child.

Not wanting to upset her even more while she was trying to calm down, Jackson didn't comment.

"Do you want me to take you home?" Eva was Tessa's rock. After getting a scare like that, she could benefit from the comfort and security her boss offered.

"No. Take me to your place."

He cast her a sidelong glance. "Are you sure?"

The last thing Tessa needed was more stress, which was unavoidable when the two of them were alone. That was why he'd been taking her out instead of inviting her over to his place.

There was too much pressure on her to push forward and overcome her hang-ups. They needed to slow down and let things progress at a pace that was comfortable for her. The last episode had set them way back.

He didn't want a repeat of that.

"I'm sure. You're not the one I should fear."

"Fears are irrational. Knowing it in your head is not enough. You have to feel it in your heart and in your gut."

"I do." There was not a trace of hesitation in her tone.

Jackson shook his head. Tessa was once again rushing into things before she was ready. "I think you need more time."

"Maybe I do, but I don't have the luxury. The sooner you change me, the sooner I can start living again."

Jackson stifled a cringe. He wanted to be wanted for himself, not as a means to an end. His grip on Tessa's hand loosened.

She pulled her hand all the way out, but instead of retracting it she clasped his. "It's not only about that, Jackson. I want you." She took in a deep breath. "After all I have been through, talking about sex shouldn't be difficult for me, but it still is."

Pushing her hair behind her ears, she looked at him.

"Before you, I'd never felt arousal, I'd never felt physical attraction toward anyone, I'd never gotten wet. Everything that had to do with sex used to repulse me. You changed all that. So don't think for a moment that the only reason I'm pushing forward is that I want to become immortal as soon as I can."

Jackson nodded, unsure what he was supposed to say in response.

Tessa had said everything he wanted to hear.

Almost.

The word love was missing from her impassioned speech. They had spoken about feelings and about falling for each other, but that particular word had never come up.

He was still afraid to say it.

Maybe she was afraid too?

There was more to her fears than the physical part. Her emotions were all over the place. The one thing that gave him hope was that he had her trust. At the moment, it was more important than all the rest put together, including love.

"We can go back to what we did in the beginning. You'll do all the touching and kissing and whatever else you want to do. I'm just going to lie down with my hands behind my head, enjoying myself without doing any of the work."

Tessa's smile was calculating. "Don't plan on being all lazy yet. Touching and kissing you was fun, but the first time I got wet was when you took over. It seems that I like it when you take charge."

Damn it. He became instantly hard and lightheaded, all the blood from his body rushing south.

Tessa chuckled huskily. "And it seems that you like it better too." The hand that had been clasping his brushed over his bulge.

He sucked in a breath. "You're going to make me crash," he croaked.

"Sorry." She retracted her hand. "I couldn't help myself."

Who was the woman sitting next to him, and what had she done with Tessa?

When he parked in front of the café, the lights were out on the second floor, which meant that Gordon and Vlad were out.

Perfect timing.

They'd better hurry up before the guys came back.

"Come on." He helped Tessa out of the car, holding on to her so she wouldn't trip on her elevator shoes. Not letting go of her hand, he opened the door, locked it, then pulled her behind him upstairs.

In his room, Jackson kicked the door closed and lifted Tessa up. Kissing her, he walked back until he had her pushed against the wall.

Letting her tight skirt ride up, she dropped her shoes and wrapped her legs around his waist.

"Kiss me again," she whispered as he came up for air.

Her red lipstick was smeared all over her mouth, looking like blood and lending his sweet little Tessa a predatory look to match the hunger in her eyes.

His woman was possessed. There was no other explanation. But he wasn't going to perform an exorcism.

Not yet.

Maybe never.

Holding Tessa up with one hand under her butt, he did something he hadn't been expecting to do for weeks to come. He cupped her breast.

No resistance.

Tessa moaned.

Encouraged, Jackson pulled her top and bra down exposing her perky breasts.

"Beautiful," he whispered.

Small pink nipples topped creamy globes that were absolute perfection.

He felt Tessa tense. But when he cupped her naked breast and then teased the nipple with slow circles of his thumb, she moaned in pleasure, and her body went loose.

"Can I put my mouth here?" He moved his hand to her other breast, repeating the gentle caresses he'd treated the first one to.

She opened her eyes and put her palms on his cheeks. "Yes, but first kiss me again."

He did, his lips and tongue gentle, unhurried, exploring and dancing with hers, not dueling.

Jackson had a feeling that this position worked better for Tessa than him being on top of her. She didn't feel trapped, and at the same time it allowed him to run the show the way she wanted him to.

Letting her drop down a little, he aligned her core with his hard shaft. She undulated against him, providing the friction he so desperately needed.

"Tessa," he whispered into her mouth. "I love you."

She opened her eyes again, and her face brightened with the biggest smile he'd ever seen her smile. "I love you too."

For a moment, they just stared at each other, until Tessa's eyes traveled south to her exposed breasts. "My nipples are cold."

"Then I must warm them up." He hoisted her higher and took one turgid peek between his lips, then flicked his tongue at the tip.

Tessa's head hit the wall behind her. "God, Jackson, I've never known it could feel so good."

The awe in her voice made him want to find those bastards who'd only taught her pain and rip them apart with his bare hands.

Tessa hissed. "Your fangs, Jackson."

Elongating in tandem with his aggressive thoughts, his fangs had nicked her unintentionally.

"I'm sorry." He licked her nipple round and round, his saliva curing the small nick in an instant. "Better?"

"Much. Let's move to the couch. You can't keep holding me up indefinitely."

He smirked. "You're a featherweight. I can stay like this all night."

She caught his nose between two knuckles. "Show off. Take me to bed."

"Yes, mistress."

Tessa giggled as he carried her over to the couch and sat down with her in his arms. There would be no getting her under him. Not tonight.

"Can I take your top off?"

She smiled coyly and pulled the tiny top over her head, tossing it on the floor, then unhooked her bra and tossed it aside as well.

"Mmm," Jackson licked his lips. "Two tasty treats. Which one should I try first?"

"This one," Tessa cupped the breast he didn't get to yet, offering it for his kisses.

"Yes." He smacked his lips again, then leaned down and took the nipple into his mouth, sucking on it gently.

Tessa's breaths were coming out in soft pants, her tiny butt restless on top of his stiff cock. Jackson knew she was aching to be touched, to be filled, at least by his fingers, but he didn't dare make a move.

Getting Tessa to this point was a monumental achievement. He didn't want to ruin it by assuming she was ready for more.

TESSA

*T*essa was discovering a whole new world of pleasure. Jackson's every touch, every lick was infused with love and care for her. He didn't paw, he didn't squeeze, he didn't hurt, and little by little her trust in him was growing, consciously and subconsciously.

That was how things between a man and a woman were supposed to be. Not the distorted, perverted version she'd been the victim of.

For the first time in memory, she felt like she could close her eyes and give in to the pleasure without fear.

Just be, just feel, just enjoy.

Tessa was floating on a cloud, and this time no drugs of any kind were responsible for the bliss, natural or otherwise.

Could she go even further than that?

Could she ask Jackson to touch her in the most intimate way?

Or should she take it slow, one step at a time?

The problem was that she was aching down there. Not the excruciating pain she'd learned to associate with everything that had to do with that female part of her, but the opposite.

Gentle fingers that would caress and entice and delve inside her with the sole purpose of providing pleasure.

Experimentally, she hiked her skirt up, exposing her thighs almost to their apex but not quite. When that didn't trigger panic, she hiked it a little more, exposing her panties.

Would Jackson get the clue, or would she have to tell him?

His attention on her breasts, he probably hadn't noticed, or if he had, thought it happened unintentionally.

Perhaps she should start by touching herself.

Tessa had never done it before, never felt the need. She touched herself there only to get clean. Often, after the brutal treatment of her tormentor, the only thing that could soothe the pain had been a spray of cold water. She would stand in the shower with the handheld pointed at her abused labia and sheath and let the cold water wash away the pain and the taint.

She remembered feeling grateful for that small mercy. Other girls like her might not have had even that.

Jackson released her nipple and looked up at her with worry in his piercing blue eyes. "What's the matter? I feel like I'm losing you."

She cupped his cheek. "A bad thought surfaced. But I'm not going to let it ruin this. I love every touch. You're wonderful, Jackson. Never doubt it."

His expression brightened, and he leaned to kiss her lips lightly. "You have no idea how much it means to me to hear you say that."

Tessa glanced at her fancy skirt that was all bunched up around her middle. "Help me get it off?"

Jackson's eyes almost popped from their sockets. "What do you have in mind? Because I don't want to guess or presume or anything. You need to tell me."

She'd figured that much. "I want you to touch me there. The same gentle way you touched me everywhere else. Then I'm going to do the same to you."

Jackson lifted his face to the ceiling and mumbled, "Thank you, sweet, merciful Fates."

She wiggled in his lap, reminding him what she wanted him to do.

He tugged on the bottom of her skirt. "Lift up for me."

She did, and he pulled the stretchy skirt off with one swift move, dropping it on the floor.

"These too?" He tugged on the elastic of her panties.

She wasn't ready to remove that last barrier. "No, not yet. But you can, like maybe put your hand inside?" Damn, it was hard to say what she wanted.

Though it shouldn't be. For the first time her wishes mattered, were heard and accommodated. No one had asked her before whether she wanted something done to her or not.

They just took and took and took...

Stop it. Tessa shook her head.

"Another bad thought?" Jackson asked.

"Yeah. It's just that I can't stop comparing between this and what had been done to me before."

Jackson's eyes glared with a dangerous glow, but she knew his anger wasn't directed at her.

"I'm going to make you forget everything that came before. I'll give you so much pleasure you won't be able to think about anything other than right here, right now."

"Yes, please."

Closing his lips around a nipple, Jackson pushed her panties aside and glided a finger over her wet folds. She felt his shaft twitch under her, but it didn't scare her. On the contrary, it aroused her.

Jackson let go of her nipple. "You're so wet for me, Tessa."

He blew on it to cool it then took her other nipple, his finger drawing maddening circles around that sensitive spot she needed him to touch.

"Don't tease me, Jackson," she whispered. "I need more."

As his finger dipped into her wet sheath, Tessa's body tightened into a bow.

He pulled his finger out, bringing the moisture up to where she wanted him, getting so very close but not touching directly. She moved against him, her bottom rubbing against the hard length under her with every undulation.

His finger moved down again, dipping into her heat, then another one joined the first and Tessa saw sparks flare behind her tightly closed eyelids.

Panting, she rode those fingers, her bottom rubbing harder and faster against him, the buildup almost unbearable. She was hurtling toward something she'd only experienced as a result of the chemicals in Jackson's venom. That had been an artificial climax, sudden and uncomfortable, it lacked the delicious buildup that was going to make this one earth-shattering.

Then his thumb made contact with that ultrasensitive, needy spot, and she cried out his name as the release rocked through her, wave after wave of violent shudders that left her limp and spent and content in a way she'd never known possible.

"So that's what a real orgasm feels like," she murmured into his sweaty T-shirt. "I can get used to that."

48

SYSSI

*S*yssi closed her eyes and tried to empty her mind.

Olga's advice during their last session was to find a quiet space for meditation; maybe it would go better after the changes Syssi had implemented.

First, she'd dedicated one of the spare bedrooms as her meditation space and informed both Kian and Okidu not to come in when the door was closed. In fact, the best time of day to practice was when Kian was still in his office down in the underground and Okidu was out driving delivery trucks to the new compound.

No distractions.

Up until her failed meditation attempts, Syssi hadn't realized that Kian's energy was so powerful it penetrated every space in the penthouse. When he was home, even in another room, a closed door wasn't enough to block it, and emptying her mind while his energy was all around her was impossible.

Still, the environment she'd created wasn't completely distraction free. The faint city sounds percolated even through the closed windows.

Top quality noise-canceling headphones took care of most of that.

Blissful quiet.

A rare experience for an immortal.

Stop thinking, she ordered herself and let her mind drift.

The vision started with the usual swirls of color, but in her relaxed state Syssi didn't tense, letting it wash over her without resistance.

The colors faded into absolute darkness. It stayed like that for long moments, until a dim light illuminated a narrow section of a scene that Syssi didn't comprehend at first.

What was it showing her?

Was it a dark corridor?

Long and wide, with doors every twenty feet or so.

Was it a hotel? An apartment building? Was it somewhere in the keep?

The dim light intensified, and she noticed something on the carpeted floor. The vision zoomed in on a woman curled in a fetal position, sleeping.

The camera zoomed even closer, and the light became a little stronger, enough so colors started showing. The vision was no longer in black and white.

What had at first appeared as a shadow cast by the woman's body wasn't a shadow at all. It was a red stain on the gray carpet. The woman was lying in a pool of blood.

Horrified, Syssi tried to pull out of the vision, but its grip was too strong, showing her another corridor and another body surrounded by a pool of blood. Again and again and again, until it all blurred, turning the dark gray corridors into red rivers of blood.

Inside the vision's grip, Syssi screamed.

Eyes popping open, she realized she must've screamed for real because her throat felt raw. Her heart hammering against her rib cage, Syssi grabbed the bedside phone with sweaty hands.

"Kian, could you please come up here?"

Worry made him sound harsh. "What happened?"

"I had a vision. I need you."

"I'm coming up."

Frantic, Syssi pulled out a suitcase from the closet and started packing. They needed to evacuate as soon as they could.

Before the keep's corridors filled with blood.

"What are you doing?" Kian found her in the closet.

"You need to issue an evacuation order before it's too late." She kept throwing clothes into the open suitcase.

Kian walked up to her and pulled her into his arms. "You need to calm down and tell me what you saw."

Syssi shivered even though his body was warm against her and his arms provided a measure of safety. "Rivers of blood, Kian. Corridors filled with dead bodies lying in pools of their own blood. Many are going to die if we don't move fast."

"Did you recognize any of the bodies? Or the corridors? What made you think the vision was about the keep and its occupants?"

His words gave her pause. She shook her head. "The bodies were all curled up on themselves. I couldn't see the faces. The ones I saw more clearly were of women, but after a while they all became a blur, so there could've been men there as well. As to the corridors, I can't say for sure. They could've been in hotels or in apartment buildings. They all kind of looked the same. I think it was symbolic and the corridors didn't really mean much. The vision communicated a warning. Many will die if we don't do something. I just assumed it was about us and the keep."

Kian snaked an arm under her knees, lifted her up, and

carried her to the bedroom. Sitting on the bed, he cradled her close to his body. And yet she still shivered from cold.

"There is no need to act hastily. Your visions don't come with a timeline. This could just as well happen in the distant future or not at all if what leads to that outcome changes."

She shook her head. "In my experience, bad visions always come true."

"Not necessarily. You saw Andrew dying. He didn't."

"No, I saw clocks ticking. He needed to take action to prevent that outcome and he did."

Kian rocked her gently. "The compound is not ready. What I can do is reinforce security. Don't forget that we are not helpless here. We have escape tunnels that lead to other buildings. If we are under attack, we can evacuate people through them. I'll arrange a drill to practice evacuation procedures."

It all sounded so rational and practical, but her gut was still churning with fear. "What if the civilian they murdered knew the location of the keep? Lately, we haven't been as diligent about keeping it secret. Someone might have told him, thinking nothing of it."

"I spoke with his friends personally. None of them knew where the keep was. Only those who move in get to know, and they are ordered to keep it a secret. The penalties I impose for breaking that rule are so severe, I doubt anyone is stupid enough to risk them."

49

KIAN

*K*ian had done his best to calm Syssi, but the truth was that her vision had disturbed him.

"Is everything ready for the drill?" He turned to his chief Guardian.

"Today at six. We sent everyone a text message and an email. I assigned a Guardian to each of our floors to sound the alarm and make sure that everything is done in an orderly fashion."

"Are we making them use the stairs?"

Onegus smirked. "Those who respond first get to use the elevators. The stragglers get the stairs. We are going to evacuate one floor at a time, starting at the top."

"Good." Tapping his fingers on the conference table, Kian looked at the assembled Guardians. "I want to speed up the completion of the Malibu project."

Bhathian put down his pen and pushed his notepad aside. "The houses are basically ready. There is still a lot of construction debris that needs to be cleared, and we need to furnish the houses. Though we can save a lot of time and expense by taking what we have here over there. It's not as if the stuff is old or in bad shape. The furniture still looks like new."

Kian waved a dismissive hand. "Once we move out, I can rent out the apartments as furnished and charge more. What I want to know is, what's more expedient?"

Onegus folded his arms over his chest. "Ordering everything new is going to be faster and more efficient, not to mention better as far as security goes. Delivery trucks leaving the keep could be easily followed if anyone is watching. We should put the orders in if we want something better than stock items. Made-to-order furniture would take months. Especially with an order that big."

"Let's ask the expert." Kian picked up the phone and dialed Ingrid's extension.

"What can I do for you, Kian?"

"I need your advice. To furnish the new place, what's better, ordering everything new, or moving what we have here? And I don't mean money-wise. What's more expedient?"

"Definitely ordering everything new. I'll call my suppliers and check how soon they can deliver."

"Thank you." Kian hung up.

Arwel lifted a finger.

"What about the special self-driving cars, and the self-washing windows, and all the other cool gadgets you told us about? I'm sure none of that could've been done since our last meeting."

True. The windows were on order and would take another twelve weeks to get delivered. By then Kian hoped to have everyone out of the keep and settled in the new place.

In the meantime, everyone could wash their own windows or leave them dirty as far as he was concerned. It wasn't a priority and replacing them later shouldn't be too difficult. They could leave one construction crew to do that and any other odds and ends that were surely going to pop up.

The transportation issue was more important. The purchase of the flying cars manufacturing facility had been a lucky coincidence. At the time, Kian had thought it a good business investment and planned to market heavily in Alaska —the best market for a multi-purpose vehicle of that kind. But Robert's idea had changed all of that. The flying aspect discarded, Kian had converted the factory to manufacture smart cars with autonomous driving technology.

The technology was available, and Kian had purchased the best and most advanced one from an Israeli company that promised to solve the special window-blocking mechanism problem as well. Incorporating it into the software was not the challenge, though. The mechanism itself was. A large research and development team was working on it around the clock.

Kian turned to Onegus. "What's the progress with the cars?"

"They promised us a prototype of the mechanism by the end of this week. If it works the way we want, they will design the car windows for us. I'm looking for a manufacturer that can take this on a moment's notice and go to work. But even if everything goes according to plan, and there are no hitches on the way, the best we can hope for is to have the first car ready in four to six months."

That was what he'd thought. In fact, Onegus's estimate was optimistic. Kian doubted they would have the cars ready in less than a year.

"Is there anything we can do to speed it up? Money is no object."

Onegus shook his head. "You should've come up with that

brilliant idea when we started building, not when the project was almost completed. Do you know how many modifications had to be done?"

"It wasn't my idea."

"Then William should've thought of it sooner."

"It wasn't William's either. All these smart solutions were Robert's ideas."

Onegus cocked a brow. "Are you serious? I thought the guy was a mere pencil pusher, taking care of the orders and other paperwork to relieve some of Shai's load."

"That's the job I assigned to him. I happened to mention the problems we faced, and he took the initiative and researched solutions. Impressed the hell out of me. I didn't even know self-washing windows existed. It never crossed my mind. Otherwise, I could've found it on the Internet as easily as he did. Knowing what questions to ask is usually half the solution."

Onegus nodded. "Indeed. The guy is smarter than he looks. What I wonder, though, now that we know he can think for himself, is whether we should trust him more or less."

"Give the guy a break," Bhathian said. "He helped Carol, and he has been with us long enough to earn some trust."

Kian dragged a hand through his hair. "I want to, believe me. I like the guy, and I'm almost sure he can be trusted, but too much is at stake. Especially now."

Bhathian's brows drew tight. "Why? Is it because of the murdered civilian? I thought we were a hundred percent sure that he didn't know the keep's location. Except for those living here, the rest of the clan members were always driven in enclosed vans and buses for clan-wide events."

Kian shook his head. "Security wasn't as tight as it should've been. Take Sylvia and her mother for instance.

They know where the keep is even though they don't live here."

"That's because they joined us on a mission. They were given the same speech and the same warnings as every clan member moving into the keep."

With a sigh, Kian scrubbed his hand over his face. "I should not have moved civilians in here. It was a mistake."

Here, he admitted what had been gnawing at him for months.

At the time, it had seemed like the right thing to do. After Mark's murder, Kian had panicked, evacuating all of the Bay Area clan members. It hadn't been paranoia. Most of them worked in high tech, and if the Doomers had figured out how to find Mark, they could've found the others.

What Kian should've done, though, was settle them in a different building, or better yet, scatter them around the city. If one was caught and interrogated, he could've led the Doomers only to a few friends, not the entire American clan population.

But Kian cared too much for his people to sacrifice even one, and in his arrogance, he'd thought he could protect them all.

What he had done instead was put all of them in harm's way.

The silence in the room was a good indicator that the Guardians agreed Kian had made a mistake. Except, none of them had voiced any opposition when he'd made his intentions known.

Not that it mattered. He was the leader and the responsibility was his.

Scratching his beard, Anandur cleared his throat. "We can still do it. Get all the civilians out and settle them in different parts of the city. At least until the compound is ready."

"We can't do that," Onegus said. "First we move them in

here, then we move them out. People will lose confidence in our ability to protect them."

Kian's jaw tightened.

Onegus was right. When people lost confidence in their leadership and in those who were supposed to protect them, they panicked and started doing stupid things.

50

AMANDA

*A*manda glanced at Syssi's pale face and shook her head.

The little get-together she'd arranged was supposed to cheer Syssi up, but it seemed that other than Phoenix no one and nothing could.

That vision had shaken her up more than any of her previous ones. And Syssi had had her share of gloomy predictions. But none of them had been so graphic in nature. Dead bodies lying in pools of blood would've shaken anyone, let alone a sensitive soul like Syssi.

"Tell me about your vision," Eva prompted, ignoring Amanda's gestures to drop the subject.

Syssi handed Phoenix back to Andrew and took a long sip of her drink. "Dark corridors, dead bodies, and rivers of blood. That's about it." She finished her drink in one gulp and handed the empty glass to Kian. "Could you please make me another one?"

He didn't argue and took the empty margarita glass to make his wife a new one.

Andrew bounced Phoenix up and down, eliciting excited gurgles and squeals. The little girl was adorable. "You could've picked up those images from the other side of the world. Or they could've been in the past or the distant future. You know how visions are. I wouldn't dwell on them if I were you."

"That's because you didn't feel what I did. It's not only about what I see. It's also about how it makes me feel. And it scared me witless." Syssi took the margarita Kian had made for her.

Amanda clapped her hands. "People, we are here to have fun, not to chew endlessly on that nasty vision. No offense, Syssi, but I'm sick of hearing about it."

Syssi shrugged, more interested in her drink than anything Amanda had to say.

"Who I want to talk about are Sharon and Nick, our two prospective Dormants. We need to hook them up with immortals."

Kian poured himself and Bhathian a drink. "Only Sharon. Nick doesn't need to hook up with anyone to go through the transition."

"True," Amanda conceded. "But having a mate will give him the motivation to go through it and ensure his loyalty. Besides, our Eva here is refusing to even consider moving to the new location before her charges are happily mated first. She is not willing to leave them behind."

Kian lifted his glass in a salute to Eva. "A true leader doesn't pick up and leave without ensuring her people's safety."

Eva inclined her head. "Thank you. At least one person here understands."

Bhathian's expression darkened. The guy took offense to that remark. Especially since it made another male look better than him. Men were funny that way, but immortal males were worse. Competitiveness seemed to be part of their genetic makeup.

Hmm. Maybe that was an indicator she could use for finding male Dormants. *Note to self—investigate the possibility of competitiveness as a possible indicator.* Maybe it wasn't limited to the males either, maybe female Dormants were more competitive than regular human women?

"Syssi, were you competitive as a kid? Or as an adult?"

Her sister-in-law cast her an exaggerated puzzled look. The girl was drunk. For an immortal, she had almost as low a tolerance for alcohol as she'd had as a human. An extra-lightweight.

"Why do you ask?"

"I have my reasons."

Syssi shrugged, too tipsy to inquire further. "I guess I was. I wanted to be the best student in my class. Then when I tutored for the SAT I wanted to be the top rated one. That's about it. I was never good in sports, so no competitiveness there."

"How about you, Eva? Were you competitive before your transition?"

"Very. I had to be the best at everything I did. But I was smart enough not to undertake things I had no talent for. Like cooking."

That earned her a few chuckles.

"Nathalie, what about you?"

Nathalie shrugged. "Sure. But my circumstances kind of dictated it. I was the poor kid on a scholarship in a fancy private school, and I knew I needed another scholarship to pay for college as well. I worked my butt off. Having no social life thanks to the ghost in my head, I had plenty of time to study. Besides, my resident ghost at the time hated school, so studying was a good way to banish him for a few hours."

There was one more ex-Dormant in the room. "Andrew?"

"Are you kidding me? My picture is next to the word competitive in the dictionary. I always had to win, even when winning didn't mean a thing and cost me friendships. It was a compulsion. Still is."

Amanda smirked. "Syssi, darling, I think we have another clue to go on."

Syssi waved a hand. "Pfft. A coincidence. Four people are not a good sample. You're making the same mistake you did before, letting optimism and hopefulness cloud your scientific mind."

Amanda folded her arms under her chest. "You don't pull any punches when you're drunk."

Syssi lifted one shoulder in half a shrug and leaned in to Kian. He wrapped his arm around her, whispering something in her ear that made her giggle.

At least the girl's mood had improved. Maybe she should make her another margarita.

Later.

They still had an important issue to discuss. "Back to what we talked about before I sidestepped into another topic. How are we going to arrange for Nick and Sharon to meet immortals they will, hopefully, hook up with?"

"Eva and I could invite people over, but we need a credible excuse for bringing different people to the house on a regular basis."

"A card game," Eva offered. "A poker or a bridge night. Sharon and Nick play poker with Tessa and me from time to time. We gamble chores."

Bhathian patted Eva's knee. "Perfect. I could bring two or three people at a time to play. Not for chores, though."

"Play for jokes." Syssi raised her empty margarita glass. "Or for margaritas." Her words were slurred.

When she tipped the glass precariously over the table,

Kian took it out of her hand. "I think you've had enough for tonight."

Syssi pouted. "One more. Pleeeease...."

Kian grimaced, but Amanda knew he wasn't going to refuse Syssi anything today.

"Fine. But that's going to be the last one."

"Okay."

He got up to make her another drink.

Amanda sat in Dalhu's lap. "You're awfully quiet tonight. Nothing to say?"

"Maybe." He pointed at Syssi who'd flopped to her side on the couch and started snoring. "Now that she is asleep. I didn't want to talk about the move and cause her more stress."

Amanda kissed his smooth cheek. Dalhu shaved twice a day just because he knew she liked his face stubble-free. What a man. And to think she'd been so torn about him being her mate. He was perfect. "What did you want to say, darling?"

Dalhu glanced Kian's way, waiting for him to come back to the couch.

Kian smiled indulgently at his wife, his love for her shining bright. Gently lifting her head, he sat down and put it on his thigh.

Without waking, Syssi sighed contentedly and threw an arm over his legs.

"When is the new place going to be ready?" Dalhu asked.

"Three months. As hard as we tried to push it to an earlier date, everything points to the three month mark. That's how long it will take for the first shipment of cars to leave the factory, the furniture to get delivered, the water pump from the ocean to be ready, the new windows to get installed, etc. The list is long. If only a couple of items were left, I would've ordered the move today. Unfortunately, that's not the case."

"Did you beef up security?"

"Of course. Turner recommended an excellent firm. I hired them to secure the area around the keep."

Dalhu nodded.

Amanda regarded her mate. "I'm surprised you're taking Syssi's vision so seriously."

A smirk lifted one corner of his mouth. "Better safe than sorry. Just to be on the safe side, I believe in all kinds of nonsense. Like good things and bad things coming in threes."

"Not crossing under a ladder," Eva added.

Andrew lifted a finger. "Lucky socks."

Nathalie winced. "Don't remind me. Lucky or not, they stank."

"You had your own superstitions," Amanda reminded her. "That whole thing about not buying anything before the baby's birth."

"True." Nathalie bent and kissed her daughter's sweet cheek. Syssi's rhythmic soft snores must've lulled the baby to sleep. "I guess it's our way to fend off the unknown and manage our fears. I would've done all kind of crazy things if there was even the slightest chance of them ensuring Phoenix's safety."

Kian stroked his wife's hair. "I believe that Syssi's visions are true. The problem is that they come with no time or location stamp. Other than that, everything else you guys mentioned is nonsense in my opinion. But whatever helps you cope with life's uncertainties is fine by me."

Amanda regarded her guests. "Am I the only one here with no superstitions?"

Syssi's snort took her by surprise. "Says the woman who wanted to dance naked in the woods."

Apparently, her sister-in-law hadn't been sleeping.

Dalhu's arms closed around her. "Care to explain?"

Damn Syssi and her big mouth.

EVA

*B*ack home in their bedroom, Eva lay on the couch. It was too early for bed, and she wasn't sleepy, only tired. The visit to Amanda's had been draining. Syssi, who was always the calm factor in any gathering, had been stressed, her anxiety permeating the very air in Amanda's living room.

Who could blame her, though?

Eva would've been disturbed too if she'd dreamt something like that, let alone received it in a vision. Being a seer wasn't fun.

A few moments later Bhathian walked in with the chamomile tea she'd asked him to make for her, and beer for himself. He set both on the coffee table and joined her on the couch, lifting her legs and putting them in his lap.

Eva pushed back to a semi-reclining position.

"You look tired." He handed her the tea.

"I am. Syssi's anxiety must have affected me."

Bhathian sighed and reached for his beer. "None of that would have worried me if we had a decent force of

Guardians. But with only seven of us, we can't defend the keep against a large scale invasion."

"What about your trainees?"

"We have one that is going to make it. Michael. The rest don't have what it takes. We keep teaching them so they won't be completely helpless."

A firearm in each adult's hand would definitely make them less helpless. "If you haven't done it yet, you should distribute weapons and teach everyone how to use them."

"Those who come to the self-defense classes get a handgun and practice in the shooting range. But that's not everyone. The classes are not mandatory, just strongly recommended."

"Then make them mandatory."

Bhathian put his bottle down and started massaging her foot. "We are not a dictatorship, but I can scare them into it. An assembly where Syssi will retell her vision should do the trick."

Eva sipped on her tea. "How do Doomers compare to Guardians in their fighting skills?"

"They are much less selective than we are. Some of their fighters are on a par with us, like Dalhu who is one of the best I've ever seen, while others are inferior. A Guardian can take on three or four average Doomers, but he can also encounter someone like Dalhu and be evenly matched or even outmatched."

She wondered how selective Kalugal had been with his platoon. If there was a way to find those immortals, there was a chance they would combine forces with the Guardians.

"Imagine you found Kalugal and his men. If they join forces with you, you'd have a much better defense in place."

Bhathian switched to her other foot, his strong fingers kneading her arch in a most delightful way. "I don't think your romantic chick flick would draw them in."

"I don't know about that. The trailer would have to be alluring to both sexes and strongly allude to your history. We can make it available in only a few select theaters first, and have a Guardian in each sniffing the audience for immortal males. It's not like with the females who we need to approach us because we can't detect them."

Bathian's fingers stilled on her foot. "Eva, you're a genius. If an immortal female is aroused, we will be able to sniff her out as easily as a male.

A grin spread over Eva's face. "Then all we have to do is make the movie hot."

"Exactly."

Eva sat up and wrapped her arms around Bathian's neck. "You're the genius, not me. I would've never thought of that."

A faint blush crept up Bathian's cheeks. Her brave warrior was uncomfortable with the compliment. "The credit belongs to you. This whole idea is yours. I just expanded on it a little."

Brave and sweet and modest, with the body of a Hercules and the face of an Adonis—a killer combination.

Not to mention the patience of a saint.

Bathian was the total package, and Eva was the lucky winner of the best partner jackpot. The word mate still sounded foreign to her, and she wasn't ready to use the word husband just yet, but the prospect no longer scared her. In fact, it was becoming more appealing by the day.

Especially at moments like this when Bathian was massaging her toes and making her eyes roll back in her head.

She'd better not squander such a precious gift by being stubborn and slow to change.

"Did I tell you already that you're wonderful?"

Bhathian pretended to check his memories. "Nope, I don't think so. Only a genius."

"Then you can add it to the cache. You're wonderful, and I'm lucky to have you."

He cocked a brow. "Are there any more?" He smacked his lips. "You've given me a taste, and now I'm hungry for more."

Eva put a finger against her lips and pretended to ponder. She could tell him what she'd been thinking before. Unlike other men, the compliments wouldn't inflate his ego to unmanageable proportions. Bhathian was too modest for that. "I was just thinking that you have the body of a Hercules and the face of an Adonis. And that I won the jackpot for the best possible man."

Her guy seemed speechless. The adorable man didn't know how to handle so many compliments even though he deserved each of them, and none was an exaggeration. In fact, they were long overdue.

"I love you." The words just tumbled out of her mouth.

Eva hadn't planned to say them, hadn't even thought them until that moment. But now that they were spoken, she acknowledged them to be true. Subconsciously, Eva had known it for a while, maybe even from the very first time, but had been suppressing the emotion, unwilling to surrender to it.

She was done fighting, though. It was time to stop swimming against the current that had been pulling her toward Bhathian for over thirty years.

It was okay to surrender.

It was safe.

Bhathian shook his head. "Am I hallucinating? Because I think I heard you say the three words that I've been craving to hear you say for what seems like forever."

Eva wrapped her arms around Bhathian's neck and pulled

him on top of her. "I love you," she whispered before kissing him for all he was worth.

Bhathian pulled back a few inches and cupped her cheeks. "You've made me the happiest man alive. Thank you."

"Don't thank me. You were so much braver than me. You told me you loved me a long time ago, while I stubbornly clung to my so-called independence and denied my feelings for you even to myself. Assuming all the risk, you made it easy for me. I'm the one who should be thanking you for believing in us and patiently waiting for me to accept what has been clear to you from the very beginning."

His arms wrapped around her in a crushing embrace. "It's not important who said what first. I love you, and you love me. That's all that matters."

BHATHIAN

*B*hathian kissed Eva's cheek. "Wake up, love." He'd been up for over an hour, waiting for Eva to get up before leaving for the keep. He'd read the morning paper and then prepared breakfast for everyone.

On most days, Eva got out of bed at the same time he did. Their day usually began with morning sex, after which they would have coffee and sometimes breakfast together before he had to leave for work. But it seemed that the marathon lovemaking they'd indulged in last night had drained her energy, and she needed longer to replenish. Which meant that he'd done a good job.

Eva flopped onto her back and opened her eyes a crack. "What time is it?"

"It's seven. I brought you breakfast. Do you want it in bed, or do you want to get up and have it out on the balcony?" She loved sitting out there, either with a cup of coffee or a glass of wine and enjoying the ocean-scented breeze.

She smiled. "You made me breakfast in bed? How sweet."

He kissed her again. "Anything for my love."

With a yawn, Eva stretched, her body forming a sinuous arc.

Sexy as hell.

Bhathian peeled the comforter off her, exposing her bare breasts.

Eva pulled it back up. "I'm cold. Could you hand me my robe?"

Obviously, sex was not on her mind this morning. A pity, but at least her breakfast wouldn't get cold.

Donning the robe he'd handed her, Eva ducked into the bathroom.

"Don't be long. Your coffee will get cold," he called after her.

She was back after a few minutes, but instead of joining him on the couch she crawled back into bed. "Breakfast in bed sounds delightful." She arranged a few pillows behind her back to hold her in a sitting position.

Bhathian brought the tray over and put it on the night-stand. "Coffee?"

"Yes, please." Eva's smile was so wide he regretted not serving her breakfast in bed more often. But he sure was going to from now on. Other than with sex, it was difficult to please Eva. She didn't like presents, or flowers, or even dinners in fancy restaurants. She didn't leave him with many options. Now he finally had something she seemed to delight in.

He handed her the mug, already fixed the way she liked it. "Toast?"

"Yes, please.'

"Butter and jam?"

"Just butter."

He smeared a thin layer of it over the bread then handed her the plate and a fork.

Eva grimaced and handed him the plate back. "Could you please take the egg off? I think it has gone bad."

Bhathian sniffed the one over-easy egg he'd prepared for her. But there was nothing wrong with it. He would've known if there was. "It smells fine. But if you don't like it, I'll get rid of it." Using his fingers, he folded the egg in two, trapping the runny yolk inside, and popped it into his mouth. "All gone."

"Ugh, gross. I don't know how you could eat it." Eva took a bite of the toast.

"Do you want something instead of the egg? I can cut up some fruit."

She shook her head. "No, stay and eat with me. This is nice."

"It is." Bhathian lifted his own plate off the tray and made his scrambled eggs disappear as quickly as he could chew them. Which was pretty damn quick.

Eva smiled appreciatively. "Thank you. That was really nice of you."

He bowed his head. "Not a problem. I have a trashcan in here." He rubbed his stomach. "Any leftovers and other unwanted food items get processed here."

"You're funny." Eva took another bite of toast and chewed it slowly. "You can add it to the cache. Being funny is good."

Bhathian pretended to open a box and drop an invisible coin inside. "Done."

Eva scrunched up her nose. "I can still smell the eggs, and it's gross. How come you didn't smell anything? Isn't immortal males' sense of smell better than that of the females?"

"It is. I can promise you there was nothing wrong with them. Maybe you should get checked over. Bridgett should take a look at you."

Eva waved a hand. "Don't be silly, I'm an immortal. I can't

be sick. Not even food poisoning. It must be stress. For some reason, Syssi's disturbing vision affected me more than it should've. It's not as if I haven't seen shit worse than dead bodies. She just projected such a strong sense of anxiety."

Bhathian wasn't convinced, but then again as an immortal, the only thing Eva was susceptible to was mental affliction, and stress was known to sometimes manifest as a physical reaction.

"What do you have on your schedule today?" he asked.

"I'm working from home doing preliminary research. Sharon and I are going to dig into the files that Nick is going to get us access to."

"Can Sharon and Nick do it without you?"

"I can tell Sharon what to look for. Why? Do you have something in mind?"

"I want to run your idea by Kian, and if he likes it we can talk to Brandon, our media expert. Pushing our agenda through books and movies is his domain, and Hollywood is his playground."

Eva's eyes sparkled with excitement. "You don't really need me for that, but I would love to hear what your Brandon has to say about my idea. I've never met someone from the movie industry."

"Then get dressed, and I'll call Kian. I hope he has a few minutes he can spare to meet with us. Depends on his schedule for today."

"And I need to make sure Sharon and Nick can manage without me."

Bhathian leaned and kissed Eva's sensual, Cupid's-bow-shaped lips. "Sure they can. These kids were trained by the best."

53

EVA

"I'm not sure it's safe," Kian said after hearing Eva and Bhathian out. "I would need to read a script or an outline to assess the risk factor first. Creating a story aimed at a Dormant who turned immortal should be safe enough because it doesn't have to say anything about us. But something that would sound familiar enough to Kalugal to prompt him or his men to check it out would also sound familiar to every other Doomer. It's too risky."

In a way it was a relief.

Eva believed herself capable of producing a fictitious romance modeled on her and Bhathian's story. With some help of course. She could come up with the general story line, and someone else could write it.

A story that would appeal to Kalugal and his men required someone who knew more about the history of the clan, the Doomers, and their shared origins. A clan historian, if there was such a person, should write that story.

"Do I have your permission to talk to Brandon?" Bhathian asked Kian.

"You don't need my permission to talk to him. See what

he has to say, and once you formulate something more concrete come back to see me and bring Brandon along."

"Yes, boss. Thank you for hearing us out."

Kian rose to his feet and offered Eva his hand. "I'm always open to new ideas. Whenever you think of something, don't hesitate to come to me."

She shook it. "Thank you."

Kian was being polite. Whether he believed there was any merit to her idea or not was another thing altogether.

"Do you think he meant it?" Eva asked in a whisper as soon as they were far enough from Kian's office. "Or was he just being nice?"

Bhathian chuckled. "Kian is never just nice. He meant it. If we show him a story he deems safe enough, he will authorize it. But we need Brandon to tell us if there is a way to make a big fuss about this kind of a story. Some obscure production will not get noticed by those we're aiming it at."

"Naturally." Eva pressed the button for the lobby. The sluggishness from last night still dogged her. She needed some more caffeine in her system to start her day.

"Do you have time for a cup of coffee?"

Bhathian wrapped his arms around her, pulling her close. "For you, I'll always make time."

It was early in the day, and with most of the keep's occupants busy at their jobs, the café was deserted.

"What can I get you folks?" Carol asked.

"Two coffees, please." Only after she'd asked, did Eva remember that there was a Nespresso self-serve center with pretty good coffee. There was no need to bother Carol who looked tired even though her day had just begun. Maybe there was something in the air affecting immortals.

"Cappuccinos or regular coffees?"

"Regular. Right, Bhathian?"

"Yes."

Carol grabbed a carafe and filled two mugs. "Here you go."

Pulling out a few bills, Eva put them on the counter, for once not getting an argument from Bhathian. Apparently, her man didn't want to rock the boat when all was plain sailing.

"You look tired," she told Carol. "Is there something in the air? Because I feel tired too."

Carol stretched her back. "I don't know what your reason is. Mine is an evil fitness instructor."

Behind them, Bhathian chuckled.

"Not funny. Brundar is killing me. He trains me as if I were planning on applying for the Guardian force. And on top of it Onidu is needed for the deliveries to the compound, so I don't have any help here."

"Maybe you should close the place?" Eva suggested. "Then reopen the one at the new location."

Carol shook her head. "I think Nathalie wants to go back to work, and I'll gladly give it back to her. There are other more interesting things I'd rather be doing."

Eva nodded, suspecting she knew what those other things were. Carol was the spy Kian planned to send to the Doomers' island. Otherwise, why would the café's temporary manager train one on one with a Guardian?

At first glance, Carol looked sweet, innocent, and deceptively young—the perfect cover for what Kian needed her to do. But even though Eva sensed the steel underneath, she was still vehemently against the plan.

"If I were you, I would stay and manage the café instead of going for interesting things that are way too dangerous."

Carol glanced at Bhathian, and from the corner of her eye, Eva saw him shake his head.

The spy-in-training blew out a breath. "I'll take your advice into consideration. Thank you."

Yeah, and pigs would fly. The woman was signing her own death warrant.

"Come on, Eva. Let's drink that coffee. It's getting cold."

She let Bhathian take her elbow and lead her to a table. "It's a suicide mission," she hissed as she sat down. "You know that."

He shook his head. "Not our decision, love."

True, and she shouldn't aim her temper at the man she loved just because he was within her firing range. "You're right."

Bhathian cocked a brow. "That was surprisingly easy."

"I told you, I'm usually a very reasonable person, and I'm not quick to anger at all. I don't know what's wrong with me lately." If she were still getting monthly periods, she would've thought it the culprit. But what she remembered from her youth was that the agitated state lasted a day or two, not months. Besides, her periods had stopped a long time ago. How she had gotten pregnant with Nathalie was still a mystery.

Theoretically, she shouldn't have been able to do so without a period.

"What are you thinking about?" Bhathian asked.

"That I would like to ask Dr. Bridget a few questions."

Worry immediately darkened his expression. "What's wrong? Are you feeling sick?"

She waved a hand. "I'm fine, Bhathian, relax. I want to ask her about immortal females' physiology. I'm ignorant about my own body."

Bhathian got to his feet. "Let's go see her right now."

"Don't we need an appointment?"

"With immortals never getting sick she is not very busy."

He had a point, but then, what was the doctor needed for?

Eva slung the strap of her purse over her shoulder and followed Bhathian to the elevators. "What does she do? Aside from delivering babies, that I understand is a rare occurrence."

They stepped inside the elevator. "She sets broken bones, stitches the more serious wounds, and spends the rest of her time, which is most of it, on research."

"Must be boring to spend long days in a lab." Eva would've hated being cooped up anywhere, even in the lap of luxury. She needed to move, to travel, to experience. As wonderful and adorable as Phoenix was, Eva couldn't have done what Nathalie had chosen to do—be a stay-at-home mom. On reflection, Nathalie didn't have much choice in the matter.

There was no daycare or full-time babysitter available in the keep.

54

BHATHIAN

"*A*re you sure you want me to come with you?" Bhathian asked.

Eva patted his bicep. "There is nothing I'm embarrassed to talk about in front of you. Are you okay to listen to talk about female anatomy?"

Bhathian knocked on the clinic's door before pushing it open. "The more I know, the better."

She patted his arm again. "That's the right attitude."

Bridget walked out from her office. "Come on in, guys, what can I do for you?" She showed them in.

"Thank you." Eva smiled at Bhathian before sitting down in the chair he had pulled out for her. "I have a few questions, and forgive me if they sound dumb to you, but I lack basic information about my own anatomy."

"Ask away."

"I stopped getting my periods a long time ago. How could I have gotten pregnant with Nathalie?"

Bridget nodded. "Immortal females don't ovulate every month like human females. We need to preserve the eggs we are born with because they have to last us a very long time.

An immortal female will ovulate only when she has sex with a compatible male, one that her body determines capable of producing a healthy offspring."

"So there is no special time of the month or any of the other known factors? Ovulation happens on demand, and it always results in pregnancy?"

"Not always. If you've ever experienced an unexpected bleeding or spotting, it was probably due to an unsuccessful insemination."

Eva shook her head. "I don't remember that ever happening. Does it mean that the only compatible male I've ever been with was Bhathian?"

"Could be. Pregnancies are very rare for us."

Casting Bhathian a contemplative glance, Eva extrapolated, "So if we are compatible, as evidenced by our daughter, the chances are good that we can have another child, and those chances are much higher than those of other immortal couples."

"That would be a correct assumption, but I don't have evidence to support it. Annani had five children with five different men, but it took thousands of years and numerous attempts."

Her fingers drumming a beat on Bridget's desk, Eva cast another quick glance at Bhathian before asking, "Do you have pregnancy tests on hand?"

Bhathian lost his ability to talk, but Bridget asked the pertinent question for him.

"Do you have reason to believe you're pregnant?"

"I didn't until five minutes ago, and it still may be nothing, but I'm unusually tired, and this morning the smell of eggs nauseated me. I remember similar sensations when I got pregnant with Nathalie. I knew within a very short time."

"Let me get you one." Bridget pushed to her feet and left them alone with the ticking bomb between them.

Eva reached for his hand and clasped it. "Breathe, Bhathian. Do you need me to get you a glass of water?"

Shame on him. He should be the one taking care of her and not the other way around. Swallowing, he brought a little moisture to his dry mouth. "Are you okay? I mean it's probably a shock to you as much as it is to me."

Eva shrugged. "I don't know. Right now I'm only curious. Maybe I'll panic later when the test confirms my suspicions."

"You don't sound as if you're expecting anything other than a positive result."

"I'm not. I'm pretty sure I'm pregnant. It just hasn't sunk in yet."

"Here you go." Bridget came back with the kit. "You can use the bathroom over there." She pointed.

Eva got up and offered Bhathian a hand up. "Are you coming?"

"You want me in there with you?"

"Yes. If I'm really pregnant, I want you with me every step of the way this time."

"Thank you." His heart swelling with love and gratitude, he took her hand.

In the bathroom, Bhathian gave Eva privacy while she used the kit, turning his back to her until he heard her flush the toilet.

When she was done, she folded a thick layer of toilet paper, put it on the counter and placed the plastic wand on top of it. She then covered it with a single paper rectangle and washed her hands. "We will go crazy if we stare at it the entire time. I'd much rather cuddle."

Bhathian opened his arms, and she walked into his embrace. "I love you. And if we've created another life then it's a blessing," she murmured into his chest.

Stroking her hair with one hand and her back with the other, Bhathian nodded because he was too choked up to speak. Eva loved him, and she was welcoming their second child. He must've died and gone to heaven or stepped through a wormhole into an alternate reality. His wildest, most optimistic dreams were coming true.

"I love you so much." He kissed her forehead. "You've already made me the happiest man alive when you told me you loved me. I could not have imagined anything better than that. But you've done it again."

The next ten minutes were the longest in Bhathian's life. "I think it's time," he said after glancing at his watch once again.

Reaching toward the vanity, Eva gripped the corner of the piece of toilet paper covering the wand. "Are you ready?"

"Yes, yes and yes. Do it." The woman was torturing him.

He held his breath as she slowly lifted the paper and glanced at the display.

"Yes! It's a yes!" Eva clapped her hands, then threw her arms around his neck. "We are going to have another baby! Can you believe it? Because I can't. Oh, God, wait until Nathalie hears about it. She is going to have a little sister or brother like she always wanted."

The big plus sign on that slim plastic wand was the best news Bhathian had ever gotten. A new chapter in his and Eva's life was about to start, and this time he was going to be there every step of the way, making it right.

He held his mate tight, showering kisses all over her smiling face. "Let's go tell her."

55

EVA

*H*olding onto Bhathian's hand as they made their way to Nathalie's, Eva retreated into her own head, thinking about her unexpected pregnancy and her even more unexpected reaction to it.

Beside her, Bhathian was quiet, either sensing her need to be alone with her thoughts or deep in his own.

There was no ambivalence.

She didn't bemoan the anticipated loss of freedom, or the inevitable loss of income as her pregnancy progressed and her ability to go on assignments diminished.

There was still plenty of time to plan solutions and strategize. Those concerns were inconsequential compared to the one feeling that permeated through every cell in her body —pure joy.

She'd been given another chance at having the family she'd always dreamed of. A loving husband whom she loved back, Bhathian would get his wish of a big clan wedding, a child who'd be raised by both its parents, and a sibling for Nathalie. She might even give cooking another try.

As Bhathian had said, she had all the time in the world to

try out any role she could imagine. She could even try playing house again and put her detective work on hold.

One thing was for sure. Her vigilante days were over. Eva wasn't going to expose the life growing inside her to such vile acts. It didn't matter that the assassinations were justified. What mattered was the taint they left on her soul, a taint that could and would affect her unborn child.

That part of her life was going to be put on indefinite hold—at least until this child grew up and had a family of his or her own.

Hopefully, by that time the cleanup services she'd provided to society would no longer be needed. It was a naive thought that went against Eva's natural pessimistic bent, but she was too happy to let pessimism ruin her day.

Nathalie opened the door, holding Phoenix in one hand and the phone in the other. "Come in." She opened the way and resumed her phone conversation.

Eva took her granddaughter and lifted the baby to plant kisses all over her adorable face.

"Hey, I want some too." Bhathian leaned over Eva's shoulder, making weird clucking noises with his tongue that had Phoenix staring at him with her tiny mouth open in wonder.

"Do you want to hold her?"

"Yes. I'd better get used to doing that."

Eva showered several more kisses on the baby's smiling face before handing her to Bhathian.

"Sweetheart, we will talk about this later. My mom and dad are here," Nathalie said into the phone.

Eva's heart swelled, and she touched Bhathian's arm. Their daughter hardly ever referred to him as Dad.

The volume of Nathalie's cell must've been turned way down because Eva couldn't hear the response.

"They had a meeting with Kian and decided to drop by." Another pause.

"Love you too. See you at home. Mwah," Nathalie finished with a kiss.

"Sorry about that," she said as she put the phone on the kitchen counter. "Andrew is trying to convince me to take Phoenix up to Annani's retreat and stay there until the compound is ready."

Bhathian tickled Phoenix's belly. "That's not a bad idea. You and the baby are going to be safe there. Besides, Phoenix needs to be exposed to Annani to transition. Girls can do it at a very young age, and there are no side effects."

Nathalie sat down next to Eva on the couch. "I know. But I don't want to take her away from Andrew for such a long time, and he can't take a vacation either. He's already used all of his many accumulated vacation days, and the situation with Roni requires close monitoring."

Bhathian frowned. "Wasn't Anandur supposed to initiate the kid's transition?"

"He was, but Roni refuses to jump ship until he can code a backdoor into the system. Can't say that he's wrong. We need the access. But the longer the charade with the martial arts class goes on, the riskier the whole thing becomes."

Eva put a hand on Nathalie's arm. "At some point you'll have to go there. The sooner Phoenix turns immortal, the better. Especially now that Syssi's vision is hanging like a bad omen over our heads. But if you're not ready to leave, you and Andrew and Phoenix should at least move in with Bhathian and me. We can have Sharon and Tessa share a room for the next three months."

"Thank you for the invitation, but it may not be necessary. I asked Bridget to find out how long a baby girl needs to be exposed to Annani before she transitions. If it can be done in a few days, we may fly to Alaska for a long weekend. She'll let me know after talking it over with the retreat's doctor."

Eva glanced at Bhathian, mouthing, you or me?

As she'd expected, he pointed at her.

"There is something we want to tell you."

Nathalie's eyes widened. "Oh, my God, are you guys finally getting married?"

Eva chuckled. "Yes, but that's not the news we came to share."

"We are getting married?" Bhathian's brows shot up.

Eva cast him a smile. "Yes, big guy, we are." She turned to Nathalie. "You're going to become a big sister like you've always wanted."

Nathalie's jaw dropped. "You're pregnant?" It was barely a whisper.

Eva nodded. "We just found out. You're the first one we're telling."

"How far along are you?"

"About two weeks. I found out very early on with you too."

Nathalie pulled Eva into her arms for a fierce hug. "Wow, just wow." She let go of her and grabbed the end of her braid, twisting the loose strands around her finger. "Do you want to keep it a secret?"

"Why? Are you embarrassed about your mother getting pregnant out of wedlock, again?"

Nathalie snorted. "Of course not. Like mother like daughter. I was pregnant at my wedding as well. I'm asking because I want to tell everyone, but not if you don't want me to."

"I'm too happy to keep this to myself. How about you, Bhathian?" Eva had almost forgotten that she couldn't make these kinds of decisions without considering his input.

"I don't want to keep it a secret either, but I'd rather that we delivered the news, at least to our close circle. I know Nathalie will share it with Andrew as soon as we leave, but we should be the ones to tell Kian and Syssi and Amanda and Dalhu."

"I can invite them over this evening," Nathalie suggested.

Eva wrapped her arm around her daughter and pulled her into a warm embrace. "Thank you." She choked up a little.

"That's nothing, Mom. I invite them over all of the time. No need to get emotional." She chuckled. "I understand, though. I still remember those pregnancy hormonal moods. I cried at the drop of a hat."

Eva shook her head. "That's not the reason for my gratitude, Nathalie. Thank you for being the best daughter a mother could have."

56

EVA

"Are you nervous?" Eva asked Bhathian as they stood in front of Nathalie's door for the second time that day.

"Excited. We need an infusion of good news right now, and there is no better news than that of another child joining our clan. It will lift everyone's spirits."

Maybe not everyone.

Eva had a feeling it would upset Syssi, adding to her already gloomy mood. The girl craved a baby of her own.

Andrew opened the door. "Come in, almost everyone is here. We are only missing Kian."

Eva was going to wait with the news until Kian showed up. Syssi would need his support.

After exchanging hugs and kisses and hellos, Bhathian brought three chairs from the dining room, for him, Dalhu and Kian. Eva, Nathalie, and Amanda took the couch, Andrew sat in an armchair with Phoenix in his arms, and Syssi sat in the other one.

A big tray sat on the coffee table, full of beers and soft drinks and small containers with nuts or pretzels. The salty snacks caught Eva's attention, and she leaned to take a fistful of nuts.

"Nathalie said that you guys have an announcement." Amanda smirked. "I think we all know what that announcement is about. We've been waiting with bated breath." She put her hand over her heart.

Eva returned a smirk of her own. Amanda was in for one hell of a surprise. "We are waiting for Kian." She glanced at Syssi.

A pair of sad eyes met hers in a silent communication. It seemed the seer already knew what this was really about, and not because anyone had told her.

There was no envy in those eyes, just sadness, and Eva felt her heart squeeze in sympathy. She wanted to go up to Syssi and give the girl some words of comfort—tell her that she was still so very young, that there was plenty of time and no reason to despair, that Eva had gotten pregnant for the first time at the age of forty-five. But she knew none of it would ease the girl's pain.

Syssi's craving was an emotion, it wasn't rational, and words, however true and well-meaning, would fall on deaf ears.

There was a knock on the door, and a moment later Kian walked in. Ignoring the chair Bhathian had brought for him, he went straight for his wife. He didn't even say hello to anyone. Lifting her up, he sat in the armchair and positioned her in his lap.

Wrapped in Kian's arms, Syssi sighed and put her head against his chest, the dark clouds in her eyes parting to let the love for her husband shine through.

"Good evening, everyone," Kian said.

They'd agreed ahead of time that this time Bhathian was going to deliver the announcement. Catching his eye, Eva nodded. It was time.

Bhathian got up. "Eva and I have good news we want to share with those closest to us."

Amanda clapped her hands, and Kian murmured, "About bloody time." Syssi said nothing, and Phoenix gurgled her approval.

Eva felt a pang of guilt for not telling her crew yet. Other than Nathalie, Phoenix, and Bhathian they were the people closest to her, with Andrew closing the short list. But the opportunity hadn't presented itself.

"We are expecting another child."

Eva watched Syssi as everyone else exploded with congratulations and claps. She showed no surprise, casting Eva a small smile.

How did she know?

Another vision?

Hopefully, it had been a good one.

"You don't look surprised, Syssi," Eva said, unable to curtail her curiosity.

Syssi nodded. "I dreamt of a little boy playing with Phoenix, and you watching over them both, but I didn't know who he belonged to. When Nathalie told me you guys wanted to tell us something, I knew right away what it was."

Kian stroked her back. "Why didn't you tell me?"

She shrugged. "I didn't want to spoil Eva and Bhathian's big surprise."

"Thank you," Eva said, thinking that Syssi was one of the nicest people she'd ever met.

Amanda pushed to her feet and clapped her hands again to get everyone's attention. "This calls for a toast. Andrew, what do you have in your bar?"

"Let me see." Andrew got up and handed his little bundle of joy to her mother.

The two came back with wine glasses and handed them out.

Andrew lifted his. "I'm sorry it's not champagne. To Eva and Bhathian, congratulations on becoming pregnant with their second child, and giving my Nathalie a brother or a sister. No offense, Syssi, but until the ultrasound confirms it, I'm going to keep saying he or she."

Syssi lifted her glass. "None taken."

"To a new life!" Amanda clinked her glass with Andrew's, then continued to clink with everyone in the room. She kept Eva for last. Leaning to kiss her on one cheek and then the other, Amanda clinked her glass with Eva's. "Your first child is awesome. Let's drink to the next one being just as lovely."

When all the clinking was done, Amanda clapped her hands again. "Wedding plans!"

"If you start talking wedding gowns, I'm out of here," Kian said.

Amanda waved a hand. "There is time for that. First we need to decide where and when. Or the other way around." She winked at Eva.

"With Nathalie, I didn't start showing until my fifth month, so if that is what you mean by when, we have plenty of time. Frankly, though, I don't care about that. As long as Bhathian and I are married before my water breaks, I'm fine. And as for the ceremony, it can be something very modest with only a few people in attendance. After all, it's not my first."

Bhathian folded his arms over his impressive chest. "But it is mine. I've waited over thirty years for you. I want a big, clan-wide celebration, with Annani presiding and making up the ritual as she goes, the same way she did for Syssi and Kian and Nathalie and Andrew."

Syssi's eyes widened. "She made it up? This is not some ancient, time-honored tradition?

Kian's lips twitched as he stifled a laugh.

Syssi slapped his forearm. "You should've told me!"

"Why? It was beautiful. Who cares if she made it up, or modified it, or whatever? It's no different from wedding vows. I think it's better than using the same speech at every wedding."

Eva shook her head. She was marrying into a clan of heathens. Her mother was probably turning in her grave.

But did she want to get married in a church again? It had seemed so important when she'd married Fernando.

And look how that turned out.

If she insisted, Bhathian would marry her in a church or a Buddhist temple or in a hippie ceremony. The only thing he wanted was to have the people he cared about share in the celebration and witness his and Eva's pledge to each other.

In the background, she heard talk about having the wedding in Scotland, like Nathalie and Andrew's. Someone even said something about renting a reception hall, but Kian shot down that idea in an instant.

"We will wait until the new place is ready," Eva said.

The room went quiet, everyone's attention on her. "Three months will give us plenty of time to plan a beautiful wedding. Right, Bhathian?" She was so used to making her own decisions, it was difficult to adjust to having a partner who had a say in them.

He nodded. "I would've liked for us to be married yesterday, but Eva is right. The prudent thing to do is to wait for the right time. Even if we could all pick up and go party in Scotland, which we can't with everything that's going on, I wouldn't want to impose on Sari's hospitality again. And having the celebration here in the keep is, if not outright dangerous, then anxiety inducing. Not the atmosphere I want at our wedding."

All Bhathian had done was explain her reasoning, and yet his heartfelt speech brought tears to her eyes. Her man always put everyone else's needs before his own.

God, she loved this man. If she could, she would've married him yesterday too...

An idea started forming in her head, and Eva acted before it even solidified.

Pushing up to her feet, she walked over to Bhathian and reached for his hands. When he clasped hers, she tugged, bringing him up to his feet as well.

"From what I've heard here today, I understand that there is no particular marriage ceremony, and that the goddess invents it as she goes. Am I right?" Without letting go of Bhathian's hands, she turned her head to Kian.

He nodded. "That's right. And if there is a ceremony written somewhere in the legal codex, Annani might simply prefer to invent her own."

"Nevertheless, the two weddings she presided over are valid in the eyes of the clan." Eva had to make sure.

He nodded again. "As long as the couple's pledges to each other are witnessed by two adult gods or immortals, it's a valid marriage. At least that's what Annani told me about her people's traditions."

Exactly what Eva had thought. Looking up at Bhathian's loving eyes, she said, "We have six witnesses. Plenty enough to vouch for our pledges to each other."

Understanding dawning, Bhathian's face split in a wide grin. "Right here, right now?"

She nodded. "Right here, right now. We can have the big party later. Do you want me to go first?" Bhathian was the dearest, most loving man in the world, but he wasn't a man of many words.

"Yes."

She squeezed his hands, holding on tight. "I love you, and I want to spend the rest of my immortal life with you. It took me a while to accept that I always did. Since the first moment I saw you on that TWA flight, you've been the only one I wanted, the only one I dreamt about. But God, or fate, or whatever higher power you believe in, had other plans for us. Perhaps we weren't ready, perhaps I had to witness a lot of failed marriages in my line of work and go through one of my own to appreciate the amazing man you are. But all of that is behind us, and the experiences we went through, good and bad, helped shape us into the people we are today. When I pledge my life to you in front of these dear witnesses, I do it with absolute confidence that our love and commitment to each other is strong enough to withstand any test, including the test of time."

Someone started clapping, then the others joined in.

Bhathian lifted her hands to his lips, kissing each one. "I'm not as eloquent, but you know that about me and love me anyway. Which I still find quite unbelievable."

His expression grew serious. "I'm humbled and grateful that such an amazing woman finds me worthy of her love. I vow in front of these witnesses that I will never take your love for granted, and that I will always strive to be the best man I can be for you, as well as the best possible father for our children. Nathalie and the one growing in here." Bhathian didn't release her hand as he put both his and hers, still entwined, on her flat belly. "And any children that we may be blessed with in the future. I pledge my love, my life, and everything I am to you."

Tears of raw emotion running down her cheeks, Eva whispered, "You may kiss the bride."

57

BRUNDAR

*O*nce again, Brundar found himself sitting in his car across from a nondescript suburban house, eavesdropping.

A better term would be stalking.

He'd been coming here for almost a year, skulking in the shadows, or sitting in his car hidden by his powerful mind control over the humans. None of them could see him. Except, on occasion, he would wait for a few moments before casting the shroud, chancing discovery. Tempting fate.

Sometimes she would look out the window as if she could feel his presence. He lived for those moments, for a chance to behold her beautiful face.

It was always a mighty struggle to stay out of her head.

Did she remember him?

Did she know he was guarding her?

At first, it had been every day, at least on the days he could get away from the keep without compromising his Guardian duties. After a month of that, he'd forced himself to limit his stalking activities to once a week. It was still obsessive, but he convinced himself that it was okay, justified, that he was just checking on her, making sure she was all right.

Total and complete madness.

There was no other explanation for his obsession with the girl.

For a man who took pride in feeling nothing, honing that cold, emotionless state since he was old enough to hold a blade in his hand, it was akin to a wide-scale system failure, a mental breakdown.

Sometimes he wanted to hate her for it, blame her for piercing his shields with such ease without even trying. Sometimes he wished he'd never laid eyes on the child.

Because she was a child.

Only twenty years old when he'd first seen her all those months ago, she believed she was ready for grown-up games she knew nothing about.

Worse.

The girl thought she was old enough to tie her future to a guy she should have stayed away from, old enough to make commitments she had no business making at such a young age.

Her childish, misguided beliefs and dreams of love had led her astray.

The jerk she was with thought he had the right to control her every move, dictate everything she did, and for reasons Brundar couldn't fathom, she'd given him that right of her own free will.

The girl believed it was love.

Which meant Brundar couldn't interfere.

The guy was a douchebag bully, who didn't deserve to be in the presence of a sweet angel like her, let alone claim her as his own. Brundar couldn't shake the feeling that one of these days the asshole would cross the line from mildly abusive to harmful—either emotionally or physically.

He'd been in the guy's head, had seen his dark side.

The irony wasn't lost on Brundar. His own darkness eclipsed the guy's in order of magnitude. But whereas Brundar's was kept in check by a strict code of conduct, the honorable rules he lived by, the asshole's wasn't.

That was the real reason Brundar was sitting outside their home, waiting for the moment the guy crossed the line and justified the death sentence Brundar was itching to deliver.

She would hate him for it, but he would be doing her a favor. Later, when she got over her misplaced grief, the taste of freedom would be so sweet on her lips that she would thank her mystery deliverer.

Her Guardian.

Perhaps once she was free, Brundar could move on and return to the cold state that had sustained him his entire adult life. The quiet zone where every move was deliberate, where his senses were perfectly attuned to his environment, where he was an emotionless killing machine—the best there was.

Except, he knew it for the lie it was.

He might set the girl free, but not himself.

he End... for now...

CLICK HERE TO FIND OUT WHAT HAPPENS NEXT!
BOOK 14 IN THE CHILDREN OF THE GODS SERIES
DARK ANGEL'S OBSESSION

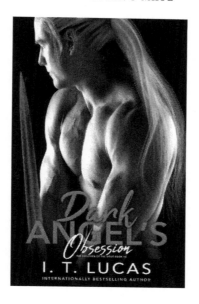

Dear reader,

Thank you for joining me on the continuing adventures of the ***Children of the Gods***.

As an independent author, I rely on your support to spread the word. So if you enjoyed the story, please share your experience, and if it isn't too much trouble, I would greatly appreciate a brief review for Dark Guardian's Mate on Amazon.

Click here to leave a review

Love & happy reading,
Isabell

skeptical and refuses Amanda's plea to attempt Syssi's activation. But when his enemies learn of the Dormant's existence, he's forced to rush her to the safety of his keep. Inexorably drawn to Syssi, Kian wrestles with his conscience as he is tempted to explore her budding interest in the darker shades of sensuality.

2: DARK STRANGER REVEALED

While sheltered in the clan's stronghold, Syssi is unaware that Kian and Amanda are not human, and neither are the supposedly religious fanatics that are after her. She feels a powerful connection to Kian, and as he introduces her to a world of pleasure she never dared imagine, his dominant sexuality is a revelation. Considering that she's completely out of her element, Syssi feels comfortable and safe letting go with him. That is, until she begins to suspect that all is not as it seems. Piecing the puzzle together, she draws a scary, yet wrong conclusion...

3: DARK STRANGER IMMORTAL

When Kian confesses his true nature, Syssi is not as much shocked by the revelation as she is wounded by what she perceives as his callous plans for her.

If she doesn't turn, he'll be forced to erase her memories and let her go. His family's safety demands secrecy – no one in the mortal world is allowed to know that immortals exist.

Resigned to the cruel reality that even if she stays on to never again leave the keep, she'll get old while Kian won't, Syssi is determined to enjoy what little time she has with him, one day at a time.

Can Kian let go of the mortal woman he loves? Will Syssi turn? And if she does, will she survive the dangerous transition?

4: DARK ENEMY TAKEN

Dalhu can't believe his luck when he stumbles upon the beautiful immortal professor. Presented with a once in a lifetime opportunity to grab an immortal female for himself, he kidnaps her and runs. If he ever gets caught, either by her people or his, his life is forfeit. But for a chance of a loving mate and a family of his own, Dalhu is prepared to do everything in his power to win Amanda's heart, and that includes leaving the Doom brotherhood and his old life behind.

Amanda soon discovers that there is more to the handsome Doomer than his dark past and a hulking, sexy body. But succumbing to her enemy's seduction, or worse, developing feelings for a ruthless killer is out of the question. No man is worth life on the run, not even the one and only immortal male she could claim as her own...

Her clan and her research must come first...

5: Dark Enemy Captive

When the rescue team returns with Amanda and the chained Dalhu to the keep, Amanda is not as thrilled to be back as she thought she'd be. Between Kian's contempt for her and Dalhu's imprisonment, Amanda's budding relationship with Dalhu seems doomed. Things start to look up when Annani offers her help, and together with Syssi they resolve to find a way for Amanda to be with Dalhu. But will she still want him when she realizes that he is responsible for her nephew's murder? Could she? Will she take the easy way out and choose Andrew instead?

6: Dark Enemy Redeemed

Amanda suspects that something fishy is going on onboard the Anna. But when her investigation of the peculiar all-female Russian crew fails to uncover anything other than more speculation, she decides it's time to stop playing detective and face her real problem —a man she shouldn't want but can't live without.

6.5: My Dark Amazon

When Michael and Kri fight off a gang of humans, Michael gets stabbed. The injury to his immortal body recovers fast, but the one to his ego takes longer, putting a strain on his relationship with Kri.

7: Dark Warrior Mine

When Andrew is forced to retire from active duty, he believes that all he has to look forward to is a boring desk job. His glory days in special ops are over. But as it turns out, his thrill ride has just begun.

Andrew discovers not only that immortals exist and have been manipulating global affairs since antiquity, but that he and his sister are rare possessors of the immortal genes.

Problem is, Andrew might be too old to attempt the activation process. His sister, who is fourteen years his junior, barely made it through the transition, so the odds of him coming out of it alive, let alone immortal, are slim.

But fate may force his hand.

Helping a friend find his long-lost daughter, Andrew finds a woman who's worth taking the risk for. Nathalie might be a Dormant, but the only way to find out for sure requires fangs and venom.

8: Dark Warrior's Promise

Andrew and Nathalie's love flourishes, but the secrets they keep from each other taint their relationship with doubts and suspicions. In the meantime, Sebastian and his men are getting bolder, and the storm that's brewing will shift the balance of power in the millennia-old conflict between Annani's clan and its enemies.

9: Dark Warrior's Destiny

The new ghost in Nathalie's head remembers who he was in life, providing Andrew and her with indisputable proof that he is real and not a figment of her imagination.

Convinced that she is a Dormant, Andrew decides to go forward with his transition immediately after the rescue mission at the Doomers' HQ.

Fearing for his life, Nathalie pleads with him to reconsider. She'd rather spend the rest of her mortal days with Andrew than risk what they have for the fickle promise of immortality.

While the clan gets ready for battle, Carol gets help from an unlikely ally. Sebastian's second-in-command can no longer ignore the torment she suffers at the hands of his commander and offers to help her, but only if she agrees to his terms.

10: Dark Warrior's Legacy

Andrew's acclimation to his post-transition body isn't easy. His senses are sharper, he's bigger, stronger, and hungrier. Nathalie fears that the changes in the man she loves are more than physical. Measuring up to this new version of him is going to be a challenge.

Carol and Robert are disillusioned with each other. They are not destined mates, and love is not on the horizon. When Robert's three months are up, he might be left with nothing to show for his sacrifice.

Lana contacts Anandur with disturbing news; the yacht and its human cargo are in Mexico. Kian must find a way to apprehend Alex and rescue the women on board without causing an international incident.

11: Dark Guardian Found

What would you do if you stopped aging?

Eva runs. The ex-DEA agent doesn't know what caused her strange mutation, only that if discovered, she'll be dissected like a lab rat. What Eva doesn't know, though, is that she's a descendant of the gods, and that she is not alone. The man who rocked her world in one life-changing encounter over thirty years ago is an immortal as well.

To keep his people's existence secret, Bhathian was forced to turn his back on the only woman who ever captured his heart, but he's never forgotten and never stopped looking for her.

12: Dark Guardian Craved

Cautious after a lifetime of disappointments, Eva is mistrustful of Bhathian's professed feelings of love. She accepts him as a lover and a confidant but not as a life partner.

Jackson suspects that Tessa is his true love mate, but unless she overcomes her fears, he might never find out.

Carol gets an offer she can't refuse—a chance to prove that there is more to her than meets the eye. Robert believes she's about to commit a deadly mistake, but when he tries to dissuade her, she tells him to leave.

13: Dark Guardian's Mate

Prepare for the heart-warming culmination of Eva and Bhathian's story!

14: Dark Angel's Obsession

The cold and stoic warrior is an enigma even to those closest to him. His secrets are about to unravel...

15: Dark Angel's Seduction

Brundar is fighting a losing battle. Calypso is slowly chipping away his icy armor from the outside, while his need for her is melting it from the inside.

He can't allow it to happen. Calypso is a human with none of the Dormant indicators. There is no way he can keep her for more than a few weeks.

16: Dark Angel's Surrender

Get ready for the heart pounding conclusion to Brundar and Calypso's story.

Callie still couldn't wrap her head around it, nor could she summon even a smidgen of sorrow or regret. After all, she had some memories with him that weren't horrible. She should've felt something. But there was nothing, not even shock. Not even horror at what had transpired over the last couple of hours.

Maybe it was a typical response for survivors--feeling euphoric for the simple reason that they were alive. Especially when that survival was nothing short of miraculous.

Brundar's cold hand closed around hers, reminding her that they weren't out of the woods yet. Her injuries were superficial, and the most she had to worry about was some scarring. But, despite his and Anandur's reassurances, Brundar might never walk again.

If he ended up crippled because of her, she would never forgive herself for getting him involved in her crap.

"Are you okay, sweetling? Are you in pain?" Brundar asked.

Her injuries were nothing compared to his, and yet he was concerned about her. God, she loved this man. The thing was, if she told him that, he would run off, or crawl away as was the case.

Hey, maybe this was the perfect opportunity to spring it on him.

17: Dark Operative: A Shadow of Death

As a brilliant strategist and the only human entrusted with the secret of immortals' existence, Turner is both an asset and a liability to the clan. His request to attempt transition into immortality as an alternative to cancer treatments cannot be denied without risking the clan's exposure. On the other hand, approving it means risking his premature death. In both scenarios, the clan will lose a valuable ally.

When the decision is left to the clan's physician, Turner makes plans to manipulate her by taking advantage of her interest in him.

Will Bridget fall for the cold, calculated operative? Or will Turner fall into his own trap?

18: Dark Operative: A Glimmer of Hope

As Turner and Bridget's relationship deepens, living together seems like the right move, but to make it work both need to make concessions.

Bridget is realistic and keeps her expectations low. Turner could never be the truelove mate she yearns for, but he is as good as she's going to get. Other than his emotional limitations, he's perfect in every way.

Turner's hard shell is starting to show cracks. He wants immortality, he wants to be part of the clan, and he wants Bridget, but he doesn't want to cause her pain.

His options are either abandon his quest for immortality and give Bridget his few remaining decades, or abandon Bridget by going for the transition and most likely dying. His rational mind dictates that he chooses the former, but his gut pulls him toward the latter.
Which one is he going to trust?

19: Dark Operative: The Dawn of Love

Get ready for the exciting finale of Bridget and Turner's story!

20: Dark Survivor Awakened

This was a strange new world she had awakened to.

Her memory loss must have been catastrophic because almost nothing was familiar. The language was foreign to her, with only a few words bearing some similarity to the language she thought in. Still, a full moon cycle had passed since her awakening, and little by little she was gaining basic understanding of it--only a few words and phrases, but she was learning more each day.

A week or so ago, a little girl on the street had tugged on her mother's sleeve and pointed at her. "Look, Mama, Wonder Woman!"

The mother smiled apologetically, saying something in the language these people spoke, then scurried away with the child looking behind her shoulder and grinning.

When it happened again with another child on the same day, it was settled.

Wonder Woman must have been the name of someone important in this strange world she had awoken to, and since both times it had been said with a smile it must have been a good one.

Wonder had a nice ring to it.

She just wished she knew what it meant.

21: DARK SURVIVOR ECHOES OF LOVE

Wonder's journey continues in *Dark Survivor Echoes of Love*.

22: DARK SURVIVOR REUNITED

The exciting finale of Wonder and Anandur's story.

23: DARK WIDOW'S SECRET

Vivian and her daughter share a powerful telepathic connection, so when Ella can't be reached by conventional or psychic means, her mother fears the worst.

Help arrives from an unexpected source when Vivian gets a call from the young doctor she met at a psychic convention. Turns out Julian belongs to a private organization specializing in retrieving missing girls.

As Julian's clan mobilizes its considerable resources to rescue the daughter, Magnus is charged with keeping the gorgeous young mother safe.

Worry for Ella and the secrets Vivian and Magnus keep from each other should be enough to prevent the sparks of attraction from kindling a blaze of desire. Except, these pesky sparks have a mind of their own.

24: DARK WIDOW'S CURSE

A simple rescue operation turns into mission impossible when the Russian mafia gets involved. Bad things are supposed to come in threes, but in Vivian's case, it seems like there is no limit to bad luck. Her family and everyone who gets close to her is affected by her curse.

Will Magnus and his people prove her wrong?

25: Dark Widow's Blessing

The thrilling finale of the Dark Widow trilogy!

26: Dark Dream's Temptation

Julian has known Ella is the one for him from the moment he saw her picture, but when he finally frees her from captivity, she seems indifferent to him. Could he have been mistaken?

Ella's rescue should've ended that chapter in her life, but it seems like the road back to normalcy has just begun and it's full of obstacles. Between the pitying looks she gets and her mother's attempts to get her into therapy, Ella feels like she's typecast as a victim, when nothing could be further from the truth. She's a tough survivor, and she's going to prove it.

Strangely, the only one who seems to understand is Logan, who keeps popping up in her dreams. But then, he's a figment of her imagination—or is he?

27: Dark Dream's Unraveling

While trying to figure out a way around Logan's silencing compulsion, Ella concocts an ambitious plan. What if instead of trying to keep him out of her dreams, she could pretend to like him and lure him into a trap?

Catching Navuh's son would be a major boon for the clan, as well as for Ella. She will have her revenge, turning the tables on another scumbag out to get her.

28: Dark Dream's Trap

The trap is set, but who is the hunter and who is the prey? Find out in this heart-pounding conclusion to the *Dark Dream* trilogy.

29: Dark Prince's Enigma

As the son of the most dangerous male on the planet, Lokan lives by three rules:

Don't trust a soul.

Don't show emotions.

And don't get attached.

Will one extraordinary woman make him break all three?

30: Dark Prince's Dilemma

Will Kian decide that the benefits of trusting Lokan outweigh the risks?

Will Lokan betray his father and brothers for the greater good of his people?

Are Carol and Lokan true-love mates, or is one of them playing the other?

So many questions, the path ahead is anything but clear.

31: Dark Prince's Agenda

While Turner and Kian work out the details of Areana's rescue plan, Carol and Lokan's tumultuous relationship hits another snag. Is it a sign of things to come?

32 : Dark Queen's Quest

A former beauty queen, a retired undercover agent, and a successful model, Mey is not the typical damsel in distress. But when her sister drops off the radar and then someone starts following her around, she panics.

Following a vague clue that Kalugal might be in New York, Kian sends a team headed by Yamanu to search for him.

As Mey and Yamanu's paths cross, he offers her his help and protection, but will that be all?

33: Dark Queen's Knight

As the only member of his clan with a godlike power over human minds, Yamanu has been shielding his people for centuries, but that power comes at a steep price. When Mey enters his life, he's faced with the most difficult choice.

The safety of his clan or a future with his fated mate.

34: Dark Queen's Army

As Mey anxiously waits for her transition to begin and for Yamanu to test whether his godlike powers are gone, the clan sets out to solve two mysteries:

Where is Jin, and is she there voluntarily?

Where is Kalugal, and what is he up to?

35: Dark Spy Conscripted

Jin possesses a unique paranormal ability. Just by touching someone, she can insert a mental hook into their psyche and tie a string of her consciousness to it, creating a tether. That doesn't make her a spy, though, not unless her talent is discovered by those seeking to exploit it.

36: Dark Spy's Mission

Jin's first spying mission is supposed to be easy. Walk into the club, touch Kalugal to tether her consciousness to him, and walk out.

Except, they should have known better.

37: Dark Spy's Resolution

The best-laid plans often go awry...

38: Dark Overlord New Horizon

Jacki has two talents that set her apart from the rest of the human race.

She has unpredictable glimpses of other people's futures, and she is immune to mind manipulation.

Unfortunately, both talents are pretty useless for finding a job other than the one she had in the government's paranormal division.

It seemed like a sweet deal, until she found out that the director planned on producing super babies by compelling the recruits into pairing up. When an opportunity to escape the program presented itself, she took it, only to find out that humans are not at the top of the food chain.

Immortals are real, and at the very top of the hierarchy is Kalugal, the most powerful, arrogant, and sexiest male she has ever met.

With one look, he sets her blood on fire, but Jacki is not a fool. A man like him will never think of her as anything more than a tasty snack, while she will never settle for anything less than his heart.

39: Dark Overlord's Wife

Jacki is still clinging to her all-or-nothing policy, but Kalugal is chipping away at her resistance. Perhaps it's time to ease up on her convictions. A little less than all is still much better than nothing, and a couple of decades with a demigod is probably worth more than a lifetime with a mere mortal.

40: Dark Overlord's Clan

As Jacki and Kalugal prepare to celebrate their union, Kian takes every precaution to safeguard his people. Except, Kalugal and his men are not his only potential adversaries, and compulsion is not the only power he should fear.

41: Dark Choices The Quandary

When Rufsur and Edna meet, the attraction is as unexpected as it is undeniable. Except, she's the clan's judge and councilwoman, and he's Kalugal's second-in-command. Will loyalty and duty to their people keep them apart?

42: Dark Choices Paradigm Shift

Edna and Rufsur are miserable without each other, and their two-week separation seems like an eternity. Long-distance relationships are difficult, but for immortal couples they are impossible. Unless one of them is willing to leave everything behind for the other, things are just going to get worse. Except, the cost of compromise is far greater than giving up their comfortable lives and hard-earned positions. The future of their people is on the line.

43: Dark Choices The Accord

The winds of change blowing over the village demand hard choices. For better or worse, Kian's decisions will alter the trajectory of the clan's future, and he is not ready to take the plunge. But as Edna and Rufsur's plight gains widespread support, his resistance slowly begins to erode.

44: Dark Secrets Resurgence

On a sabbatical from his Stanford teaching position, Professor

David Levinson finally has time to write the sci-fi novel he's been thinking about for years.

The phenomena of past life memories and near-death experiences are too controversial to include in his formal psychiatric research, while fiction is the perfect outlet for his esoteric ideas.

Hoping that a change of pace will provide the inspiration he needs, David accepts a friend's invitation to an old Scottish castle.

45: Dark Secrets Unveiled

When Professor David Levinson accepts a friend's invitation to an old Scottish castle, what he finds there is more fantastical than his most outlandish theories. The castle is home to a clan of immortals, their leader is a stunning demigoddess, and even more shockingly, it might be precisely where he belongs.

Except, the clan founder is hiding a secret that might cast a dark shadow on David's relationship with her daughter.

Nevertheless, when offered a chance at immortality, he agrees to undergo the dangerous induction process.

Will David survive his transition into immortality? And if he does, will his relationship with Sari survive the unveiling of her mother's secret?

46: Dark Secrets Absolved

Absolution.

David had given and received it.

The few short hours since he'd emerged from the coma had felt incredible. He'd finally been free of the guilt and pain, and for the first time since Jonah's death, he had felt truly happy and optimistic about the future.

He'd survived the transition into immortality, had been accepted into the clan, and was about to marry the best woman on the face of the planet, his true love mate, his salvation, his everything.

What could have possibly gone wrong?

Just about everything.

47: Dark haven Illusion

Welcome to Safe Haven, where not everything is what it seems.

On a quest to process personal pain, Anastasia joins the Safe Haven Spiritual Retreat.

Through meditation, self-reflection, and hard work, she hopes to make peace with the voices in her head.

This is where she belongs.

Except, membership comes with a hefty price, doubts are sacrilege, and leaving is not as easy as walking out the front gate.

Is living in utopia worth the sacrifice?

Anastasia believes so until the arrival of a new acolyte changes everything.

Apparently, the gods of old were not a myth, their immortal descendants share the planet with humans, and she might be a carrier of their genes.

THE PERFECT MATCH SERIES

PERFECT MATCH 1: VAMPIRE'S CONSORT

When Gabriel's company is ready to start beta testing, he invites his old crush to inspect its medical safety protocol.

Curious about the revolutionary technology of the *Perfect Match Virtual Fantasy-Fulfillment studios*, Brenna agrees.

Neither expects to end up partnering for its first fully immersive test run.

PERFECT MATCH 2: KING'S CHOSEN

When Lisa's nutty friends get her a gift certificate to *Perfect Match Virtual Fantasy Studios*, she has no intentions of using it. But since the only way to get a refund is if no partner can be found for her, she makes sure to request a fantasy so girly and over the top that no sane guy will pick it up.

Except, someone does.

Warning: This fantasy contains a hot, domineering crown prince, sweet insta-love, steamy love scenes painted with light shades of gray, a wedding, and a HEA in both the virtual and real worlds.

Intended for mature audience.

Perfect Match 3: Captain's Conquest

Working as a Starbucks barista, Alicia fends off flirting all day long, but none of the guys are as charming and sexy as Gregg. His frequent visits are the highlight of her day, but since he's never asked her out, she assumes he's taken. Besides, between a day job and a budding music career, she has no time to start a new relationship.

That is until Gregg makes her an offer she can't refuse—a gift certificate to the virtual fantasy fulfillment service everyone is talking about. As a huge Star Trek fan, Alicia has a perfect match in mind—the captain of the Starship Enterprise.

FOR EXCLUSIVE PEEKS AT UPCOMING RELEASES & A FREE COMPANION BOOK

Join my *VIP Club* and gain access to the VIP portal at itlucas.com

CLICK HERE TO JOIN

(or go to: http://eepurl.com/blMTpD)

Included in your free membership:

- **FREE** Children of the Gods companion book 1
- **FREE** narration of Goddess's Choice—Book 1 in The Children of the Gods Origins series.
- Preview chapters of upcoming releases.
- And other exclusive content offered only to my VIPs.

Printed in Great Britain
by Amazon

54715271R00192